Tappin'
on
Thirty

Tappin'
on
Thirty

CANDICE DOW

KENSINGTON PUBLISHING CORP.
http://www.kensingtonbooks.com

DAFINA BOOKS are published by

Kensington Publishing Corp.
850 Third Avenue
New York, NY 10022

All Kensington titles, imprints and distributed lines are available at special quantity discounts for bulk purchases for sales promotion, premiums, fund-raising, educational or institutional use.

Special book excerpts or customized printings can also be created to fit specific needs. For details, write or phone the office of the Kensington Special Sales Manager: Kensington Publishing Corp., 850 Third Avenue, New York, NY 10022. Attn. Special Sales Department. Phone: 1-800-221-2647.

Dafina Books and the Dafina logo Reg. U.S. Pat. & TM Off.

ISBN-13: 978-0-7582-1937-4
ISBN-10: 0-7582-1937-7

First Kensington Trade Paperback Printing: February 2008
10 9 8 7 6 5 4 3 2 1

Printed in the United States of America

Acknowledgments

First and always, I give thanks and honor to God for allowing me to touch people through my words and for granting me the ability and desire to do it over and over again. To my readers, you make this journey worthwhile, and I thank you for showing up at signings, picking up my books and giving me your feedback. You are my inspiration!

I can never take for granted how blessed I am to have such a strong support system: Mommy, Daddy, Mr. Randolph, Lisa, Crystal, Tara, and my nieces: Morgan, Macey, Candice, and Ashley—you are my peace, my backbone, and the best family in the world. To my tight circle of good, good girlfriends, thank you for giving me more than enough material to write about! Sean, you are truly a rare man and I thank you for your love and support.

Special thanks to book clubs and reviewers for your constant support. Special thanks to Turning Pages, RAWSISTAZ, Conversations Book Club, ASIS, Circle of Women, O.O.S.A., PeoplewholoveGoodBooks, Books2Mention Magazine, APOOO.

My editor, Selena James, and the entire Kensington team: Jessica McLean, Adeola Saul, thanks for everything. My agent, Audra Barrett, thanks for helping me fulfill my dreams.

Thanks to all my good author friends: my Homie-4-Life . . . Daaimah S. Poole; my Scorpion-Twin . . . Janine A. Morris; Latrese Carter, Darren Coleman, Lissa Woodson, and so many more. It's great to have coworkers like you.

Many thanks to all the bookstores and distributors. Much love to Brother Nati and Andy from Afrikan World. You're the best!

And, as always, if I failed to mention your name, please forgive me and know that I still appreciate and love you!

1

TAYLOR

Toni and I sat on the steps outside my parents' house playing Name That Movie, a silly game that we started when
we were kids. One person would say a quote from a movie
and the other person would have to shout the title of the
movie.

She said, "No good's going to come from what you're
thinking about doing."

I laughed. "I don't know that line. What movie is that
from?"

"Knucklehead. I'm talking about what you're about to tell
Scooter."

"What should I do if I'm not happy?"

She gasped. "Taylor, you need to figure out why you're not
happy." Her eyes searched mine for an explanation. "Is it because you're getting so much attention now?"

I snapped, "No."

With an affirmative nod, she said, "You're going to regret
it. Watch."

"See, this is why I don't tell you anything. Why you always
got to judge me?"

"I'm not. I'm just trying to tell you to think about this."

"I have." An arrogant I-know-what-I'm-doing smirk sat

posed on my face momentarily. "I think I'm too young to be in a committed long-distance relationship."

"Young is relative. Maturity is the only thing that matters. Maybe Scooter's just too mature for your wild butt."

I laughed. "Why I got to be wild?"

She rolled her eyes. My family had unofficially adopted Scooter during our five-year relationship. How could I explain to him that I wanted to see other people? After three months of contemplation, I was still uncertain. It just never seemed like the right time to explain that I'd fallen victim to all the fine black men lurking on campus.

As I fretted over what to do, Toni hissed, "That's the problem with you. You don't care about anyone's feelings."

"If I didn't care about his feelings, I would just cheat on him, right?" I paused. "At least I want to break it off first."

When we noticed his car cruising into the cul-de-sac, Toni's eyes pleaded with me. If I'm not being true to myself, how will I ever be true to him? As I provoked my conscience to sympathize with my reason, I nodded. If not today, then when?

He pulled into the driveway and Toni grunted, hating the thought that I would crush Scooter's world. I tapped my knee into hers apologetically, as he stepped out of the car and walked toward us carrying a McDonald's bag. I half-heartedly hugged him. He kissed my cheek. "Hey Tay."

I sighed. "Hey."

When I sat, Toni stood to hug him. "Hey, brother."

Her eyes scolded me as she sat down. He handed me the bag. "I got sundaes for y'all."

Toni giggled. "Yea, Scooter."

He laughed and patted the top of Toni's head. He looked at me. "Are we hanging out here or do you want to go to the movies?"

"It doesn't matter. We can go to the movies."

When I stood, he admired the long, fitted cotton-striped dress that he'd given me as a just-cause gift. "I like that on you," he commented.

"Thanks."

He asked Toni if she wanted to tag along, but my expression demanded that she decline. She chuckled, and said, "Y'all go ahead. I'm okay."

I asked her to put my sundae in the freezer, as he opened the passenger side door. When I sat in the car, Toni's expression criticized me. My eyes begged for her empathy. He started the car and pinched my cheek. "I made a tape for you."

He popped the tape in and the first song to play was Tanya Blount's, "Through the Rain". Scooter sang the lyrics as if he meant every word, while he held my hand. "Through the rainy storms together. We can last." He nodded and smiled. "Gonna make it last."

I winced. *No, actually we're not.* When the song finished, I turned the stereo down. "Scooter, why do you always make stuff for me and . . ."

He looked baffled. "I've always made stuff for you. We make stuff for each other."

"What's the last thing I've made for you?"

His eyes questioned my disposition. I said, "Have you noticed I haven't wrote any poems or made any tapes since . . ."

He tapped on the brakes. "Since spring break."

I dropped my head and allowed the sting to resonate. We pulled up to the Bowie Movie Theatre. We sat in silence for a minute. My face crumbled into a sympathetic frown, pleading for his understanding.

Finally, he asked, "What's wrong?"

"Scooter, don't you think we're too young?"

His temples popped out. His silence scared me, but I forged on. "I think this long-distance thing is too much for us."

He snapped, "For who? For you?"

"It just seems like I . . ."

Tears formed in his eyes. Ooh, this wasn't going so smoothly. My eyes shifted back and forth. What the hell was I supposed to say to make this better? I frowned.

As I studied the expression in his face, I winced. Finally, the tears fell. Not one or two. An endless stream flowed down his strong jaw structure.

"Taylor, I love you."

Dumbfounded, I asked, "Don't you want to explore first?"

He snickered through his sniffles. "I guess that's what this is about. You want to explore."

"Uh-huh."

He banged on the steering wheel. "I'm on campus with a bunch of white girls. I don't want to explore. I want to be with you."

Was this all about our options? He had few. I, on the other hand, was on a campus full of fine-ass black men. My lips curled with confirmation. No one told him to go to Princeton.

"Scooter, I do. I do want to explore."

This six-foot-five boy that I loved so much wailed like a chick in the confines of his small car. Where was his pride? Although I was repulsed by this episode, I asked, "Are you okay?"

He growled, "Do I look okay?"

My eyes danced in my head. I wanted to ask if he didn't mind taking me home and we could talk about this when he was in better shape. Instead, I sat there and endured his begging. Needless to say, my stubborn ass did not surrender. The more he cried, the less I cared. *Speed on, Scooter.*

The propellers of my ceiling fan played episodes of my immature stupidity. The aroma of a humid summer's eve and an insect symphony outside my patio door contributed to my delusions. My contact lenses blurred as I watched my life play out before me.

In less than three hours, my ten-year class reunion would take place. Anticipation left my restless body fatigued. In the midst of my daydream, the phone resting on the pillow startled me as it rang in my ear. I jumped up. "Hello."

My partner-in-crime sang into the phone, "Make me loose my breath."

I giggled. "Girl, turn that music down."

"Whatchu doing?"

"Just lying here."

Courtney huffed. "Girl, you better start getting ready."

"I am."

"What are you doing?"

"What are you doing?" I snapped.

She chuckled. "Trying to get Mark's ass to stay home."

"You're crazy. Here I am, wanting to pay somebody to go with me, just so I don't look desperate and your crazy butt wants to leave your fiancé at home."

"Girl, you never turn down meeting ops."

"You're stupid."

"I'm honest." She chuckled sneakily, adding, "Hell, I'm single until I tie the knot."

"No, whore. The theory is you're single until you get the ring."

She laughed. "Yeah, whatever. I'll let you know if he's coming or not. Either way, I'll be there at nine."

A piece of me prayed he'd decide not to come. I didn't want to be a part of the threesome strolling into the reunion.

My body peeled up from the bed. No more dress rehearsals. The full stage production approached. The tangerine-and-coral satin dress pinned neatly on the dry cleaner's hanger decorated my closet door. I looked at it for the millionth time. When I first tried it on and when I tried it on an hour ago, it fit perfectly. Still, I hoped it made the impression that the $300 price tag made in my pocket.

After I showered and flat-ironed my ear-length layered flip, I stood in front of my dress once again. Courtney would be here in about thirty minutes, but I was scared to have more time than necessary to critique the finished product. Instead, I played with makeup for twenty-five minutes. Putting on my false eyelashes took longer than expected, but I was still on schedule. Finally, I washed my hands and stepped into my strapless dress. While I zipped up the side, I sucked in my already flat belly and stepped over to the full-length mirror.

The subtle sparkles from my lotion glistened on my full cleavage. My makeup added to the striking effect of the dress. The zigzag hem complemented my long get-it-from-my-mama legs. I winked at the five-foot-nine cutie staring back at me.

Courtney rang the doorbell and interrupted my self-absorption. I took a second to slip on my four-inch strappy sandals. Then, I rushed to the door, peeping at anything resembling a mirror. When I opened the door, I was careful not to rub up against it. Standing nearly six inches below me, Courtney reached her arms out for a hug. Midstream in the embrace, she adjusted the straps of her tight black spaghetti-strap dress. Bronze sparkles glistened on her pale skin.

I warned her, "Be careful girl. Don't get any makeup on your dress."

Courtney batted her lashes, obviously proud that she could glue them on as well. "Trust me. I won't."

Simultaneously, we sang, "Damn chica, you look good."

After hanging around someone for fourteen years, it's second nature to speak the same words together. We laughed.

"You look real bronze," I commented.

"It's this Neutrogena Sunless Tanning."

Like galloping horses, we strutted across my hardwood floors. "I guess you made Mark stay home."

"I told him he probably wouldn't enjoy himself."

We laughed. "You are no damn good."

She tossed my clutter around. "When are you ever going to clean this messy room?"

"When I marry Dr. Evans and stop practicing law."

Courtney plopped down on my bed without a response. She kicked her heels up on the wicker trunk at the foot of my bed pretending to admire her reflection. Then, as if she could no longer restrain her thoughts, she jumped up and walked into the bathroom. She stood beside me. Ignoring her inquisitive eyes, I patted my lips together and used my pinky to fix a makeup mistake.

"Taylor, I hope you haven't filled your mind with fantasies of hooking up with Scooter."

Attempting to minimize my obvious anticipation, I chuckled carelessly. "No girl, I'm not stupid."

She folded her chiseled arms, "Yeah, but I know you did your research," she said.

She knew me all too well. From preliminary research, he was no one's daddy or husband. He was in his third year of residency at Yale Medical Center. The big question was, is he still single? And not Courtney's interpretation of single.

"Look, I'm taking all numbers tonight. I'm not tripping about Scooter."

I shrugged my shoulders and flicked my fingers through my hair. Despite my show of aloofness, she continued, "You still feel like there's unfinished business, right?"

I sighed and exited the bathroom. "Not really."

She followed, as I headed into my walk-in closet to get my purse. "Whatever, Taylor. You need to stop faking. Remember *I* was the one Scooter cried to when you left him. Remember *I* was the one you cried to when he got over your ass. If you remember, you two never told each other how you felt."

As to confirm the answer to what was supposed to be a question, she proclaimed, "There is unfinished business."

She stood in the doorway with her hand on her hip. I returned the gesture. Face to face, she wanted me to confess. Instead, I brushed past her. "Girl, I'm not trippin'."

As she compiled her case, I checked all the electrical appliances. I turned the light off in the bathroom. "So, how are we going to close this chapter of your life tonight?"

I giggled. "Girl, whatever, we're going to have a good time."

I headed for the stairs. She followed and made her closing argument. "All right chica, don't say I didn't try to help you when you get there and loose your cool."

I giggled again. This time because I knew she was probably more afraid of me loosing my cool than me. For her sake, I reminded her that I would not forget the ground rules we set in tenth grade. Before we walked out the door, I smiled at her and said, "Rule number one: Always be cool."

As if I'd lifted my foot from her chest, she sighed and together we said, "Rule number two: If you think you've lost your cool, refer back to rule number one."

She bumped her side against mine. "All right chica, all eyes are on you."

I kidded. "Lights, cameras, action."

2

TAYLOR

When we pulled up to the Newton White Mansion, cars laced every inch of the parking lot. Courtney had the 5 Series sparkling. I felt like a diamond, even though I didn't have one propped on my finger. Courtney opted to remove her ring. I was tempted to rent a ring so I wouldn't have to endure the sympathetic expressions that I get when people find out that I'm still single.

As we waited in line for the car to be parked, we were trying to recognize people going inside. Courtney pointed. "Ooh girl, that's Yolanda." She winced and added, "Damn. She's huge."

I laughed. "Ooh, look at her. She was in the honors program with us. What's her name?"

Courtney laughed. "I don't know, but she's big too."

We amused ourselves as we pointed out all the people that had fallen off. Somehow a part of me needed to know that others failed in areas that I hadn't.

A muscular white guy, wearing a yellow T-shirt labeled VALET finally found his way to our car. He opened Courtney's door. When I put my hand on the handle, my heart sank. I took a deep breath and stepped out.

As we trudged onto our virtual red carpet, we heard others making similar observations. "Is that Taylor? That's Courtney.

They look the same. Do they still hang together?" As my eyes searched for Scooter, the photographer practically shoved us up to the background and snapped the flash.

Scooter's old football teammates guarded the entrance like bouncers. I hoped their quarterback stood in the midst of their huddle. I quickly gravitated toward them. We hugged the guys. Courtney gave unemotional hugs. I gave anticipatory hugs, hoping the next arms to circumvent me would be those of Scooter Evans. As I wrapped my arms around the final guy, I peeped behind him and there was no Scooter. My eyes wandered in circles as the guys shouted flattering praises to us.

"Damn, y'all still fine."

"Y'all still the smartest, finest chicks I know."

"Look at the paid-ass attorneys."

"How y'all still in shape? Everyone else has blown up!"

We walked into the foyer of the mansion and stood in an endless line to get name tags. My eyes scoped every inch of the room. When I glanced up the stairs in the middle of the foyer, he stepped down. Scooter. My heart thumped, and my nerves began to percolate. His black slacks fell neatly on the top of his shoes. I tugged Courtney's arm. With my teeth clenched together, I mumbled, "Oh my God, Courtney. Do you see who I see?"

She nodded nonchalantly. Her expression said, "I told you so."

I sucked my teeth and rolled my eyes, saying, "You make me sick."

She didn't acknowledge my hysteria. My insides were flipped upside down. As if it would help, she mumbled, "Rule number one."

Before she could finish, I gasped. The last thing I could think about were a couple of childish rules.

My heart sank deeper as he neared the bottom of the stairway. My head drooped lower and lower. I closed my eyes and said a silent prayer.

Finally, I lifted my head. His looks startled me. The cute

boy was now a handsome man. His tall slim body had transformed into lean bulk. I gasped for air and quickly dropped my head again. I took a deep breath, inhaling a dose of courage. Then, I raised my head. Finally I was ready to face the love of my life. I looked left. I looked right. Scooter was gone.

Courtney shook her head as if she was already disappointed in my actions. I huffed anxiously, hoping the line would hurry. Before I began biting my nails, I stepped out of line. Heck, whomever I wanted to see should know my damn name. Courtney called out for me, as I stormed away.

When I rushed into the dining area, he stood there. I inhaled his presence. Detecting me in his peripheral vision, he turned and smiled. I smiled nervously. He smirked. His facial expression intimidated me. As the space between us disappeared, so did my words.

I stood face-to-face with the only man I have loved in my twenty-eight years on this earth. He grabbed me and hugged me tightly. Momentarily the embrace settled the volcano erupting inside of me. He pulled back, held both of my arms out. He smiled and shook his head as if to grant his approval.

"Taylor, Taylor, Taylor . . ."

Still lost for words, I followed his lead. "Scooter, Scooter, Scooter . . ."

"Tay-Bae."

"Scootie-Boo."

We burst into laughter as we reminisced on our teenage pet names. He complimented me, "Girl, I'm not surprised that you are still fine as hell."

Hoping he was flirting, I blushed. He quickly jumped into superficial conversation.

"How's the Bishop?"

"He's still the same."

"Your mom? Your sisters?"

"Everyone's good. Toni got married like six years ago. She has two kids." I smirked, acknowledging that we all knew that she'd get married early. "And Turi is in Atlanta."

"We used to have fun in Zion Temple."

Not wanting to remember all the sins I committed in my daddy's church, I smirked. "Shut up!"

Trying to lead on that there has been no one of significance since our breakup, I said, "You know my daddy still asks about you . . ."

He nodded. "Bishop was my man."

Hoping to keep him in a reminiscent mood, I added, "Yeah, he was definitely grooming you for the ministry."

He smiled proudly. "I ain't mad. He wanted his girls to be with God-fearing men."

"I know. He's funny. You know Toni's husband is a minister."

"What?"

"And Turi's getting her Masters in Divinity at Emory and she's dating a guy in the program." I shrugged my shoulders. "So, chances are."

He smiled as if he were proud of my youngest sister's accomplishments. "Yeah, I was watching your dad's broadcast and he mentioned that Turi was going to Divinity School."

"You still watch daddy's sermons?"

"Whenever I can catch it, I definitely watch. He always has an inspirational word."

I smirked. "You're right. Whenever I can catch it, I watch it too."

We both laughed. He put his hand on my shoulder. "Taylor, you don't go to your father's church anymore?"

I wrinkled my nose. "On holidays."

"That's a shame. I'm not surprised though. You've always been the rebel," he said, laughing.

Directing conversation away from the imperfect girl with the perfect family, I asked, "So, how are your parents?"

"They're good."

I paused, waiting for him to say they asked about me too, but he didn't. He nodded. I nodded. We exchanged smiles.

Neither of us said a word. The thoughts of his parents rewound us back to our last encounter.

When I'd returned to school that fall after the breakup, I quickly learned that bad boys are called that for a reason. By December, I wanted the big crybaby back. I sent letters to no avail. Out of desperation, I showed up at his family's home on Christmas Eve. His parents hosted an annual party, and I was certain they'd all be glad to see me.

I rang the doorbell and his Aunt Cynthia was the first to greet me. She stuttered, "Hello, Taylor. How are you?"

Her words were cold, but I didn't think much of it. I invited myself in. Everyone in the room paused. Even the kids stopped running around. I waved. "Merry Christmas, family!"

The realization that I was no longer a member of the family was immediately obvious when only a few people mumbled a response to my greeting. They looked at me as if I were an intruder. Scooter gave me a blank stare and walked into the kitchen. My eyes followed him, but the bodyguards sitting around the living room told me my feet better not bother.

His mom sat propped on the edge of the couch, staring at me like I was a mistress who crashed her party. Her wrinkled fingers grasped tightly on a small goblet. She swirled her drink. Her dark lips turned upside down. Feeling the need to make a U-turn, I crossed one foot over the other. She cleared her throat, "Taylor, what are you doing here?" she asked.

Six months prior I referred to this woman as Mommy. Now, she was glaring at me like I was a traitor. Suddenly, I questioned my own presence and began to back up. She stood. Her war stance affirmed that I was standing on enemy ground. My back leaned against the foggy glass door. Mrs. Evans forged toward me. I stumbled out of the door and she came out with me.

In a disgusted tone, she said, "Taylor, you don't belong here."

"I—"

"My son did not deserve to be treated like that."

I flinched as she got closer.

"Your parents raised you better than to have no remorse for people's feelings."

I stuttered, "I'm sorry. I . . ."

She pointed her finger. "When my baby went back to school, he couldn't even concentrate. He wasn't eating. He wasn't sleeping. Depressed over your fast ass." Sprinkles of spit smacked me in the face. "When I saw his midterm grades, this became personal."

She stepped closer to me and my eyes bugged out of my head. Her arm sprang up and I quickly ducked. When I didn't feel the effect of the blow, I peeped up to find her posed as if she were pledging to God not to kill me. Seconds passed and the ready-to-fight rumble barked in my belly. Finally, she pumped the palm of her hand into the air and blew out some frustration before she continued. "I ain't paying twenty-five thousand dollars a year for some floozy to break his heart and make him flunk out of school. I told him to stay as far away from you as possible."

I began to cry. "Mrs. Evans, I didn't mean it. I—"

"You don't deserve my son's friendship. He has been a loyal friend to you and you just stomped all over his poor little heart. You are evil."

Scooter never came out of the house to rescue me. She stormed back in, leaving me out in the cold. That was the last time I'd seen Scooter, and that encounter has haunted me ever since.

He interrupted my daze, "Yeah, they ask about you from time to time."

I wanted to jump up and down, hoping his mother didn't still think I was some evil witch. "Really?"

"Yeah, they always talk about how much I used to love Taylor Jabowski."

I took that opportunity to segue into my plan of action, "I loved you, too."

"Not as much as I loved you."

I laughed, saying, "What do you mean? I did love you."

"Man, you played me."

"I didn't play you."

He laughed and gave me an I'll-catch-you-later hug. "Yes, you did, but you made me the man that I am, and I still love you for it."

Just like that, he walked away. He didn't give me a chance to spill my heart and ask him if he'd be willing to consider an intimate relationship. It was late in the third-quarter in the game of love and happiness. Thirty was coming fast and Scooter was one of the few good men standing. My bottom lip drooped as I watched the game clock time out.

Courtney walked up behind me, "Girl, shake it off. You look stunned."

Didn't I deserve more? Or were the five years from freshmen year of high school through freshmen year of college just that insignificant?

Courtney grabbed my lifeless hand, "Let's go to the bar and get a drink."

"Okay."

As we walked, Courtney whispered through clenched teeth, "Taylor, you have to chill. You look like you don't even want to be here. We look too good for this."

I rolled my eyes. "Courtney, whatever."

The smell of old books distracted me momentarily as we wandered past a library. After playing bumper cars with our bodies to squeeze through a narrow passage, we arrived at the open bar. I sighed. Every second or so, Courtney would look up at me and chuckle. Finally a cocoa-colored bartender greeted me.

"What do you need gorgeous?"

Courtney chimed in, "Advice."

I smiled thinly and checked his name tag. "Magnus. I do not need advice."

She put her hand on her hip. "Magnus, yes she does."

Others hovered over our shoulders and shouted their desires. "Two Coronas." "Remy." "Patrón."

I huffed. "No, I don't."

She giggled, "Don't get all feisty with me. You know you need advice."

As we had our mini-spat, Magnus served others and ignored our call for help. I needed something strong to counter the effects of rejection.

"Magnus, I need Grey Goose and lime juice. More goose and less juice."

We all laughed at my corny line. Courtney pushed her body into mine, trying to apologize for upsetting me. I pouted a little and added, "Hit her off with the same." I smirked. "Maybe then she won't be able to pay attention to what I'm doing."

Courtney said, "Actually, Magnus, since we're celebrating our class reunion, I think I'll have something with Crown Royal in it."

"Crown Royal?" I snapped.

"Don't act like we didn't used to sneak my father's Crown Royal and ginger ale."

"I guess you're right, but that's not exactly what I had in mind," I said, half-heartedly.

She slightly rocked side to side to the beat of the music. Her head nodded in unison as she said, "I don't know about you, but I'm taking it back to the roots."

Magnus monitored our spat, and impatiently offered a solution. "I make a drink that I call the Royal Red Apple Martini."

Both of our necks snapped in his direction and he explained, "It's Crown Royal, Sour Apple Schnapps, and Cranberry Juice." His eyes shifted from me to Courtney and back again. "Does that sound like something you'd like?"

I winked at Magnus. "You know what, maybe going back to my roots will help me out tonight. Hook me up."

Courtney shrugged in agreement and Magnus' shoulders relaxed making him appear a little less agitated. Maybe he was just thankful that we'd come to a decision. Before we could change our minds, Magnus was mixing, shifting from hand to hand, shaking, and pouring. In a matter of seconds, he handed us our much-anticipated drinks in disposable martini glasses. I took a sip and looked at Courtney as she put it up to her lips. Our smiles became all-out grins as there was no doubt that we'd discovered our signature drink for the night. Courtney's bob-haircut swung around as she shouted, "This is slammin!"

I reached in my gold clutch purse and put five bucks in the tip jar. Magnus swirled the remainder in the shaker. Assuming that he was offering to put it in my glass, I gulped down enough to make room for more. He poured the rest and it nearly hit the rim. "Thanks Magnus," I said.

I raised my thumb at Magnus, deeming him my best friend for the evening. After a few more sips, I was convinced that the Royal Red Apple was clearly my new drink of choice. When it was gone, I turned to Magnus and told him to shake me up another one. Courtney said, "See, I told you Crown Royal is what we needed."

Magnus said, "I'm glad you like it."

"Well, I love Crown Royal. It's my father's drink. He swears that black people need to drink dark liquor, because white liquor makes you crazy," Courtney said and Magnus' eyes wandered aimlessly, as she continued to invite him in on my dilemma. "And I need her to be as sane as possible."

"Courtney, please leave Magnus alone so he can hurry up and make the drinks."

Courtney shook her head at me. She wasn't feeling what I felt, and not to mention she was the designated driver, so I ignored her insinuation that I should slow down. My desperation for the drinks to soak up my emotions was successfully relayed, because this time Magnus handed me two glasses and I rewarded him with another five-dollar tip. My eyes toured the room to check if anyone else noticed my rapid consumption of alcohol. No one cared.

We played the whole happy-to-see-you game with everyone that came to the bar. After standing around and noticing everyone else wearing rings and introducing their husbands, I peeped over and found Courtney slipping her band on. What happened to the damn single-and-satisfied attitude she instructed me to adopt? Maybe she was tired of the questions that I'd become tired of hearing?

Married? Any kids? No and no. I ordered another drink and decided to keep count of how many times I was asked. Okay, I'm on number eighteen. Finally, I slapped my left hand on my forehead. Would that stop them from asking? Nope. Then, they began to ask, "Do you have a headache?"

Even the single men brought dates. Did pairing up somehow mean you succeeded in life? Luckily, I had yet to see Scooter's date as I observed him congregating with his friends. Hearty laughter escaped their circle. Were we the only two without a date? My neck turned back and forth scrutinizing my graduating class.

People seemed sincerely happy to see me. Wishing I had more to talk about than my prestigious job, I made general statements about my life thus far. Although I didn't mention it, they still asked. I was on number twenty-seven. Why do people ask stupid questions?

As I contemplated how I could kidnap Scooter from his friends, in walks this tall brown-skinned woman. She had high cheekbones and small Asian-shaped eyes. Her hair was in a short, boy cut. I was immediately jealous. Maybe it was my intuition. She headed toward Scooter's crew and she kissed my man directly on the mouth. As if my brain was no longer in control of my motor skills, I needed someone to pull the plug. My bottom lip hung loosely. My shoulders sagged. If not for pride, I would have stormed out of the reunion.

I pinched Courtney, who was having a perfectly fulfilling conversation with an ugly duckling turned hunk.

She screeched, "Ouch!"

"Come on. We have to go in this room."

She frowned. "Why?" she asked.

My eyes begged her. Reluctantly, she followed. "Did you see that?"

"What?" She paused and put her hands on her hips. "First of all, calm down."

"I think Scooter has a date."

Irritated at my naiveté, she huffed, "Did you think he wouldn't?"

"You're right. I guess I got excited when it looked like he didn't have one."

We stepped onto the dance floor and camouflaged my disappointment with our rendition of Salt 'n' Pepa. The DJ was spinning all the high school hits. As we bobbed and weaved, did the cabbage patch and raised the roof, I almost forgot that I had no date. That is, until he mixed the slow jams. My head hung. Courtney laughed, "Whatever, remember we used to slow dance like this."

She wrapped her arms around herself and turned her back to me. Her hands sensually touched her shoulders to simulate they belonged to her dance partner. I followed her lead. We giggled and slow danced solo. She gave doses of encouragement, saying, "Don't feel bad about being here alone. Half of the married assholes are miserable. At least you're happy."

"You got that right."

Mary J. Blige's "I Never Wanna Live Without You" pumped through the speakers. Scooter tapped my shoulder, and asked, "Excuse me. Can I cut in?"

I pouted. "Your girlfriend doesn't mind?"

"Well, she's not here. And I won't tell, if you won't tell."

"Why are you lying? I just saw you kiss her."

"You just saw me kiss Phil's wife. She went to medical school with me."

I unfolded my arm barrier. He laughed, and said, "You are so crazy."

When he wrapped his arm around me, he asked, "Where's your date? I'm not trying to get into a scuffle."

"I didn't bring a date," I huffed.

"You're still a player."

No! I mean let me correct that. "I didn't have anyone to bring," I said.

"You expect me to believe that." I nodded, and he continued. "You probably didn't have anyone you wanted to bring, but I'm sure someone would have loved to come with you."

How could I explain that the market wasn't that good anymore? I just shrugged my shoulders. He held me close. We grinded to the song. I could feel the beat of his heart. Hoping to interpret each beat, I leaned closer. When the song ended, he grabbed my hand and we walked into the lounge area. We both grabbed a shot from one of the hostesses' trays. I gulped down the shot of vodka and grabbed a lemon. My lips puckered and I made a sour face. Scooter shook his head. "You haven't changed."

I silently yelled, *No! I really have changed. Now, I know how to appreciate a good guy.*

I placed the shot glass back on the tray and repeated the process, hoping that two shots would give me the courage to say all the things that I'd waited nine years to say.

He was first to sit. Slightly stumbling, I immediately followed. I scooted my hips close to him and he wrapped his arm around me.

"Scooter, do you remember how close we used to be?" I asked.

He laughed, not like he was laughing with me, but rather at my dumb-ass recollection. "Yep. I remember. We were way too young to be that serious."

"I know, but do you think it was real?"

"Taylor, I know it was real. At least it was for me."

"Do you ever think about how things would have been if we'd stayed together?"

"Not really."

He lifted his arm, disconnecting our closeness. He readjusted and folded his hands on his lap. "I used to," he added.

"When did you stop?"

Taking a deep breath, he said, "When I realized that it just wasn't meant to be."

I sighed. "Scooter, I think it was."

"Trust me, it wasn't. If we didn't break up when we did, it would have happened sooner or later. We were five hundred miles apart."

We sat in silence for a moment. I asked, "Scooter, how many times have you been in love since we broke up?"

Without hesitation, he responded. "Once."

Before I could ask my next question, he cut in, "And you?"

My answer wasn't so simple. "Scooter, I never stopped loving you. I haven't been in love since. I've been practically single since the moment I told you it was over. And I . . ."

He interrupted my confession, "Taylor, you still got game."

I waved my hand. "I'm not saying I haven't been in relationships." Laughing at myself. "Too many to count, but I haven't been in love. Hell, I haven't been in a relationship longer than sixty days."

He laughed, saying, "Sixty days?"

Embarrassed, I nodded.

"Damn, Tay-Bae."

I blushed. "Yeah. It's rough."

He put his hand on my knee. "Are your expectations too high?"

"Maybe." I paused. "No one has measured up to you."

"Taylor, don't play games with me."

"I'm serious."

"You must be kidding me."

I looked at him. "No, I'm not. I think about us all the time. I feel like if I could rewind the hands of time, we would be together. Or . . . if . . . you . . ." My words slowly exited my mouth, because I didn't know what I really wanted to say. "Still feel the way I—"

He placed his index finger over my lip, "But it's too late."

I pleaded, "Why?"

"Because I don't move backward and I really don't want to think about something that happened so long ago." He placed his hand on my entangled fingers. "Let's go have a drink for old-time sake."

"Scooter, I have waited nine years to let you know how I feel."

He stood up, clearly acknowledging that he wasn't interested. "It couldn't have been that serious if you could wait nine years to say it," he said.

He took a few steps and I shuffled behind him, "Scooter, I was afraid."

His smirk dismissed my sincere plea, "Are you trying to have fun or are you trying to sit here and reminisce all night?"

He swiftly walked away from me. Feelings of regret fluttered in my tummy. I needed to vomit. I felt like a fool trying to resolve issues from a high school relationship. I rushed to the bar to search for Courtney. After practically snatching her away from Dexter again, I recruited her to the dance floor.

As we two-stepped to the old-school hits, she laughed at me. "I don't believe you played yourself like that."

"I figure he's here alone. I'm here alone. I was thinking maybe it was a sign."

"I knew it. I know you like a book."

I curled my lips. "He's the only guy I ever loved."

"And."

"And I figured we could probably hook up again."

She shook her head. I shrugged my shoulders. Though I fronted for my girl, my feelings were hurt. After pretending that I was exhausted, I convinced Courtney that we should go. My reunion wasn't what I dreamed it would be. My confession made me feel worse. I should have just shut the hell up. But, no! I go in for the kill. Of all songs to be playing as we headed to the door was Biz Markie's "You Caught the Vapors."

Courtney looked at me and we burst into laughter. Just as I pulled the doorknob, Scooter pulled my arm. "Tay-Bae, where you going?"

"Home."

Courtney stepped out the door. "See you outside." She smiled at Scooter. "Good seeing you again. Keep doing your thing."

He smiled. "Okay, Courtney. Take care."

"What's wrong, Tay-Bae?"

Abandoning all dignity, I confessed, "I must look stupid."

He frowned at me. "Why?"

"I guess because I wanted more from our reunion."

He pointed back and forth between us. "*Our* reunion?" I nodded. We laughed and he said, "Like what?"

"I hoped you'd be single, too. I hoped you'd ask me out. I hoped you hadn't loved anyone else either."

He pulled me to him, his hands cupping my elbows. He looked in my eyes. "Taylor, it took me a long time to get over you. It took me a long time to love someone else. I didn't get into another relationship until I was in Medical School." He sighed. "I swore I would never love another woman ever again. Then, I grew up. I couldn't hold what you did against all women."

He continued, "I'm in love with a good girl now." As if he heard my heart shatter, he said, "Taylor, I will always love you. I always have."

I hugged him one last time. Our lips were reacquainted. He pushed his tongue into my mouth and passionately swirled it around. The consistent thrashing of his tongue sent chills up my spine. I snatched away and rapidly walked toward the valet. With a bewildered look on his face, he let me go. Neither of us was prepared for what hid behind our lip-lock. He waved. I stood at the bottom step, watching him disappear into the party.

3

SCOOTER

The vestibule of Zion Temple was in full swing when I entered the church. Like two opposing football teams, the congregation transitioned from people entering for 9:30 service and those exiting 7:30. Once I fought my way into the sanctuary, I saw Taylor. She was even sexy wearing her usher uniform. She waved anxiously. I waved back.

She blew a kiss. I nodded. She sent another message using sign language. Her persistence that we master the art of sign language was solely for this purpose. Her graceful hand gestures were more distinct in her white church-lady gloves. She said, "Hello, handsome."

I responded, "How are you beautiful?"

"Dreaming of you."

She communicated a poem while we patiently waited for the crowd between us to disperse. Finally, we stood eye to eye. Her sparkly braces beamed into my glasses. We stood speechless, admiring one another as if we hadn't seen each other just hours ago. Spurred by the passion rising between us, she grabbed my hand. "C'mon. Let's go downstairs into the fellowship hall."

People seemed to make a pathway for us. Taylor pulled me into the kitchen of the fellowship hall and kissed me. Her fearless spontaneity sucked the strength from me. She owned my heart. Fireworks crackled in my pants. Self-conviction forced me to end the connection with a small peck. She smiled.

In the midst of the commotion surrounding me, I day-dreamed of the young girl who sparked flames in me the way no other woman has been capable of since. I sighed. Boy, did I miss the good ole days when love was so trivial. Until her soft lips touched mine two nights ago, these memories were buried.

Tackling my way into the sanctuary, I sat down ten pews from the front. After reviewing the program, I looked up to find Taylor's mom waving at me. I waved back. She constantly peeped at me throughout the service. Her anxious expression screamed that she needed to talk to me. I mouthed, "I'll see you after church."

She nodded, but didn't stop turning around every fifty seconds. I'd smile each time our eyes connected. After a while, Toni, Taylor's older sister peeped from the choir stand to see what was causing her mother's distraction. Her huge smile embraced me. I smiled back.

When Bishop said the benediction, Mrs. Jabowski nearly leaped over the crowd to come and hug me. She touched my face delicately. "You look so good, Scooter." Tears welled in her eyes. "Where are you now?"

"I'm in Connecticut at Yale."

She shook her head, asking, "What are you doing at Yale?"

"I'm an anesthesiology resident."

She smiled. "So, you went to Medical School?"

I nodded. Releasing air from her lungs, she squealed, "I'm so proud of you. You know Taylor graduated from GW Law. She works for the Train Workers' Union." She nodded. "Labor law."

"I know. We actually had our class reunion on Friday night."

She raised her eyebrows. "You know Taylor's so secretive."

That was weird. The Taylor I remember told everything. One of the deacons went over to the speaker. "Please make your way out of the sanctuary so the eleven-thirty people can come in."

She grabbed my arm. "C'mon. We have to go speak to Bishop."

She towed me through the crowd. As we traveled through a quiet hallway, leading to the pastor's study, Toni ran up behind us. She sang, "Scooter."

I hugged her. The Jabowski girls were all slim as toothpicks. Their boney knees replayed in my mind. As I recalled their weekly dances, I chuckled. Taylor would do the choreography and the troop would sing to me. As we rocked back and forth, I laughed. "SWV."

Mrs. Jabowski stood impatiently while we reminisced. Toni laughed. "You're crazy boy. You still remember that."

"Yep." Sweeping my arms left and right, I imitated the Jabowski sisters, "I get so weak in the knees. I can hardly sleep."

Mrs. Jabowski interrupted our laughter. "Toni, I'm taking him to see your daddy. We have to hurry, before eleven-thirty service starts."

Toni hugged me again. "Okay, brother."

That evoked more memories. This was my family. "Okay, sister."

She waved and turned to walk in the opposite direction. "Keep in contact, Scooter. We miss you."

"Okay. I will."

I didn't tell her that I missed them too. When we stood at the pastor's study, my heart thumped. Trying to calm the rumble in my stomach, I took a deep breath. Could I feel the power of the man behind the door? He was the reason I was so committed at such a young age. Either you treated his girls like princesses or you had to step. After thirty seconds or so, the door swung open and the overweight man that I thought was larger than life was even larger up close. I stretched my arms out. "Bishop."

"Scooter?"

Mrs. Jabowski nodded. "Honey, this is now Dr. Evans."

He draped his arms around me. The sleeves of his robe hung down my back, as he began to pray silently. He thanked God for me. After telling me how proud and happy he was to see me, he was forced to rush back into the church. Their love revived suppressed emotions.

Bishop left us standing in the hall and Mrs. Jabowski wouldn't stop smiling at me. She asked, "Are you married, Scooter?"

I shook my head. She cackled, "Oh, goodie."

"I have a girlfriend, though."

She nodded, but didn't acknowledge what I said. "Did you and Taylor exchange information?"

"Actually, we didn't."

"Why don't you give her a call while you're here?"

I was skeptical of Taylor's single proclamation, but her mom's anxiousness squashed all doubt. "Actually, I will. Can you give me her number?"

She dug in her purse for a pen. I chuckled and opened my cell phone. "I can just put it in here."

She rambled off Taylor's home and cell number. I entered the information. *Definitely no man.* What happened? How could Taylor Jabowski still be single?

4

TAYLOR

Shortly after one in the afternoon, the phone rang. I stretched over to the nightstand to read the caller ID. My jaw nearly dropped to the floor. My eyes stretched in amazement. I pinched myself to confirm that I wasn't dreaming and I took a deep breath. "Hello."

After a long pause, he said quietly, "Tay-Bae."

I looked up in the air and mouthed. "Thank you, Lord." I smiled and replied, "Scooter."

He chuckled slightly. "I just got your number from your Mom."

"My mother?"

"She still has the same number. Right?"

Thank God. I blushed. "You're right. When did you call her? She leaves for church at . . ."

"The same time she went to church ten years ago."

"So, how did you—"

He cut me off, saying, "I went to nine-thirty service and—"

"You saw her there."

Surely this wasn't his first visit home. What made him stop by Zion Temple today? I held the phone tightly, awaiting his next sentence. His next breath. Maybe I wasn't losing my mind. Maybe we did share something more than puppy love.

He continued, "You've been on my mind since Friday and I . . ."

I sighed. I prayed. I imagined that he wanted me. He needed me. He missed me.

Then he finished, "I want to hook up before I leave on Tuesday."

I bit my bottom lip. As much as I wanted this, I didn't know what to say. I stumbled over my thoughts. "Uh, um." I slowly rolled out, "So when are you trying to hook up?"

"I'm chillin'. I don't have much on my schedule. You tell me."

Internally, I shouted. *Today! Right now! Hell, five minutes ago!* But my mouth spoke, "Um, tonight and tomorrow are both good for me."

My nerves tingled because I felt him smile. "That sounds like a plan. Let's shoot pool for old-time sake."

My overactive emotions wanted to have candlelight dinner and talk about the future. Instead, I obliged.

"I haven't been in the area for a minute. Where's a good place to go?" he asked.

Hmmm. I pondered. I mumbled, "There's a place in Arundel Mills, Dave and Buster's."

"Oh yeah, I went there with some of the fellas a while back."

Confused as to how I should proceed, I asked, "Do you want to meet there, or would you like to come here first?"

He paused. "I'll come through your spot first. We can go together." He chuckled, obviously recognizing my nervousness. "Is that cool?"

"Yeah, that should be fine."

"I hope you don't have some dude hiding in the bushes," he kidded.

Flattered by his insinuation of jealously, I smiled and sucked my teeth. "Boy, please."

We both laughed, and he finalized the plans. "So, I'll come through around eight. I'll call to get the directions when I'm on my way."

I stood up to browse through my closet before I said goodbye. "I'm actually not far from my parents."

"You're still in Bowie."

"Yeah, right off of 450."

"That should be easy. I'll call you anyway."

After I hung a few tops over my arm, I grabbed my infamous Citizens for Humanity Kelly-Cut jeans. They were the best of low-rise, adequately covering my cotton-picking booty. I dumped the tops on my bed and began playing dress up. My final selection was a black shirt that drooped off the shoulder, one of those that could be dressed up or dressed down. With my outfit perfected, I danced anxiously around the room to the music in my head. I plopped down on my bed, bounced up and down, and chanted, "I'm going out with Scooter. Out with Scooter."

My juvenile behavior forced me to laugh. I contemplated calling Courtney, but I refrained. Instead, I gloated in my own excitement until it was time.

I stepped out of the shower around seven-thirty. My heart thumped with anticipation. When I finally stood at the mirror, polished from head to toe, I began to feel silly.

The bell rang and startled me. My knees buckled. "Oh my God!"

Coaxing my nervous system to simmer down, I meditated. *Just breathe. Be cool. Don't trip. Act normal.* Without further hesitation, I skedaddled down the stairs. My fists were balled tightly to dry the sweat. With my hand clamped on the doorknob, I took one more deep breath. Rhythmically, I exhaled and slowly turned my wrist. I paused. I prayed. The door creaked open. Scooter smiled. I melted. He wore jeans, a polo shirt, and a pair of Pumas.

He opened his arms and stepped toward me. Our bodies

met. He wrapped his arms around me, "Are you going to invite me in or what?"

His presence made me speechless. I inhaled and trapped his scent in my lungs. Afraid to let go, I swallowed. How was I going to survive the whole evening? Finally I was resuscitated and exhaled, "C'mon in."

He ended our embrace and walked in. He paced in short steps around the living room, commenting, "So this is how you're livin'?"

He nodded approvingly. Then, he put his hand out to give me five. "You're doing all right Ms. Jabowski."

He was calm, composed. I stood bashful and nervous in my own home. To alleviate the awkwardness, I asked if he wanted a drink. He shook his head no. Still, I rushed into the kitchen and mixed my version of the Royal Red Apple Martini. I took a gulp and asked casual questions from afar. "So, have you had a good weekend?"

He responded with one-word answers. "Yeah."

"What did you do?"

"Nothing."

"Did you hang out with any of your old friends?"

"No."

I slipped past him. As I scampered up the steps, I announced, "I have to grab my purse. I'll be back."

I glanced in the mirror again and sprayed Gucci perfume on my hot spots. I mouthed, "Taylor, work your magic."

After taking a few more gulps of my drink, I touched up my makeup. Then, I skipped down the stairs and put my glass in the sink. My body was warm, but I tried to remain cool. "Okay. I'm ready."

He opened the front door and pointed. "You first."

Indecisively, I stepped toward him, than backward. He chuckled. "Um, I'm trying to remember if I put my keys in my purse. Uh. You go ahead out. I need to set the alarm."

He smiled and stepped out of the door, closing it behind

him. I took another deep breath before setting the alarm. Then, I stepped out of the house and admired him standing patiently at the end of my walkway. When I got closer to him, I noticed his old car. "Oh my God. You still have Shameka."

Shameka was a 1991 charcoal Honda Civic that Scooter's parents bought him the summer before senior year. Scooter smiled and shook his head. "I can't get rid of Shameka." He tapped the hood. "This is my baby girl."

"Yeah, she was always number one."

He punched my cheek softly, and said, "Whatever. You were number one."

"Are we driving Shameka?"

"Hell yeah, we're driving Shameka."

Shameka was spotless. "Did you drive this car from Connecticut?"

He stopped and looked at me as if I'd smoked some weed. "Girl, my father takes care of Shameka. He keeps her clean for when I visit."

When he started the car, the engine hesitated a little. I raised my eyebrows. It coughed for a few moments. This car didn't sound like it could make it out of my development. The automatic seatbelt rapidly came up and choked me. I laughed. "I forgot that cars used to have these stupid seatbelts."

We replayed our Shameka stories during the ride. Unconsciously, I rested my hand on top of Scooter's on the gearshift. When I finally realized it, I snatched it back. Before I could pull away, he grabbed my wrist. "Keep it there."

When we arrived at Dave and Buster's, we immediately ordered drinks. As the circus of people scurried around us, Scooter appeared irritated. He wrapped his arm around me to protect me from the crowd. He whispered in my ear, "You really want to stay here? It's kind of busy."

"It doesn't matter. I thought you wanted to play pool."

"I did, but I was having a good time just reminiscing."

Feeling that our memories would reconnect us, I blushed. "So, do you want to just reminisce?"

"Yeah, let's just chill. We can grab a movie and go back to your place."

As I put the key in my front door, Scooter was so close I could feel his breath on my neck. My stomach felt queasy. I fumbled with the door. Finally, it swung open.

To calm the intensity rising between us, I quickly turned on the television. Scooter sat on the couch and got comfortable. I went into the kitchen and poured two glasses of wine. I gulped some rapidly before I returned to the living room. When I handed Scooter his drink, I sat Indian style in front of the television. After rummaging through my DVD drawer full of chick flicks, I pulled out *Bad Boys II*.

"You want to see this?"

"I don't care. It's whatever."

I popped in the movie and grabbed the DVD remote. After slipping out of my shoes, I sat beside Scooter. He asked, "Remember we thought we were going to be the Huxtables?"

I reminded him, "Well, we both stuck to our plans. We're just not together."

"You're right."

I was curious about this female he labeled his girlfriend. Where did he meet her? What did she do for a living? What was her name?

Instead, I concluded not bringing attention to her would make him not think about her. The movie began and the surround sound blasted through the speakers.

He looked around. "I could chill in here. You have it hooked up like a guy."

"Well, I have a lot of movie nights." I added, "Alone."

"Whatever, Tay-Bae. You probably have dudes all over you."

"It's not the number of dudes on me. It's how many I want on me."

"Yeah, it is hard out there. That's why I—"

As he was about to acknowledge why he settled down, I cut him off. I laughed hysterically when Martin Lawrence got shot in the behind. "He is so silly."

His bottom lip sort of dangled as if he really longed to complete his sentence. I jumped onto conversation that would keep him close to me.

"Remember we used to watch *Martin* faithfully?"

"Yeah that was our show."

I nodded. "Yep, every Thursday."

"We used to sit on the phone and only talk during commercials."

"Yep."

We laughed. Our "remember-when" session continued. Whenever we stumbled onto uncomfortable territory, I would steer us back into our past in hopes to unite us.

After intoxication conquered my senses, I moved closer to him. He turned to face me. And just as he did at the reunion, he opened his mouth and kissed me. I didn't resist. I couldn't resist. I was lost in the moment. My mind fast-forwarded to me walking down the aisle with him. In slow motion, we made love with our mouths and I fantasized about the possibilities with each twirl of the tongue. He backed up and landed a few kisses on my face, then finally on my forehead. He held my face in between his hands. "You asked me a question the other night."

Still entranced, I nodded.

He said, "No."

No? I asked a whole bunch of questions. He smiled and said, "No, I've never loved anyone like I love you."

Confused as to how I should react to the response that I prayed to God for, I smiled. Then my mind began claiming victory. So, I wrapped my arm around his neck and embraced him tightly. His arms made their way around my lower torso. He lifted my shirt and rubbed my back. "You're still so soft."

Seductively, I straddled him. He held my waist and slowly pushed it back and forth. I searched his eyes for answers.

He fumbled with my pants. I climbed off of him and pulled my jeans down. He shook his head. "You still got it."

He ripped his clothes off. "We staying down here?"

As I led the way to my quarters, his nature boldly protruded from him. I was anxious to feel him. We entered my bedroom and he cupped my girls with his hands and massaged them. I fell to my knees. He kneeled in front of me and kissed my breasts. He stretched me out on the floor and asked, "Do you have any condoms?"

I told him to get one from my nightstand. He quickly returned with a strip of three. Hopefully, he wasn't planning on multiple rounds. It had been a long time since I could do that. He masterfully rolled the condom on as he stood over me, arousing me, making me anxious to feel him. Finally, he carefully spread my legs apart and playfully tantalized me. Pushing my hips upward to receive him, my body begged him to end my despair.

Finally, he fully submerged. My eyes watered. I wrapped my arms around his body and welcomed him. Slowly, deeply, my first love glided inside of me. Hesitant breathing. Expectations. I raked his back. He kissed my face. Harmonious lovemaking landed me on cloud nine. I floated in the moment. Then, I came down. He lay on top of me, but I felt empty. I couldn't speak. He was first to break the silence, saying, "I need some water."

I slid from beneath his moist body and he rolled on to his back. Though I thought I wanted this to happen, I instantly regretted the encounter. I sat up and slowly rose to my feet. How could I be so vulnerable?

I took slow, concentrated steps to the kitchen. What the hell was I thinking? When I returned to the room, Scooter was lying in my bed with the remote control in his hand. I handed him the water and he flipped through the channels. He mumbled, "Thanks Tay-Bae."

For the water or the sex? I climbed in the bed beside him. I pulled the covers up to my chin. When I reached over to rub his arm, he didn't reciprocate. I began to talk, but realized I had very little to say. We chatted about miscellaneous issues. He eventually dozed off. I sat there staring at the ceiling. Time swiftly escaped. Just as the sun rose, Scooter's cell phone rang three or four times in a row. I fumed, because I knew the person on the other end had to be his girlfriend. Scooter squirmed. I folded my arms and replayed our night.

Finally, he grabbed his phone and scrolled through the call log. The alarm clock buzzed. I jumped up and darted for the shower.

As the water ran down my face, my tears blended in. It was as if Scooter came over to see if he could still hit it. After he achieved his goal, our communication down-shifted to neutral. I scrubbed my skin like a rape victim.

When I finally opened the bathroom door, Scooter was gone. My heart dropped. Then, I heard him walking up the steps. He walked into the bathroom to join me.

He stretched. "I'm on vacation. I'm not supposed to be getting up this early."

I rolled my eyes. "Well, somebody thought you should be up this early."

"You know how it is."

I gave him a puzzled look, and replied, "No, I don't know how it is."

He kissed my cheek. "Tay-Bae, you're a trip."

I closed my eyes, breathed deeply and rummaged up enough courage to ask, "Scooter, where do we go from here?"

He answered with a question. "Did you enjoy being with me last night?"

Like a dummy, I nodded. He said, "Well, that's all that matters. I enjoyed myself too."

"Scooter, why did you call me?"

He took a deep breath and didn't answer. I was pressured to ask everything before we parted. "You said that you didn't want to risk what you had. Why did you call?"

He folded his arms and leaned on the sink. "Taylor, I guess I needed to know too."

"Needed to know what?"

"If I still cared about you. I hadn't thought about us for years. When you put it out there Friday, I thought you were trippin'. When we kissed, I felt like . . ."

He shrugged his shoulders like it was so simple. I longed to hear him say he needed me in his life. I desperately asked, "What did you feel?"

"What did I tell you last night?"

As I struggled for each response, I felt guilty. His ability to communicate his emotions is what separated him from every other man I've dated. Was this a result of me hurting him? Did I create this stoic man in front of me? I pouted. "I don't know."

"I don't think I'll ever love anyone like I loved you."

He stressed the past tense on his statement. Still, I clung to his every syllable. I gazed into his eyes. "So, what's next?"

He hugged me. "I don't know. We'll see. You know I'm in a relationship."

The sting from his honesty silenced me. He was a grown-ass man and not the little sucker who used to be madly in love with me. I proceeded to get ready for work. Scooter watched TV until I was done and didn't appear interested in discussing our future.

We had coffee and debated current events. I scrutinized his words and gestures and found nothing but a man who belonged to someone else. Who is she? Finally, I grabbed my things and we walked out through my garage. Outside, he grabbed me and held me tightly. I searched for more in the embrace. Offering me just an inkling of hope, he kissed my cheek and promised to call.

5

SCOOTER

Just when I settled with not having it all, the full package waltzes back into my life and claims she still loves me. For the life of me, I had no plan to be driving to my parents' house this morning overwhelmed with confusion. Guilt stricken, I read Akua's messages. WHERE ARE YOU? WHAT ARE YOU DOING? CALL ME.

How could I come home for three days and find myself questioning if she's even the person I want to be with?

When I walked into my parents' house, my mother was up and ready for work. As soon as I opened the door, she grunted. I walked into the kitchen and kissed her cheek. She twisted her lips. "Where have you been, boy?"

"Am I grown?"

"Yeah, you're grown, but when your little girlfriend starts ringing my phone at seven in the morning . . . she put her hand on her hip. "Then, I got the right to ask where you been."

My eyebrows wrinkled. "She called here?"

She nodded inquisitively.

"What did she say?"

"I didn't answer. Hell, I didn't know what to tell her."

I kissed her cheek. "You're my girl."

She rolled her eyes. "Uh-huh."

I laughed. "I drank too much last night and I crashed over my boy's house."

She rolled her neck. "You don't have to lie to me."

"Ma, you're a trip."

She grabbed her keys and walked to the garage door. "Look who's talking."

I smirked, and she said, "Boy, don't you come here and lose your mind."

I contemplated calling Akua with the scent of another woman reeking on me. Instead, I hopped in the shower first. The urge to smoke a cigarette kidnapped my senses. Smoking is a habit I picked up in medical school as a stress reliever. Knowing its effects forces me to try to kick the habit, but I can't seem to shake it. Akua's constant warnings have decreased my intake, but still in stressful situations, I revert back to my dependency.

I carried the cordless phone outside, along with a pack of Marlboro Lights. I took a puff to dismantle my guilt before dialing my girl.

After a quarter of a ring, she picked up. "Where the hell have you been?"

I took another puff. "Where do you think I've been?"

"If the hell I knew, I wouldn't be asking you. Would I?"

The nicotine had totally taken over as I attempted to reverse the blame on her. "Man, I paged you before I went out last night. Where were you?"

She huffed. "You know I was on call last night."

"All right then, I didn't expect to hear from you until this morning."

"Why didn't you answer your phone?"

"Akua. I'm off work. Why would I be up at seven in the morning?" I huffed.

"Whatever. You're always up."

"I went out with the fellas last night. I was asleep."

"Whatever."

"You miss me?"

"What do you think?"

She never responded positively to mushy questions, but I needed it at the moment. I needed her to reaffirm why I'm planning a future with her.

"I don't know. Tell me."

"Do you miss me?"

I chuckled and tried to give her what I wanted. "Yes, baby, I miss you. I miss you and I love you."

"Uh-huh."

"Are you ready for me to come home?"

"Uh-huh."

"What time are you going to sleep?"

"I was about to go to sleep. I'll call you when I wake up."

"A'ight. Call me when you wake up."

"Make sure you answer."

She hung up and I shook my head. That's my girl. She's a little abrasive, but that's her style. I played with the phone. Then, I began to feel bad for just thinking about leaving her. I can't leave her. Despite her flaws, she's committed. That's more than all the superficial things that constitute what I declare as my ideal mate.

6

DEVIN

Life couldn't get any better than this. Clark and I danced in an empty room. All the money in the world couldn't replace what we shared. Our relationship was like a melody that didn't need lyrics, like exercise that didn't require movement. Side to side, back and forth, we swayed. The disco ball served as a compass as we spun on our own axis.

When my alarm clock buzzed in my ear at 8:00 A.M., my real life was spinning out of control. Here I was, dreaming about a long-gone relationship that ended more than six years ago. I'd been married to someone else and divorced. The third beautiful woman in one week lay beside me in my bed, and still I yearned for something more, something real.

She wrapped her arm around me. I slid it to the side. She moved it back. I took a deep breath. Staring at my high ceilings, I wonder why I even subject myself to this. It would make more sense to just take women out, go to their house, get my rocks off and leave before the sun comes up.

She moaned, "You okay?"

I cleared my throat. "Are you okay?"

When I slid out of bed, she stretched out, like she'd been asked to stay longer. If not for dignity or my political aspirations, I'd pay for sex. I stood at the foot of my bed and watched her lie there peacefully. I grabbed the remote from my armoire and turned on my stereo. The bass blasted through the speakers.

Her head popped up and she whined, "Devin."

As I lowered the volume, I apologized. That strategy works with most women. Instead, she lay back down. I decided to jump in the shower and hoped she'd get up and begin gathering her things. Wishful thinking. Even after I'd gotten dressed, she slept.

I shook her arm. "Hey, sleepyhead."

"Yeah."

"I'm about to get out of here. So . . ."

She plopped her head back down. "I'll lock the door. I'm exhausted."

Isn't this just great? Why do I feel the need to play nice guy? Women take that nice stuff to the extreme. This chick has spent two or three nights and each time, we go through this. I sat on the side of the bed. "Look, baby. I'd rather you leave now."

"Devin, why don't you trust me?"

Maybe cause I don't know your ass? I rubbed her back. "It's not that I don't trust you. I don't really like to leave people in my house."

She grumbled and I massaged her shoulders. "I hope you're not upset."

She tossed the comforter back and jumped out of the bed. While mumbling under her breath, she scampered around the room. It was obvious she was offended by my stance, but I wasn't in an appeasing mood. Finally, she stood in front of me with her high heels and low-rise Capri jeans. With her huge lime-and-brown Louis Vutton bag propped on her shoulder, she put her hand on her hip.

"I'm ready."

The wrong head throbbed and I said, "I hope you're not upset with me."

"It's okay. I just want to get some rest."

"I'm sorry."

I asked for a hug and she half-heartedly obliged. I kidded, "You can do better than that."

"Look, I'm tired. Can we go?"

Her irritation decreased my obligation. It meant that she thought I was a jerk, so she wouldn't be blowing my phone up later. She'd be a good girl and just disappear. *Hopefully*.

When we walked out of my building, I kissed her on the cheek and hailed her a taxi. I walked to my ex-wife's apartment to pick up my daughter, Nicole. I called from outside the apartment and Jennifer's live-in boyfriend answered. "I'll bring her down," he said.

"Where's Jennifer?" I asked.

"She left early."

All of a sudden, my anger elevated. "She left?"

An irritated sigh came through the phone. I took a deep breath. "Just bring her down."

Before they came down, I called Jennifer. "Didn't I tell you not to leave her alone with him anymore?"

"Devin, grow up."

My anger vanished when I looked up and saw my baby. "Daddy," she screamed.

Stooping down to catch the cannonball of excitement flying into my chest, I closed my phone. Aaron ducked back into the elevator without speaking. Nicole crashed into me. "Daddy."

I kissed her cheek. "Hey princess."

When I stood up, she pulled off her backpack. "Here, Daddy."

I laughed. "Why do I have to carry it?"

"You're stronger."

My cell phone rang. Jennifer sighed in my ear. "Devin, when will you understand that Aaron is going to be her stepfather and there will be times when I'll need to leave her with him? He would never do anything to hurt her."

"Okay. Can I call you when I drop her off?"

By the time I dropped her off at camp, my issue seemed selfish. How could I control what Jennifer did in her home?

I strolled into my office a little after ten. My assistant smiled. "Hi, Mr. Patterson."

"Hey, Lisa."

"I made your travel arrangements to DC. You'll be staying in the host hotel."

I frowned. "Are you talking about for the Black Caucus?" She nodded.

"I have to go down next week. I have some meetings with the legislative division of the Train Workers' Union."

She shrugged her shoulders. "That's not on your calendar."

I pointed to my head. "I keep it all up here."

"That's the problem."

We laughed. It's not funny, though. I have a whole bunch of damn problems.

7

SCOOTER

When I walked into the house, my heart sat in my throat. I'd done some things early in our relationship, but since we moved in together last year, I've been faithful. Hoping my infidelity wasn't spray painted on me, I took a deep breath before calling her name, "Akua."

"I'm in the office, baby."

I peeped in the hall mirror before walking into the office. After running my hand over my face a few times, wiping away the evidence, I stood in the doorway of the office. She twirled around in the office chair. I smiled. "Hey, sexy."

She smirked. "Hey."

Her eyes scrutinized me. "You smell like cigarettes."

"Can I get a hug?"

"I don't hug nicotine junkies."

I walked up to her and grabbed her hand, yanking her from the chair. "Give me a hug, girl."

I pulled on the waist of her scrubs. She reluctantly swung her arms around me. I tilted her head back and kissed her lips. She frowned. "You stink."

I cuddled her head into my chest. "I'm sorry."

"You don't have to apologize to me for trying to kill yourself," she grunted.

As her head lay on my chest, I thought I did owe her an

apology. She didn't deserve to be a part of the battle inside my head. She stepped backward and plopped down in the chair. Her arms folded and she looked me up and down. "So, I take it you had a good time." She curled her lips. "What made you start sticking those cancer sticks back in your mouth?"

"I don't know."

She spun back around to face the computer. "When the cats away, the mice will play?"

I chuckled at her analogy. Was I the mouse and she the cat? Resting my elbows on the top of the chair, I stood behind her. "Whatchu looking at?"

"Buying some new work shoes." She clicked the shopping cart. "I figured we needed some new ones."

She selected the Drew Deersoft shoes I'd been eyeing since I began my residency, but the $200 price tag prohibited me from ever finalizing the transaction.

"Aren't these the ones you like?" I nodded and she said, "I got you a thirteen. You think that's good."

I twirled the chair around. "Baby, you're buying me some shoes?"

"Uh-huh."

I kissed her and she pushed my face away. "Yeah, I still take care of you even though you're trying to kill yourself."

Guilt filled my lungs and I coughed. "What would I do without you?" I verbalized what I was asking myself.

"You tell me."

I kissed her again. "Thank you, baby."

She smiled. "Yeah, I can't have my man walking into the hospital with those run-down Darcos you have in there."

I laughed and headed to the bedroom to unpack. "What's for dinner?"

"Frozen dinner. I'm going to work. I signed up for a moon-lighting shift tonight."

When I walked into the bedroom, my laundry was folded neatly in a basket. I dropped my head. How could I question if she was my ideal mate? Thoughts of her insensitivity and arrogance I'd pushed to the forefront of my mind on the drive home began to drift away. They were just excuses for my selfishness.

I plopped down on the bed and stretched out. Taylor whispered into my ear, "Scootie-Boo."

Her vulnerable eyes pierced through me. "I've never stopped loving you."

She climbed on top of me. Her waist gyrated. She purred. My hands traveled around her and groped her inner thighs from behind. As I guided her strokes, she pounded on me.

When Akua slammed a textbook on the dresser, it startled me. I discovered my hand inside of my sweatpants. Trying to appear composed, I didn't stop groping myself. Instead I reached my free arm out for her, "C'mon baby. Lie down with me," I said.

"Didn't I tell you I had to work?"

I begged, "C'mon. Just let me feel you."

She packed her backpack. "I have to go to work."

I watched her maneuver around the room. Hoping my body would transition in accordance with my mind, I pleaded, "C'mon baby. I need it."

She sucked her teeth. "I'm only working until midnight. I'll give it to you when I come home."

I stopped fantasizing and sat up on the bed. Akua is too punctual to play. Since this sexual encounter was not on the agenda, it was best that I take a cold shower. As it began to deflate, she kissed me on the cheek and patted my nature. "I'll take care of you later. I gotta go."

She rushed from the room. I lay back on the bed. When the front door slammed, I returned to making love to Taylor.

8

TAYLOR

Isn't it funny that we know they're not going to call, even when they promise they will? I woke up to a text message from Scooter. THINKING ABOUT U. WILL CALL SOON. After nearly a month passed, this was the best I could get. Why would he send a message like that on a Friday night at 11:43? Was this message a result of a damn lovers' quarrel? Call me because you think I'm the greatest, not because your damn girlfriend has gotten on your nerves! I shouted at my cell phone praying that somehow my thoughts could be telepathically communicated to Scooter. Text messaging is the closest thing to blatantly saying, "I'm not interested." I refused to respond. If he was sincerely thinking about me, he would have called me. Huffing and puffing to myself still would not erase the truth, Scooter had no score to settle. He'd given me his best ten years ago and he owed me nothing.

When my mother called a few minutes later, I picked up but all I was thinking about was his text message. "Taylor, are you there?" My mother asked, in a concerned tone.

I cleared my throat. "Yeah, I'm here."

"How are you?"

"I'm good. Nothing much going on. Just working a lot."

She sighed. "I can only imagine."

"How's Daddy?"

"He's good."

Then, her normal questions followed. She didn't have much to say to me. Nor did I to her. I was this independent single woman and she was Bishop Jabowski's wife, nothing more, nothing less. The spice of our conversations had long been extinct. Finally, she asked about Scooter. The day after he came to church was the last time we had a decent chat.

In an attempt to give her a slice of my life, I said, "He actually sent me a text message last night."

She perked up. "Really?"

Trying not to overestimate the intent of the message, I just said, "He said I've been on his mind and he'll call soon."

She chuckled sneakily, "Really, Taylor?"

"Yeah."

"He was always such a gentleman."

"Ma, please."

"God is good."

With a smirk on my face, I responded to the Black Christian motto. "All the time."

As if she'd gotten a quick dose of the Holy Spirit, she said, "Whew." Then she finished the motto. "All the time." I could hear her hand bang on the table to add thunder to the last three words. "God is good."

"You sound real happy to hear from Scooter," I said, nonchalantly.

My mother rarely went above level two on a ten-point excitement scale, but right now she was tipping the scale. As if the words wouldn't come out. She would begin, "I . . ." Then, that would stop with a "Whew."

Finally, she said, "I had been praying for months for God to send you a good man."

I frowned and looked at the phone. Was this really my mother? We hadn't discussed relationships in almost six years. Her desire for me to settle down was this sort of unspoken mountain that kept us distant. Before she could finish, I interrupted, "Ma, Scooter is not who you've been praying for. He has a woman. A woman that he's in love with."

"He ain't married." Again, I gawked at my phone. Completely ignoring my desire to be a woman with dignity, she continued, "A few months ago, I decided to get descriptive about your husband."

Why wasn't I consulted on her expectations for my husband? My head shook in disbelief as she explained. "I asked Him to send you a Christian. I requested him to be tall, brown, and equally educated. The ladies in my prayer circle said I was asking for too much. But I kept praying anyway."

Not as if it took a whole lot of convincing, but maybe the man she prayed for was Scooter. Maybe God heard both of our prayers. I said, "I know that's real, Ma."

"I was fasting the week Scooter came to church, too. See, sometimes you got to give up something to get something."

Assuring her that I still knew the Bible, I egged her on. "Uh-huh. I know."

"When I saw that boy, it was as if God said, 'That's him.'"

The spirit ran through my veins, too. We were on one accord and I never even said anything to her about Scooter. "Are you serious?"

"And not only that. When your father saw him, he said the same thing."

"What did he say?"

"He said, 'That boy is supposed to be Taylor's husband.'"

I slipped under my covers and talked to my mother like she was my girlfriend. "Ma, no he didn't."

"Girl, you talking about praying. Me and your daddy prayed that night."

It's a damn shame that my parents were praying while we were tossing around on my bedroom floor. "I don't believe y'all."

"Huh."

Imagining her rolling her eyes and adjusting her thick

glasses, I chuckled. This conversation was bridging the sea that had grown between us. With my phone stuck to my ear, I felt the warmth and sincerity escaping from my mother's mouth.

"When two touch and agree, God said it shall be done."

Actually warning myself, I said, "Ma, don't get all wrapped up in believing Scooter is the guy you've been praying for."

"Taylor." Before I answered, she asked. "Do you know anything about faith?"

I snapped, "Yes, I know about faith."

"It is the things hoped for and not seen."

"I know. But . . ."

"If you know, you better act like it. I have a brunch to go to. I'll talk to you later."

That meant next Saturday. Never in the last five years did I want my mother to stay on the phone with me, but I needed her encouragement. I needed to hear all of her prophesies. If the bishop's wife condoned me getting my man back, it had to be the right thing for me to do. I wasn't the only one convinced that Scooter was the one. Maybe he did intend to call. Maybe I was on his mind. Maybe my mother's phone call was confirmation for me to keep hope alive.

9

DEVIN

I rummaged through my apartment. My cleaning lady had taken my laundry and left me dangling in the wind with no clean underwear. This is just what I get for doing things last minute. After I put a couple of dress shirts and suits in my garment bag, I jumped in the shower.

Aside from my business meeting, I planned to meet with a realtor in DC. Having another home base should decrease the stress of city-flopping and suitcase-swapping. I stuffed some casual clothes in my duffle bag. Still, I hung free, debated whether or not to stay that way or put on some dirty drawers. As I pulled out every garment I owned, I tried to find at least one pair of clean boxers. During my frantic search, I stopped and took a deep breath and checked the time. Unless I found something in the next minute, I would miss the 1:05 P.M. train into DC. When I opted to let it hang, a pair of spandex shorts appeared on top of one of the many clean clothes piles on my bedroom floor. I swiftly slipped them on and threw on my jeans and Nike T-shirt.

Finally, I rushed out. As I lugged all my junk into the elevator, the two young ladies inside huffed. I chuckled, certain that they wondered why the hell I was always dragging luggage. I nodded and smiled. "Good morning."

One chick smiled and returned my greeting. The other

smirked. *To hell with you, too.* The driver chuckled as I hastily walked toward the car. "Rough day again, Mr. Patterson?"

After tossing my bags in the trunk, I nodded. "Always."

Since I used the same car service, Joseph frequently transported me. Somehow we always get into "the talk." When I got in the car, he wasted no time, asking, "Mr. Patterson, have you found yourself a nice young lady yet?"

"Not yet, Joseph. Not yet."

"I don't know how you young guys do it. My wife and I have been married for thirty-three years. I can't imagine what I'd do without her."

"I understand."

It was funny to watch him dance around asking what he was really curious about. Was I gay?

"So, are you interested in marriage?"

"Been there. Done that."

"That was a long time ago."

Why do people want to shove marriage down your throat? Nothing compares to a miserable marriage. I damn sure won't do it because it's the damn right thing to do anymore.

As to confirm my negative feelings about my marriage, my ex-wife rang. "Yes, Jennifer."

"Devin."

I rolled my eyes. "Yeah?"

"Nicole said you were going out of town today."

"Yes," I huffed.

Jennifer has access to my Yahoo calendar so we can schedule pick-ups and drop-offs without too much conversation. So, I wondered why this question surfaced. She mumbled, "Friggin' great."

"Is there a problem?"

She huffed, "Yes, it's not on your calendar." She paused. "We have a problem."

Lisa didn't have it on her calendar so it never made it to Yahoo. I covered my face and sighed. "What kind of problem, Jennifer?"

"Never mind. I'll just ask Aaron."

Blood shot to my head. Reluctant to give her the glory, I went for the high road, I said, "Okay, if Aaron can't do it, I'll have to call Adrianna."

"You don't even know what it is?" she snapped.

I took a deep breath. "What is *it* Jennifer?"

"I need someone to take her to swimming lessons on Tuesday and Thursday. I have to work late."

The vision of Aaron helping my baby in and out of her bathing suit infuriated me. Adrianna is my on-call nanny. This was an obvious on-call moment.

I chuckled. "Nah. Don't ask Aaron. I'll take care of it, since it was my mistake. If Adrianna can't do it, I'll catch the train back after my meeting tomorrow."

"Thanks Devin. Let me know what you decide. I think Adrianna still has the key to my apartment."

I nodded my head. "She does."

"Okay, well it's all clear. Thanks Devin. Don't forget to call me."

I smirked at my phone. Sometimes I scared myself, because I can't explain how many times a day I envision strangling her.

Joseph looked in the rearview mirror. "You coming back to New York tomorrow?"

"I don't know, man."

We pulled up to Penn Station. He said, "Mr. Patterson, you're going to have a heart attack by the time you're forty if you don't slow down."

After handing him a tip, I said, "Man, thanks for the prophecy."

His West Indian accent intensified. "Not prophecy. Just warning."

"Thanks, man."

After dashing into the station, grabbing my ticket from the kiosk, and rushing to the gate, I sat on the Acela Express headed to my other hometown. I tilted my head back and breathed. Just as my heart rate decreased, it dawned on me. Damn. I have to call Adrianna.

I dialed her number and left a message. I dialed her several times during the ride. Still no answer. By the time I arrived in DC, I left one more desperate message. I concluded that it was highly possible that I'd be commuting back and forth for the remainder of the week.

As I sat in my hotel room, purchasing my ticket on the all reserved 3:00 train to New York and returning on the 10:00 train, I loosened my tie. When I printed the reservation confirmation, I caught a glimpse of myself in the mirror. The clean-cut guy on the outside was no representation of the hurricane swirling inside. I brushed my hair and readjusted my tie. Finally, I tossed my suit jacket over my shoulder and rushed out of the hotel.

When I arrived at the Train Workers' Union, the hospitality was just what I needed. A friendly receptionist escorted me to a conference room. Fresh cookies, croissants, bagels, juices, a variety of teas, and coffee were there to greet me. I smiled. "Wow, you guys do it big around here," I said.

She covered her giggle. "Yeah, they do."

I joked, "If you don't mind, I think I'll help myself to this."

"Be my guest. They'll be here in a minute."

I stood over the spread. I wanted everything. Maybe it would appease me somehow. I grabbed a bagel, four cookies, and a blueberry muffin.

I looked at my watch. Where were these people? 10:25 and still I was the only one there for the 10:30 meeting. If I planned to be on the train in time, I had to leave no later than two. The members of the legislative team began trickling in a few minutes later. Another consultant came in. I looked at my watch. Maybe I was the only anxious one. It was 10:35 and I felt like it had been an eternity.

Though we'd had several conference calls, some of us had never met in person. We went around the room for introductions and the presentation began shortly after. The focus of this meeting was to strategize for salary stabilization for workers as a result of increased gas prices.

The young man giving the presentation appeared nervous and flustered. When asked a question, he turned beet red and mumbled. I looked at my watch. Damn if I can afford to have timid responses when we're trying to make things happen. Suddenly, I found myself taking over his presentation and responding to questions without giving him the opportunity. He didn't seem to mind. In fact, he looked as if a weight had been lifted from his shoulder. Prior to responding, I'd given him an I-got-it nod. During our first break, the administrative assistant taking the notes approached me.

She extended her hand. "Hi, Mr. Patterson."

I smiled. "Hi."

"I'm Katherine. I'm actually the assistant in the legal department. I'm filling in for the legislative team's assistant."

I squinted. And why the hell do I care? She chuckled. "You're really covering a lot in there. Can you slow down?"

I laughed and patted Katherine on the shoulder. "I'm sorry, I'll slow down."

She joked, "I would ask if you needed more coffee, but you're already wound up."

Since Katherine came off as real down to earth, I reciprocated. "Look, I'm trying to get out of here. They got that young white boy up there fumbling around."

She cackled loudly. "That's the truth."

I looked at my watch. "I need to be out of here by two."

She frowned. "But the meeting isn't over until three."

"I know. I have a 3:00 train back to New York."

She nodded inquisitively. "You're not a part of the meetings all week?"

"Yeah. Something came up, so I have to shoot up there this afternoon and come back tonight."

"That's a lot."

I smiled. "I know."

She smirked. "Must be really important, huh?"

"Yeah, she is."

She put her hand over her chest. "Your wife?"

"My daughter."

She laughed, asking, "Are you married?"

"Divorced."

People began congregating in the room, and we stopped talking. During the meeting, I caught her smiling at me from across the table. Did she think I was interested in her old ass? Why didn't I say I was married?

When we broke for lunch, she came up to me. "Mr. Patterson, I'm sure you don't like to mix business with pleasure, but . . ."

"Nah, definitely not."

She blinked bashfully. "Okay, let me explain."

As she waved her hand to help with her explanation, I noticed a ring. Good! I'll just tell her I don't date married women. She chuckled. "Another young attorney, Taylor Jabowski, she works in our legal department." She continued to wave her hand wildly. "She's tall and gorgeous. She's about your age."

Taylor walked up. She was tall, white, and bleach blond. She was a size zero and my stomach turned. As I shook my head to erase the vision of Taylor that just tiptoed into my mind, I chuckled. "Nah, I'm really not interested. In fact, I'm in a serious relationship."

She shrugged her shoulders. "Oh, I'm sorry. I love to play matchmaker." She bobbed her head from side to side like she felt silly for asking. "Please excuse me."

Relieved that she wasn't the one interested, I blushed. "Nah, you're cool. Don't worry about it."

10
TAYLOR

My administrative assistant ran into my office. I peeped behind her to see if she was being chased. My forehead wrinkled. She blushed and fanned herself. "Taylor, girl."

"What?"

"The man of your dreams is downstairs in the conference room."

"Katherine, just because there's a single man in the building does not mean he's the man of my dreams." I chuckled. "Where have you been all day?"

She clenched her teeth together. "Downstairs, girl. You need to get your butt down there."

"What have you been doing down there?"

"I had to fill in for the damn legislative admin."

"You're a trip."

"Girl, this man is fine. Trust me."

"I've trusted you before."

She lifted her glasses and looked at me. "Don't even try it. I told you that young boy was cute. And I saw you . . ."

She laughed. I shooed her. "Whatever."

"Taylor, I know you better than you think I know you."

"Anyway. Are you done downstairs?" I huffed.

"No, we're meeting until three. Come down there around one-thirty so you can meet Mr. Patterson."

"Katherine, I'm not thinking about Mr. Patterson."

She turned to leave my office. When she reached the door, she leaned back in. "He's finer than the last guy I told you about."

"Good bye, Katherine."

At quarter of three, I got the urge to go downstairs and just check out what Katherine was raving about. I went into the conference room corridor. I peeped in all the closed doors. Finally, I saw her. Through the slim windowpane, I surveyed the room. There weren't even any black men in the room. Who the hell was she talking about? I saw two white guys that I didn't recognize. Now, she must think I'm desperate. Just as I was about to walk away, it looked like they were adjourning. I stood in the hall waiting for Katherine.

I jokingly said, "We need to cut out right now and go to happy hour, because you are crazy." I pointed into the conference room. "Who in there is supposed to be my dream guy?"

"Taylor, you really think I'm crazy, don't you?"

I stretched my eyes. "Yah!"

"He left early. He had to go back to New York with his daughter."

"His what?"

She grabbed my arm. "C'mon let's walk to the break room." She continued, "His daughter."

I frowned and she added, "What am I going to do with you?"

"Leave me alone and stop trying to find me a man."

"Trust me. This one is fine."

As I perused the vending selection, I said. "And he has a daughter. I don't even deal with my own niece and nephew. Hell if I'm trying to play stepmom." I chuckled. "I don't even know if I want kids of my own."

She nodded. "Yes, you do. All women do."

"Don't put us all in a box. Some of us are different."

She ignored my declaration of independence. "Taylor, I really do want you to meet Mr. Patterson. I think he'll be back to-morrow."

"I'll be out of the office tomorrow and Thursday."

She gasped. "Dang! You're going to miss him."

11

SCOOTER

Speaking in an unacceptable decibel at five o'clock in the morning, Akua stood over top of me, "Why did you leave the television running all night?"

My purpose for sleeping on the couch was so she would not wake me when she left for work. Couldn't we discuss this when I got to the hospital at seven? I covered my ears. She grabbed my jeans from the floor and stomped away. She spoke to herself loud enough for me to hear, "He doesn't think. Does he even look at the electric bill? This is ridiculous."

I pulled the quilt over my head. Like, really. How much does it cost to run the television all night? It's easier to ignore her, than to respond. Slinging things around the room, she continued to argue. Finally, I yelled out, "Akua, shut up! I'm tryna sleep."

She stormed from the room. "I wanted to sleep too, but you"—she pointed her index finger at me—"left the television on all night."

I sprang up. "Are you satisfied now? Are you happy that I'm up?"

She stormed back into the room. "That's not the point. I want you to pay attention to what you're doing."

Does she even realize how ignorant some of the things she says sound? I stomped behind her in my mind. In reality, my knees conked out and pushed me back onto the couch. Lacking the energy to bicker, I dropped my head in my hands. Slowly, I wiped my face. "What makes you think I'm not paying attention?"

When she didn't respond, I knew my voice was too low for her to hear. After a few deeps breaths, I staggered into the room. "Why don't you come out there and cut it off for me if it bothers you that bad?"

I plopped on the bed. She stomped around me throwing her scrubs and clean underwear on the bed beside me. Her neck moved in the same zigzag motion as her pointed finger. "My man shouldn't be out there every night. You should be in here with me."

Too exhausted to sympathize with her, I stretched out on the bed and huffed, "Akua, don't even try it."

She headed to the bathroom and yelled, "Go to hell!"

I chuckled at her last words. She slammed the bathroom door, and I was asleep by the time she finished.

When I got to the hospital, my head was still throbbing. As I reviewed my charts, I winced. My attending physician stood beside me, "Is everything okay?"

I nodded. Damn. I had two surgeries with Akua. Her nasty moods last all day. I sighed. The first surgery was scheduled for 9:30. I checked the clock on the wall. Should I try and catch her between surgeries just to settle our beef? As I got into the mix, time slipped away. Akua and I ran into each other, both running a few minutes behind schedule.

She surprised me with a stiff peck on the lips. "Hey, Doc."
"Hey, baby."
She laughed. "Did you turn the lights off in the house?"
"Don't start that shit with me this morning."

After we scrubbed down we headed into the operating room. I thought she said something, so I asked, "What?"

She smirked. "Don't *start* with me."

I put my finger up to my mouth. Last thing we needed was to walk into the OR in the middle of a squabble. I smiled. She didn't. The nurses had already prepped the patient. I asked my required questions and told the patient what I'd be doing. Finally, I did my part, and the patient drifted off into a deep slumber. My attending physician gave me a nod of approval. I nodded back in appreciation.

It takes a certain kind of arrogance to perform surgery. Every time I watch her with that scalpel, it scares me. Her adrenaline pumps through her veins, but her hands remain steady and focused. This was one of the few things that excited her. I stand there studying her and she doesn't even realize I'm here. She and her patient are the only people in the room.

Nearing the end of the surgery, the patient squirmed. Akua's eyes pierced through me. Without exchanging words, I knew she was furious. I bit my lips. *C'mon, man. Stay asleep for five more minutes.* My fists tightened, as I prayed. Thankfully, Akua said, "All done."

I uncrossed my fingers, my legs, and my arms. That was a close one. As we exited the operating room, I heard someone with an accent say, "You need to get your shit together."

I turned around to my girl's stony look. I frowned. I can respect her style, but not in front of my colleagues. I'd obviously misjudged his weight and didn't give him enough to last the length of the surgery, but did I really need her smart-ass mouth? That had nothing to do with getting my shit together.

On my way into the second surgery, she chuckled, adding, "Don't mess up in here, too, Doc."

I frowned at her and didn't comment. During the surgery,

I found myself reflecting on how we'd gotten to the point that Akua felt she could say whatever she wanted to me. Why did I settle? Maybe I concluded I should take the good with the bad, but is her bad really worth her good? When the surgery was done, we scrubbed down and I still didn't say anything. I couldn't help thinking about Taylor.

12

TAYLOR

The phone startled me as I coasted down the highway in a daze. I looked at the caller ID. I smiled when I saw my little sister's name. "Hey Turi. What's up, girl?"

If she hadn't dialed me, her monotone voice would have made me question if she even wanted to talk. "Hey, Tay."

"When you coming home?"

She sighed. "Dunno. Maybe Thanksgiving."

"Maybe?"

She snickered. "Yes. Maybe."

"So, are you trying to disown us?"

"Look who's talking."

"They disowned me. What am I supposed to do?"

She laughed again. "Nobody has disowned you." She kidded, "They're just concerned about your spirituality."

"Whatever, Turi."

"For real. They pray for you like you're the devil himself."

"Shut up. Just cause I don't go to their church doesn't mean I'm a devil."

"You're right," she agreed. "Enough about that, you know they love you all the same. What's going on in your life?"

"Nothing."

"I heard that you been talking to Scooter."

"Who told you that? Mommy?"

She teased. "I can't reveal my sources."

"It had to be Mommy."

"Psych. It was Toni." She laughed. "She said you would have thought God walked in the church when they saw Scooter."

"Stop playing, Turi."

"Look, I'm only telling you what I heard."

I laughed. "What did she say?"

Why are the religious ones the biggest gossipers? She hummed to expand my curiosity. I begged, "What did she say?"

"She said he was fine as ever."

I gasped. "Tell me about it."

"So have y'all hooked up since he went to church?"

How was I to explain I'd been awaiting his call for over a month? Acting as if it wasn't so serious, I said, "No. You know he lives in Connecticut."

"Between Mommy and Toni, they got all the info. They know all his vital statistics. Mommy got you on the prayer list."

"Turi, Mommy is crazy."

She laughed. "Taylor, don't miss your blessing. You better start praying, too."

"Whatever."

"You better recognize the power of prayer."

"All right, Daddy Junior."

"Whatever, I'm on my way to Bible Study. I was just calling to see if you want me to add you to our prayer circle."

I snapped, "Turi, I'm not a charity case. I don't need y'all praying for me to find a man."

"A husband, Taylor. We're not praying for you to just find a man."

I laughed. "I don't believe y'all."

"Contrary to what you believe, we love you."

"I never said y'all didn't love me. I know *you* love me."

"So does Toni."

"Yeah okay, Mother Theresa." I chuckled. "I guess that's why you're the one who was called into the ministry."

She laughed. "Yeah, cause my big sisters are crazy."

"Forget you."

Just as I was pressing the END button, my phone beeped. Assuming it was Courtney, I didn't bother checking the caller ID. I clicked over and said, "Hey."

"Hey. It's Scooter."

Oh shit. My heart dropped. I looked at the cloudy sky. Powerful was an understatement, prayer was the bomb! Before I could respond to his greeting, I mouthed, "Thank you, Jesus."

Then I took a silent deep breath and cleared my throat. "Hey Scooter. What's up?"

He immediately began to spit excuses as to why he hadn't called. "I've been under a rock since I got back from Maryland. They have me working like a slave."

Just as I was tempted to roll my eyes, I thought about the Angel that called to forewarn me that my blessing was coming. I responded pleasantly, "Yeah, I know how it is. I've been working a lot lately too."

He sighed. "Plus . . ." He paused.

My mouth hung open, waiting for him to crush me. When it didn't come out fast enough, I snapped, "Plus what?"

"It's kind of hard to call you when, you know . . ."

I knew what he was saying, but I refused to accept it until he explicitly verbalized it. I huffed, "No. I don't know."

Without hesitation, he said, "When my girl is around."

Again, my bottom lip dangled from my face. As all my blood shot to my head, my right foot was left without enough energy to press the gas pedal. Going about forty mph, cars zoomed past me. I crawled into the right lane. Maybe I should surrender. If a man claims his woman like that, nine times out of ten, he has no plans to leave her. I absorbed feelings of defeat. Then, I confidently asked what I was afraid to ask when we spent the night together, "So, it's like that?"

"Like what?"

"I mean, are you two like always together?"

He seemed hesitant, but he said it, and I wanted to faint as I swerved off on the Ardmore/Ardwick Exit. "We live together."

As I slowed to stop at the red light, I finally released the breath that I was unconsciously imprisoning in my lungs. What was Plan B? How could I move in on a chick that he slept with every night?

Despite all of those people praying for him to be my husband, I decided to throw in the towel. As Scooter went on to explain how tied at the hip he was with his girlfriend, my decision became much easier.

"Plus, she's a resident at Yale, too."

Not only did they live together, they worked together. It was clear that Operation Sneaky Devil was over. With disappointment dribbling from my lips, I pretended to sound friendly and unfazed. "Oh. That must be nice."

"Not really."

Though I was awfully tempted, I didn't feed into his downplay of his obviously troubled relationship. "Yeah, I'm sure it could be stressful, but all relationships are stressful." I quickly switched topics before he gave me an excuse to justify pursuing him.

"Guess what happened to Courtney today."

As I pressed my garage door opener, he interrupted me before I got too into the details. "Tay-Bae."

I paused to shake off the strong attraction tingling in me. Then, I said, "Yes?"

He laughed. "I used to hate when you said 'yes' like that."

"Like what?"

"Like Mrs. Cleaver or something." We both laughed and he proceeded to end our conversation. "I'm on the hospital phone. I'll call you when I get home."

"What about your girlfriend?"

"She's working nights for the next two weeks. So I'll call around nine. Is that okay?"

I wanted to say no, but my mouth spoke louder than my brain. "That's cool. I'll talk to you then."

When I pressed END, I shouted loudly in the confines of my garage. "Damn!"

I'd already opened myself up to entertain a man with a live-in girlfriend. Shit! And I was already anticipating nine o'clock. I grabbed my cheap boxed wine from the shelf, rushed upstairs and poured a tall glass.

I flicked through the channels and *Entertainment Tonight* happened to be telling me what I wanted to hear. "Pictures of Angelina Jolie and Brad Pitt back in LA months after the birth of their daughter . . ."

As if it would make the television louder, I scooted closer to the screen. I was inspired. I found myself praising Angelina for having the skills to conquer such a happy home. Just a year ago I was angry as hell to hear about the Brad and Jen breakup. What kind of woman have I become? What could be the cause of my distorted state of mind?

I showered and got into my bed. My slight intoxication sedated me and I slipped into a light nap. The loud sound of my cordless blazed in my ear. My head sprung from the pillow and I rubbed my eyes. Who was calling me in the middle of the night? I cleared my throat and pretended to be awake as I answered. Simultaneously, I glanced at the clock. 10:12.

I quickly pressed TALK. "Hello."

"Are you asleep?"

His soothing voice calmed my pounding heart. I took a deep breath and lied, "No, I'm up watching the news."

"I remember you used to hate watching the news."

I laughed. "I know, right?"

"That's why you claimed you'd never do criminal law."

He seemed to remember just about everything about me. Could it be that memories of us were as fresh in his mind as they were in mine? I said, "You got it. You know I hate crime. I ain't trying to work those long hours and prosecute them for no money. And you know I could never defend them."

He kidded. "You're still bourgeois."

"Call it what you will. I have to pay my loans off."

We both laughed. He said, "Courtney looks like she's doing okay."

"See, Courtney was born to prosecute criminals. I was just born to make a lot of money and shop."

"I love that you haven't changed," he said, laughing.

Was that a good thing or a bad thing? I smiled nervously. He snickered and repeated, "I love that."

If he loved it, it couldn't possibly be a bad thing. I was lost for words, but he saved me. He continued, "It's really hard to find women who are focused, but still youthful."

"What do you mean?"

He searched for the words to explain the term youthful. "Women." He paused just as he realized he was attempting to lump us all into one category. "Most professional women are uptight."

Needing the encouragement, I asked him to explain. "I know y'all think it's hard for women to find men, but it's just as hard for men to find women," he said.

"Whatever."

He laughed. "Trust me. You got the fun women who don't have anything going for them. Then you got the women who are tight on paper but boring as hell. It's not every day that you find women like you and Courtney. It seems like y'all handle your business and still have fun. It just doesn't seem like you guys let age or responsibility get the best of you."

Instead of taking the opportunity to gloat about how Courtney and I were "Ride or Die" chicks, I took a deep breath and prepared for the worst. "So which kind of woman is your girl?"

He laughed hard. "She's the smart, boring chick." His humor subsided. "All her friends are uptight, too."

He'd left his front door wide open and I was ready to go in and clean house. "Are you serious?" I gasped.

"Yup."

"I can't imagine you with an uptight girl."

As if he didn't believe it himself, he grunted, "Yeah, I couldn't either."

"So how did y'all get together?"

"She was persistent." As if he needed to correct it, he added, "And consistent."

Men make the craziest decisions. I rolled my eyes. "And . . ."

"And she's attractive." My heart sank. I wasn't sure if I could handle the rest. He continued, "She was someone I could learn from as well. You know, I was tired of dealing with the fine, dumb chick."

"You used to mess with dumb chicks?" I grunted.

"Not like that Tay-Bae. I had a girl all through medical school, so I didn't have to deal with dating. We tried to couple match," he explained.

"Huh?"

"That's when you and your significant other get into the same hospital for residency."

"Oh, okay. Go ahead."

"Anyway, we didn't match together. She went to UCLA, I ended up here. We knew going in that we couldn't make it work." He sighed. "She was the fun, smart type."

Good thing I wasn't competing with her. I nodded as he continued with his relationship journey.

"When I got here, I realized fun and smart isn't always a package deal. I had to choose. I either had to go with fun or smart. Like a dummy, I chose fun." He chuckled again as if he explored his wild side. "I figured I would make enough money to compensate for her shortcomings."

Damn. Was being fun that valuable? I looked at the receiver in disbelief.

"I was just sowing my oats. The fun chick was cool for that, but not for raising my kids. When I got serious about settling down, I changed my thinking. My girl was right there all along watching me chase the dumb chicks and I knew that I'd rather marry smart and boring any day opposed to fun and dumb."

Did he ever think about coming to find me? I'm not taken! I'm smart *and* fun. Trying to manipulate his psyche, I asked, "So besides being ready to settle down, what attracted you to your girl?"

Without a second's hesitation, he responded, "She was tight, in all aspects of the word. We started out as friends. I respected her. She respected me. One day, we just hooked up and it's been that way ever since."

He sighed, as if he were feeling guilty for talking to me. Finally, he finished, "Plus, I knew she loved me for me."

After I swallowed all of his endearing words, I cleared my throat. "As opposed to . . ."

As if he awaited my question, he quickly said, "As opposed to being interested in the American dream."

I wanted to yell, "I loved you when you didn't have a dream." Becoming a physician was my dream for him. Instead, I said, "I understand."

Moments of discomfort sat on the line with us. Finally, I said, "I guess she's the one, huh?"

"I don't even know."

Hating on the love I heard in his voice, I sighed. "Whatever, Scooter."

"For real, Tay-Bae."

"Does she know that you aren't sure?"

As if his uncertainty bothered him, he huffed. "Nope. She's just waiting for the ring."

Needing a little more evidence before I threw away my reunion possibilities, I asked, "What's stopping you?"

"Number one, her family has issues with me."

"Issues with *you*?" I asked.

"Akua's from Ghana. She was raised traditionally." He

chuckled. I took a mental note of her name. "Her parents aren't down for me like that."

"Wow, that's crazy. Is her family in the states?"

"Yeah, they came here when she was sixteen. They've been here about thirteen years."

I nodded. "Does it bother her that they don't like you?"

"She claims she doesn't care and she can't live for them, but I know she does." He sighed. "I hate it. I feel like I'm forcing her to choose between me and them."

I asked, "So, if you could get rid of Akika's parents, would she be the one?"

He laughed and pronounced her name. "Ah-Coo-Ah. Akua."

I envied how cute he said her name. In my mind, I made it my business to give her an insensitive nickname. I chuckled at the thought. From this moment on, she'll be referred to as coo-coo, spelled Kuku. As if her name was insignificant, I said, "Whatever, would she be the one?"

"Ah, she's very controlling. That's one of our major issues. Sometimes a man needs someone who'll let him lead." He sighed. "Someone who's sensitive and doesn't have to always be right." He huffed, "Shit, I know you're smart. You don't have to prove it to me."

Take me. Pick me. I'm strong. I'm sensitive. I don't need to prove that I'm smart. I asked, "Why is she so controlling?"

"She's a female surgeon." He snickered. "An orthopedic surgeon at that."

Ignorant to the implications, I asked. "And that means what?"

"She's a black woman in a white, male-dominated field. She had to be ten times tighter than everyone in her program to get in, but she still has to fight for respect." He sighed. "Every day. So, she's constantly on this power trip. Most surgeons are like that, though." He paused. "I used to find it cute but as it gets closer to that time—"

I interrupted. "What time?"

"Time to buy the ring." Awaiting a response, he paused. My lips were paralyzed. He continued, "I'm starting to wonder if I can deal with that forever." He sighed. "I wish she could just flip the script at home, but her strong personality is what's going to make her one of the best female surgeons. Is it fair for me to ask her to change who she is?"

"I guess not." Then, I asked, "So what was it that attracted you to her again?"

"I don't know. We used to butt heads when we first started our residency. Then, you know . . ."

"No actually, I don't. So, what happened?"

"When you're in the hospital eighty hours a week, all you get a chance to see are people in the hospital. We ran in the same circle. We were black and single. Other residents started suggesting things, and I think we both concluded why not."

Innocently, I asked, "So, it wasn't like you guys fell in love."

"Yeah, I guess you can say that. I mean, I definitely feel like we make good partners."

I wrinkled my forehead. "Meaning?"

"She's smart and focused. She'll be a great mother." He chuckled. "We'll make a shitload of money together."

I promised not to harp on the ignorant money comment. In a sarcastic tone, I said, "So she sounds great." I tilted my head. "So, what don't you like about her again?"

He chuckled. Then, he sighed. "Her personality. Her family."

Could this intelligent man actually know how stupid that sounded? "So, you really don't like her."

I frowned as he attempted to explain those issues were outside of her. "Scooter, those are what make her who she is," I said.

He tried again. "I mean we get along, but . . ."

"She has no clue that you don't like her personality. Does she?" I huffed.

"Maybe I shouldn't have said her personality. I like being with her. I just don't like that she's so bossy."

"So, tell me. What is the biggest issue, her bossiness or her family?"

"Both."

"So why have you stayed so long?"

"Probably because I'm comfortable and I thought she was the best thing going."

Running water echoed through the phone. I asked, "Are you in the bathroom?"

"Yeah, I'm about to get in the shower."

I visualized his Hershey-colored body, standing naked. I imagined his large endowment just hanging freely and before I realized it, my right hand was tucked between my tightly closed thighs. I grunted.

He laughed. "I wish you could get in here with me."

My mind warned me not to entertain him, but my libido yelled obscene responses. I tucked my bottom lips in and snickered. "Whatever."

Replaying him inside of me, I moaned. Satisfied that he'd aroused my interest, he laughed. "Have you been with anyone since I was there?"

I moaned, "No."

"Be honest."

"Honestly. I haven't been with anyone. I've been working and—"

He cut me off. "And thinking about how good it felt with me inside of you."

My vagina tingled and my eyes rolled into my head. Pressing my inner thighs tightly together, I coaxed myself to fight the feeling consuming my body. Again, I tried to finish my statement, "I haven't had time to think about sex."

He kidded. "I know 'Ms. Gotta Have It' has at least thought about it."

I reminded him that he was referring to a horny little teenager whose parents didn't allow her out of the house.

"Yeah, but women usually want sex more with age."

Thinking of our early days, I moaned. To be young and ex-
plorative. I sighed.

"What are you thinking about?" he asked.

"How we used to act like animals."

He laughed. "And it's still the best I ever had."

"Don't patronize me."

He hesitated and then admitted, "I swear I wish I was just
playing, but ever since I left Maryland, all I can think about
is—"

I interrupted him. "Scooter, stop—"

"Every time I think about you, I get hard."

Although I wanted to resist, I let my hand explore myself.
"What about your girl?"

"You know our chemistry has always been strong."

My panties were drenched, my senses blurred. I needed to
hear more of how I made him feel. "It's too late now."

"I'm not married. It ain't never too late."

I sighed. "Why are you doing this to me?"

"Why did you do this to me?"

My face frowned with suspicion. "What did I do to you?"

"Made me think about leaving my girl."

Maybe all of my parents' prayers had been answered.

I stuttered, "What?"

"When I settled down with Akua, I thought I'd done all I
wanted to do. After the night I spent with you, I can't shake
it. I keep questioning my relationship." He paused. "I want
to see you."

"Why did it take you so long to call?"

"I didn't want this. I didn't want to hurt her. Then, I realized that I have to be happy before I can make anyone else
happy."

I nodded. He added, "Right?"

"Yes."

The busy signal came through my phone and startled me
as it lay tucked between my ear and my pillow. I sat up and

looked around. It was four o'clock in the morning. Did I fall asleep on Scooter? Trying to remember the last few things we discussed, I rubbed my eyes. He asked me to come see him this weekend.

Possibilities danced in my mind as I thought about what we talked about and how he repeated that I was his ideal mate. I sighed and tried to go back to sleep. I couldn't recall when I actually fell asleep, but when the alarm clock went off at 7:00, it felt like I'd only slept for fifteen minutes. Cursing at the clock, I pounded on the snooze button. Finally, I peeled myself out of bed and prepared for work.

On my way to work, Courtney and I chatted on the phone about nothing. We agreed to meet for drinks later and got off the phone. I was surprised to find a text message when I hung up. I quickly opened it.

Scooter wrote: HAVE A GOOD DAY, BABY. WILL TALK 2 U LATER ABOUT THIS WEEKEND.

As I sat waiting for Courtney and her coworker, Rachael, to arrive at Red Tavern, Scooter called. I swirled my martini glass and simultaneously answered. My syllables rolled slowly off my tongue. "Hello."

He sounded preoccupied. "Hey, what's up?"

"Nothing much. How was your day?"

He shuffled papers and huffed, "Stressed."

"Yeah, I'm sure. What time did you get to work?"

"Seven."

"I'm so sorry."

He fumbled more and said, "It's not your fault. Time just slipped away. We could always talk all night."

I sipped my drink and agreed, saying, "You ain't lying."

"So how was your day?"

"I guess it was okay. Work is work. I'm at a restaurant waiting for Courtney."

"Where's she?"

"She's supposed to be here."

He chuckled. "The odd couple."

"Yep, we're still together."

"Courtney was my girl. I used to feel like I belonged to the both of you."

"Yeah, I remember you always said that. Her fiancé always claims he has two women, too."

Engulfed in my conversation, I hadn't noticed Courtney's arrival. Courtney wrapped her arms around my shoulders and leaned her head in toward mine. "Hey girl."

I jumped, practically closing my phone as I spoke, "Hey, can you call me a little later."

As he rambled on as to when he'd be able to call again, I shooed him off of the phone. "Okay. That's cool. It's whatever. Bye."

I quickly closed my phone and looked at Courtney, who sat beside me with her face twisted in a knot. I attempted to ignore her inquisitive look. Without giving Courtney eye contact, I greeted Rachael.

"Hey, Rachael. How you doing girl?"

Rachael reached over Courtney to touch my hand. "Girl. I'm fine."

The quick exchange allowed me to evade Courtney's expression one second longer. I offered to buy a round of drinks.

When I pointed to Courtney to take her order, she smirked. "Who were you talking to?"

I waved my hand and proceeded to Rachael. She answered, "A cosmo."

Courtney asked again, "Who were you talking to hooker?"

"What are you having?"

After she ordered her drink, she returned to the question at hand. "Who were you talking to when I came in?"

"This guy."

Courtney shook her head and looked at me with a suspicious grin. "Don't you think I know you better than that? I called you two times from the parking lot and you didn't answer. Then, when I came in here, you tried to rush off of the phone."

I laughed and turned my attention to Rachael. "What brings you out this evening?"

Rachael laughed knowing I was trying to avoid the question. Courtney rolled her neck, "Hooker, who the hell were you talking to?"

Embarrassed by my own silliness, I pouted. "It was Scooter."

"Where the hell has he been? What took him so long to call?"

Exactly what I didn't want to discuss. I smirked. "Girl, he lives with his girlfriend."

Courtney scooted to the edge of the bar stool. She grabbed my forearm. "Did you know that?"

Rachael added. "Girl, leave that shit alone."

"No, I didn't know he lived with her," I answered.

Then, I looked at Rachael. "And I don't plan on messing with him."

My mind was saying *at least not until he leaves his girlfriend like he said*. Courtney's eyes pierced through me, as she demanded, "Don't get caught up with Scooter."

Chuckling, I suppressed the desire to announce that he wanted to leave his girlfriend for me. "Whatever. I'm not stupid."

Courtney added. "I know you're not stupid, but you're human."

Growing tired of being the center of the lecture, I got the attention of the bartender. "They need another drink. Fast."

My cell phone vibrated. Afraid to look at the message, but too excited to contain myself, I flipped my phone open. Courtney tried to grab it. We arm wrestled momentarily and Courtney surrendered. I BOOKED YOUR FLIGHT. FRIDAY – DCA @ 5:15.

I blushed and Courtney shook her head. The spinach dip came just in time for me to dodge any questions. As I anxiously ate, I carelessly put my phone down. Courtney grabbed it and read the message.

She rolled her eyes saying, "I hope he's not talking about this weekend." She chuckled. "You're gonna have to refund his money."

I frowned. "Why?"

"Girl, it's the Congressional Black Caucus weekend." It had completely slipped my mind. "Whatever. We don't miss the CBC for nobody."

Scooter was definitely tempting, but Courtney was right. CBC is our must-attend event. I nodded. "You're right."

"So, what are you going to do?"

"I'm staying here."

She looked at me. "Taylor, promise me that you're in control of this situation."

I placed my hand on top of Courtney's and lied, "I promise."

When you start lying to your tight-girl, you know you're headed down the wrong path. Rachael piled her hand onto the promise stack. "Here's to finding our own men."

I nodded in agreement, but that statement didn't include me. Scooter *is* my man.

13

SCOOTER

When I got in from the hospital, Akua had candles burning throughout the house and relaxing music playing. I walked into the bathroom and found her soaking in the tub. When she noticed me, she smiled. "Hey, baby."

I sat on the toilet to have a few moments with her before she left for her night shift. I leaned in for a kiss. "Hey. You look relaxed."

"Looks are deceiving. Last night was murder. I hate working at night."

"I know you do."

She analyzed my expression. "Why do you look so sleepy? You should have slept well since I wasn't here to wake you this morning."

I poked her damp shoulder. "I knew it. You try your best to wake me up in the morning."

"It's not fair."

"Don't hate the playa, hate the game."

"We'll see who laughs when I bring home all the bacon."

We laughed, but in reality that joke was never quite as funny as she found it. She changed topics. "How was your day?"

"Regular stuff."

"Pray that I have a better night tonight."

"I will."

She stood up and water glistened all over her body. I was momentarily mesmerized. She smiled. "Hand me my towel."

I reached toward the towel rack. Then, I changed my mind. "I want you to stay wet."

She looked at the clock, but I put her mind at ease. "You got time. Don't worry."

I stood up and flicked the light off. The candles made for a romantic setting. I sat back on the toilet. When she stepped from the tub, water slung from her body and onto my scrubs. I pulled her in front of me, letting my face slip and slide on her stomach.

I made love to her navel. She wrapped her arms around me and stroked my back. My hands massaged her slippery body. I reminded myself, "I love you, Ku."

She nodded. I stepped out of my scrubs and she climbed on me and slowly lowered herself onto me. With one hand around her back to stabilize her, I dug as deep as I could go. She moaned. Her eyes fluttered. I examined her sound, her movement. She balanced her feet on the floor and rode me like I was the last train in the station. Her body soaked me. I leaned my head into her moist breasts. She wiped the sweat from my face.

She abruptly ended our post-sex embrace by jumping off of me and letting the water out of the tub. I watched as she frantically turned the shower on. "Look what you made me do."

Looking down at my drenched scrubs, I joked, "Look what you made me do."

She rolled her eyes. I took my shirt off and climbed in the shower behind her. Suds covered her chocolate skin. I massaged her neck. She said, "Don't start that shit, Doc. I have to go to work."

"All right, Ku. Go ahead. Go to work."

She rinsed off and hopped out, leaving me there to ponder

my emotions. The water ran down my face and blurred my vision. What if this is how all women act once they have you?

I blew air from my jaws and my lips vibrated. Akua. Taylor. How could I be confused after one weekend away? After I dried off, I went to the room and threw on some sweats. Nicotine was calling my name. I chuckled. Now, I have three women. When I stepped out to light my cigarette, my fatigue had taken over.

I sat outside of the building when Akua left for work. "What am I supposed to do if you kill yourself?"

"You'll live."

"That's what you think. I'll have to quit my residency and die too."

I smiled. "It's going to be a while before I develop lung cancer."

"Now, you're talking crazy." Her face turned serious. "I don't care how long it takes you to develop lung cancer. I'll still be the one taking care of you. I don't want you to die on me."

How was she so certain of our future? Was this my fault? Guilt forced me to put my cigarette out. She kidded, saying, "I would give you a kiss, but you smell like smoke."

"Have a good night."

She turned around. "If I get some free time, I'll call you."

I watched her drive off and wondered if and when it was time to let go, how could I destroy her confidence in us? I hung my head between my knees. Here I was embarking on a new relationship and the one I'm in is perfectly fine. I kicked myself in the ass all the way into the house.

When the phone rang, Akua's mother shouted into the phone, "My daughter, please!"

"She went to work."

"To work?" she asked.

"Yeah. Work."

"Tell her to call me."

She slammed the phone in my ear. I stood in my living room, wondering if I could really live like this. I had to laugh at her parents. Akua gave me the impression they would grow to like me. Here we were two years later and they hate me as much now as the day they first met me. Any American family would be proud to claim me as a son-in-law, but I'm not good enough for them. It was as if that phone call came to remind me why I'd just spent four hundred dollars for Taylor to come visit this weekend.

After I studied, I called Taylor. She picked up on the first ring. When she said hello, all of my questions were erased. Her joyful voice brought a smile to my face.

"Hey, Tay-Bae."

She sighed. "Scooter, guess what?" she asked, sounding disappointed.

"What?"

"This weekend is the Congressional Black Caucus. I have to go. My job requires me to go."

I sighed. "Damn."

"Give me the reservation number. I'll change it to next weekend."

Before I agreed, I walked into the kitchen to view our big calendar. If Akua was no longer on night shift, this wouldn't work. I pumped my fist in the air. "Yeah, that'll still work."

"Are you mad at me?" she whined.

"Nah. Just a little disappointed that I can't see you this weekend."

She laughed. "Don't worry. Next week will be here soon enough."

14

DEVIN

After a full day of looking for houses, I walked into the Convention Center to pick up my CBC registration. I stood there for a second absorbing all the beautiful black people scurrying around me. I sported a black T-shirt stating, I LOVE MY PEOPLE and a pair of jeans. I decided to save the professional attire for the following days.

A smile sat on my face, as it always did when I attend the CBC. I get enough numbers here to last me throughout the year. This is my restocking conference.

After I picked up my registration package, I headed to the exhibition hall. I called a few of my boys to see where they were. After I'd taxied around the floor speaking to all the vendors, I ran into one of my line brothers.

We hugged and he said, "What's up, Dawg?"

"Nothing man. What's up with you?"

"Man, I'm 'bout to tie the knot."

I sympathized and lied. "That's all right."

"So, what's up with your boy Jason?"

"About to tie the knot."

We burst out laughing. "What about you?" he asked.

"I'm good."

"Yeah, you did it too early. You should've waited on us."

"You ain't lying. Why didn't y'all stop me?"

"Nigga, your ass was married by the time I found out."

We laughed again. "You ain't lying. I'm looking for B and 'em. You seen 'em?"

He pointed. "Yeah, they're over there." He patted my back. "All right man, I'll catch you a little later."

I proceeded to walk in that direction. Two young ladies walked toward me. They both wore black suits. The short one wore a blue button-down shirt. The tall one had on a white T-shirt that read, SIX-FOOTER. I smirked. After giving me a once over, the short one commented, "I like that shirt."

I smiled. "Thank you."

The tall chick looked me up and down. Her lips curled up. Suddenly, mine curled down. Why do the fine ones always have to have attitude? I took a deep breath. Then, to destroy my inaccurate perception, a bright smile spread across her face. She pointed at me. "Oh, that shirt."

Her girl rolled her eyes. "What shirt did you think I was talking about?"

Her eyes shifted around translating to her girl that she'd rather not explain at the moment what shirt she thought she was talking about. We all laughed. The model nodded at me. "That shirt *is* hot."

I smiled. "Thanks," I said.

"Where'd you get it from?"

"New York."

They giggled and I frowned. "What?"

The short one said, "We were just saying yesterday how when we were teenagers, if you didn't want someone to know where you got something from, you'd say New York."

That didn't occur in my hood. I clearly missed the joked. They laughed again. Then, the model asked, "C'mon, where'd you get the shirt?"

Feeling the need to defend myself, I repeated, "I got this shirt in New York. I'm from New York."

The model chuckled. "Don't mind us. We're just being silly."

They passed and their amusement twirled my head in their direction. I grinned. It's good to see happy people. I stuck my chest out. Damn right! I love my people.

15

TAYLOR

I talked to Scooter on the phone, while I waited for Courtney to come out of the house for CBC's Annual Black Party at Sequoia's on the Waterfront in Georgetown. He asked what I was wearing. "Why?" I asked.

"Cause I want to picture you with it on."

"So you want me to describe it."

"Please."

I looked down at my dress. "Um, it's a black washed-silk BCBG dress."

He laughed. "Huh?"

Obviously, his girl was not into fashion. I huffed. "Well, it fits tight through the midsection. The sleeves are wide and they come to like my elbow, but they kinda hang off my shoulder."

"So, you're showing your little bit of cleavage."

"Whatever. I have on the bomb push-up bra."

"Okay, finish."

"Okay, so you figured out it's cut really low in the front and the bottom has an asymmetrical hem."

"I know you look good."

"Thank you."

"Remember you used to take pictures every day and send them to me at the end of the month. That was your way of letting me see you every day."

"Uh-huh."

I tried to stay off the college days. Instead, I focused more on our high school stories. He yawned. I quickly asked. "Are you ready to go to sleep?"

He yawned again. "Nah, I want to talk to you."

"I'm about to go out. If you want to go, it's okay really."

"Your voice relaxes me. I'm cool."

"So anyway, what are we going to do when I come up there?"

"We're going to just enjoy each other's company."

When Courtney peeked out of her front door, I began to rush him off of the phone. "Scooter, baby. I'm going to have to go. We're about to leave."

His good-bye lingered. "Yeah, this is going to be the first night all week I fall asleep before four."

"Uh-huh."

"I've already gotten used to talking to you all night."

"Uh-huh."

"The crazy part is, I don't even mind waking up in the morning."

Courtney plopped in the car, handing me a sippy cup, labeled TAYLOR. I sipped and responded to Scooter simultaneously. "Uh-huh."

Courtney frowned and whispered. "Who the hell is that?"

I smiled. "I'm going to miss you tonight," he continued.

"Me too."

Courtney's eyes stretched. I giggled. Scooter didn't pay attention. "Yeah, I'm already addicted."

Trying my best to make this conversation sound platonic, I said. "You'll be okay. I have to go."

"If it's not too late, call me when you get in."

"Okay, I will."

"Talk to you then."

"Okay."

"All right."

"Okay."

When I closed the phone, Courtney rolled her eyes at me. "Who the hell was that?"

"Nobody."

"Nobody, as in Scooter."

"Shut up."

"You think I'm joking. You better leave that shit alone."

"Look, we're just kicking it."

"One day you'll be kicking it and next your ass will be caught up."

I shook my head. "Whatever."

By the time we walked in the party, it was already live. This was like the Black GW Law School Alumni party. As soon as we walked in, we were hugging and greeting people. The music was jumping. I took my one free drink ticket up to the bar aka drink station.

"Um, I'll have Merlot."

He filled my cup with three-fourths ice and the other one-fourth of wine. Can you really complain about a free drink? I turned to see Courtney doing just that. She argued, "Sir, you only put a smidgen of Crown Royal in here. I may as well get a coke."

The bartender topped her off with more. I frowned. She giggled. "They are tripping."

"It was free Courtney."

"Oh, hell no it wasn't! I paid fifty dollars to get in this joint. I don't see any food." Her eyes circled the room as if she was really looking. "At least they can give us a real drink."

"You're right." Then, I reminded her, "Good thing we drank those strong-ass martinis you made before we got in here."

Michael Jackson's *Off the Wall* came on. I grabbed Courtney's arm and pulled her onto the dance floor. My hands waved in the air as we rocked side to side. We danced and danced and danced, while the DJ played all the hits from the eighties. If it wasn't my song, it was Courtney's. Just as I'd be tempted to sit, she pulled me back and vice versa. Guys usually notice how much fun we have dancing together, so no one usually bothers to interrupt.

When someone tapped on my shoulder, I thought for sure it was a mistake, until Courtney's eyes lit up. She pointed. "Remember him, Tay?"

I turned around and frowned. "No."

He smiled. "I love my people."

"I know that's right. Me too."

As the revelation came where I knew him from, I put my hands up to my head. "Oh, my goodness, you're the guy from today."

As I began to drop my hand, he grabbed it. I pumped our clasp up in the air as I sang, "I ain' sayin' I'm a Gold Digga, but I ain' messin' with no broke . . ."

I smiled and let the crowd finish my sentence. He chuckled. "Go 'head girl, go 'head, get down."

When my long legs stooped down to the floor and sprung back, his jaw followed. He smiled. "You got skills."

Appreciating his admiration, I seductively teased him with a few more drop-it-like-its-hot dance moves. He raised his arms in the air and enjoyed the ride. As my squeaky knees began to tire, I hit the hitchhiker dance. Courtney caught on, and we faced each other. My thumb went right hers went left. "I Love My People" rocked side to side behind me. From a side glimpse, I saw a huge grin on his face. I slowed down and asked. "What are you laughing at?"

"You and your girl. You two are funny."

I turned to face him and smiled. "We aim to please."

Before asking my name, he said, "So, what do you do?"

I joked. "Not a whole lot."

"Are you a model?"

"Yeah, I'm a model."

He nodded. "Six-footer."

"No, actually I'm five-nine."

As our dance became a conversation in the middle of the floor, Courtney's song came on. She sashayed behind him and put him in a dance sandwich. Watching her dance so hard forced me to join her party. He remained cool with a two-step in the middle. I asked, "What's your name?"

"Devin. What's your name?"

"Taylor."

"Do you do runway or print?"

"A little of both."

"You're fine. I know that."

"Thanks. So are you."

He blushed. We danced for a while longer and finally Courtney pulled me off the floor. She joked. "Girl, 'I Love My People' is fine as shit."

"His name is Damon or Devin." I chuckled. "Something like that."

"What does he do?"

"I dunno. You know I hate the what-do-you-do, who-do-you-know questions."

"You're so crazy girl. That's how you start a conversation."

I smirked. "By calculating how much money I make."

"However you want to look at it, it's a conversation starter."

"Well, all I know is he's from New York and he thinks I'm a model."

We giggled and she reminisced on the time I told someone I was a rapper. "Remember he asked you to spit some rhymes," she said.

I shook my head. "Girl, yeah. That was funny. At least with claiming to be a model, all I have to do is walk sexy."

When it was time for us to switch locations, I practiced my runway strut. Courtney poked me. "Stop. You're making me laugh."

Before we left, Courtney asked, "Did you exchange info with 'I Love My People'?"

"No, dummy. I'm a model remember. My business cards will blow my cover."

"You're silly. He could hit it in a heartbeat."

"He was all right. And come to think of it, he didn't offer to buy drinks. No wonder I didn't get his information. I only exchange digits with drinks."

"We shook him before he could offer."

"We danced long enough for him to ask. Anyway, I have ten other numbers to make up for his."

16

DEVIN

When the few people trickled out of the party, it was obvious that I'd missed my six-foot cutie. My neck stretched over and in between the crowd, searching. Where could she have gone? I had my eye on her all night. As the crowd herded to exit, I lost her.

One of my boys asked, "Damn man, who are you waiting for?"

"This chick."

He laughed. "You better come on. We're going to Ozio's. There'll be a bunch of chicks there."

"You right. Let's go."

Still, I scoped every tall woman as we walked to the car.

I walked aimlessly through the exhibit hall the next day, searching for the six-footer. Why was I tripping on her? Was it because she wasn't tripping on me? I tried to shake it, because as of late I've been shooting for looks and ending up with nothing more. Maybe it was the way she bent over to the floor and touched her toes. I chuckled as I minimized the attraction to merely sexual.

I ducked in and out of all the Emerging Leaders sessions. She was nowhere to be found. I began to think she just was here styling and profiling, picking up numbers like me. Around two, I decided to continue my house hunt. When I hopped in a taxi, I heard someone say, "Hey, 'I Love My People.'"

Walking toward me was the model's home girl. She waved her left hand. A huge rock that I didn't notice the night before sat propped on her finger. I chuckled to myself. As I contemplated hopping out, it hit me that the model may have been wearing a rock, too. I frowned. Usually I'm more in tune to rings. Why hadn't I seen it? Maybe she wasn't wearing it. She walked up the Convention Center steps and the taxi hadn't moved. Just as I looked at the driver, he looked at me in the rearview mirror. "Where to, sir?"

My brain apologized to the driver and threw my body from the taxi. It pushed my legs up the steps and back into the Convention Center. Once inside, I looked around. Home girl was no where in sight. Feeling slightly silly, I walked toward Starbucks to grab a coffee. When I passed the couches on the left, someone said, "I thought you were gone, 'I Love My People.'"

I smiled. "Actually, I forgot to pick up my ticket for the Gospel Brunch on Saturday."

She giggled. I laughed too. "Honestly, when I checked in they didn't have any more tickets. They told me to . . ."

As my words collided with her you're-faking smirk, I chuckled. "All right. I needed some coffee."

"It really doesn't matter to me. I was just surprised to see you back here."

I decided to scrap the explanation. "Yeah, where's your girl?"

She looked at her watch. "She may not make it here today. She's working. She was trying to get off, but some things came up."

"Oh really. Where does she work?"

"She's a labor attorney for the Train Workers' Union."

I frowned. "What?"

"No, she's not Naomi Campbell. She doesn't like to career drop when she's out."

She misinterpreted my shock. Could this be the Taylor with the Polish last name? "Yeah, I understand that. I'm actually a consultant for the Train Workers' Union."

"Really."

"Yeah, what's her last name?"

"Jabowski."

I started to explain to her that some old lady tried to set me up with her two weeks ago, but I didn't bother. Instead, I said, "Is she married to a white guy?"

She chuckled. "No, she's single. Both of her parents are black, and we have no clue where that name came from."

"I'll have to look her up the next time I'm in her building."

"Yeah, why don't you do that?"

I would have attributed it to fate, but I downgraded it to luck. I whipped out a card and decided to put the ball in Taylor's court. "Here you go. Good seeing you again. I have to get my coffee."

We both laughed. I'm not certain she knew I'd rushed back in to get Taylor's information or not, but she was clear that it wasn't strictly for coffee. She didn't offer her card. As I pretended to rush off to Starbucks, I said, "Make sure y'all keep in touch."

She gave me a "whatever" nod. I waved. She waved and said laughing, "Keep the love alive for our people."

My detour caused me to be fifteen minutes late for my appointment with my realtor. The taxi pulled up to newly built condominiums in the Potomac Place; I nodded approvingly. My realtor stood outside. He smiled like he knew this was the one. I stepped from the taxi and extended my hand. "What's up, man?"

He nodded. "Man, these are the ones."

"A'ight. We'll see."

He went on to describe the amenities and the details of the building. "The one we're going to look at is an investment flip. The owner has never lived in it, but you know . . ."

"Yeah, he's selling it for twice the amount."

"Exactly."

We entered the chic building and went to the third floor. He pointed, "It's an end unit."

"Okay."

He opened the door to the condo and Taylor sat on the counter. She smiled. "Hey Devin. You like it, don't you?"

I nodded. She hopped off the counter and music began playing. She danced seductively. I smiled. She motioned for me to join her. I stepped into the living room with her. She wrapped her long arms around my neck, just as she did at the black party. We danced in front of the fireplace. She whispered, "Wait 'til you see . . ."

My realtor finished the sentence and ended my daydream. "The bedroom. It's huge."

I followed him into the master bedroom. It was definitely larger than all the rest I'd seen. This was the place. It was near the South West Waterfront, close enough to Union Station that I could transport back and forth from New York. This was it. A part of me wasn't sure why this place felt more like home than all the others, but I was sold.

"I want to put a contract on it."

My realtor looked surprised. "You sure?"

"Positive."

"I had a few other things to show you. Do you want to see them first?"

"Nah man, I think this is it."

"Okay, it's a great building. I definitely think it meets all your requirements. The people in the building seem pretty cool."

Why was he still giving the sales pitch? I nodded. "Yeah man. I think this is it."

I heard my mother in my ear telling me to buy a house instead of a condo. I blocked her voice. Splitting my time between two cities was not conducive to managing a house.

We went to his office to process the contract. He forewarned me, "Yeah man, the market is crazy right now. People are out-bidding each other like crazy."

I nodded.

"So, if this contract isn't accepted, how much are you willing to go up?"

"I'll go as high as I need to as long as it's still market value."

"I got you man. It's my job to educate you."

I signed the contract. Now, I have to explain to Jennifer that we're going to have to flip-flop weeks, instead of days. I took a deep breath. Some things you're never prepared for. Life would be so much easier if I'd had a kid with someone I actually loved.

17

TAYLOR

When my alarm clock sounded, I banged on the snooze button. I pulled my comforter over my head and stretched. Conversations with Scooter had me up until almost three o'clock for the last two weeks. How did he manage to make it to work at seven every day?

I lay motionless hoping time would completely stop. I looked at the clock and 10:00 A.M. was rapidly approaching. "Shit!" I muttered.

I contemplated calling in sick. Finally, I got my exhausted butt up and into the shower. Luckily, I'd packed my luggage while we chatted last night. Once I was up and moving, adrenaline pumped through my veins. I rushed around the room to find the right mix between professional and sexy. I put on my black Tahari suit and a wife beater underneath. Planning to switch after work, I packed my denim blazer.

My cell phone buzzed. I looked at my morning greeting. GOOD MORNING TAYLOR. CAN'T WAIT 'TIL YOU GET HERE.

I responded. CAN'T WAIT EITHER, SEE YOU SOON.

By the time I got to work, it felt like it was time to leave. Was it my excitement that fast-forwarded the clock to 3:15? I peeped into my MAC compact and went for my last run to the restroom.

After rushing through the terminal, through security, and to my gate, I sat there awaiting the flight to my future. Finally, the flight attendant's voice came over the speaker. "We will be boarding flight 423 to Stamford, Connecticut, in just a few moments. Please have your IDs out."

My heart dropped. I looked at the time. Thirty-five minutes before take-off. Two hours from my destiny. I imagined our greeting. Our departure. The magazine that sat on my lap, slowly slid down my legs, as I explored the possibilities.

"Rows fourteen and higher."

I looked around wondering if anyone noticed me daydreaming. Then, I stood up and walked over to the gate. As I walked through the tunnel, I sent Scooter a text message. GETTING ON THE PLANE. WILL C U SOON.

I turned my phone off before he could respond. Once I had my carry-on stowed away, I sat in the window seat. As I always do, I watched the baggage carriers rip and run, loading luggage and riding around, transporting thousands of dollars worth of goods in their little carts. They deserved more money.

Temporary diversions were welcomed, because when my mind reverted to Scooter, nerves danced around in my chest. I attempted to close my eyes, hoping to block the visions of what I expected to happen. Surprisingly, I drifted off to sleep and woke up midflight, questioning why I was here. I sat up in my seat, looked at the balding white man beside me, rubbed my eyes, and looked out of the window. One mile high and I was not sure if I should continue the journey. I grabbed the *Sky Mall* magazine from the seat-back pocket to calm my nerves. I flipped anxiously through it. The pilot came over the speaker.

"We're about 100 miles outside of Stamford. It's sixty degrees Fahrenheit. Winds are light. You're in for a nice evening. In just a few moments, we'll begin our descent."

As the plane descended, so did my confidence. Why was I headed to creep with another woman's man? I shook my head. I'm too cool for this. Just as the wisdom would seep in, my desire to find Mr. Right would bully it out. When the plane hit the runway, my heart sank. I took a deep breath and prayed. "Lord, I need your help. I know this ain't right . . ."

I stopped midprayer. Letting the prayers of my ordained family intercede seemed like a better option.

When the pilot turned off the seatbelt sign, the other passengers popped out of their seats, grabbing luggage from the overhead bins. Everyone was in a rush to nowhere. It's always funny to watch the hysteria that leads to standing still at baggage claim. While everyone else stood up in line to exit, I peeped out of my window and enjoyed the sunset. When the passengers behind me were all out, I got up.

I called Scooter when I got to baggage claim. He picked up and said, "I'm outside waiting for you. I'm driving a silver Honda Accord."

"Y'all love those damn Hondas."

We laughed and got off of the phone. I gave Courtney a safe-arrival phone call. To my surprise, she answered almost immediately. She sighed. "Hey girl."

"I'm here."

"Thanks for calling."

"I'm waiting for my luggage." A man nearly tackled me as he went to get his luggage. I frowned and sucked my teeth. "Dang!"

Courtney asked, "What happened?"

"People kill me in a rush to nowhere."

"That statement is profound."

My bag came around the carousel. I grabbed it before I responded. "What the hell are you talking about, girl?"

"In a rush to nowhere."

"What's so profound about that?"

She grunted, "I'll text you, okay. Have fun."

Baffled by her comment, I shrugged my shoulders, closed my phone, and put it in my back pocket. I headed out of the airport and Scooter was leaning on his car in blue scrubs. He smiled. I smiled. I wanted to run, but I floated instead. As the cloud graciously carried me to him, a stun gun trembled through me, bringing me back down to earth. I jumped and realized it was my phone vibrating in my back pocket.

Scooter smirked as he tried to decipher the confusion on my face. I laughed, as I stood in front of him. He reached out to hug me. I leaned into him and felt like I could melt. "Hey, Dr. Evans."

He kissed my cheek. "Hey Tay-Bae."

We held on for a few more seconds. I could have stayed there, but he let me go and grabbed my luggage. He opened the car door and I sat in the passenger seat. I pulled my phone out to see who'd just sent me a text message. It was Courtney. The subject was THE RUSH. I contemplated not opening it, because I didn't want to deal with any warnings. My curiosity would not rest, so I read it.

RUSHING N2 THIS RELATIONSHIP WITH SCOOTER IS THE SAME AS RUSHING 2 BAGGAGE CLAIM. TAKE YOUR TIME. DONT GET 2 INVOLVED 2 SOON. -C.

Was she trying to say I was headed to nowhere? The anxious look on Scooter's face was spoiled by the baffled look on mine. He asked, "What's wrong?"

"Nothing." Trying to reaffirm, I repeated, "Nothing."

He asked, "Are you hungry?"

The jitters in my stomach filled it to capacity. "Um, not really."

"Well, let's go to the hotel so I can change. Then maybe you'll be ready to eat."

"That's cool."

My mind was on Courtney's message. God only knows where Scooter's mind was, but we had nothing to say. After hours and hours of phone conversation, we sat confined in his car exchanging silly smiles. We pulled up to the Westin Hotel and stopped at the front door. He got out and pulled my roller bag and his backpack from the trunk. He sat it on the side. The older bellman pulled his cart over and placed the bags on it. He was a handsome black man, about fifty with mixed gray hair and a pleasant smile.

"Good evening, young lady."

I smiled. "Good evening, sir."

He pulled the cart toward the automatic doors, and I followed. He asked, "Is that your husband?"

"No."

"Boyfriend?" he asked.

Suddenly, I felt like an asshole. No, he's not my husband. No, he's not my boyfriend. But here I am going into a hotel with him. I obviously looked like I was worth having a title. Feeling rather insecure, I nodded.

"He's a very lucky man."

I blushed. "Thank you," I said.

Scooter came rushing into the hotel. He smiled at me. The nice man smiled. "A doctor, huh? You're a lucky lady . . ."

Hoping my discomfort wasn't obvious, I nodded. Scooter checked in and grabbed our bags from the cart. He handed the man a few dollars. "I got it from here, man. Thanks."

"You guys have a great time here in the marvelous town of Stamford," the man said.

We laughed, as he was clearly joking. I pressed the elevator button and turned around to Scooter's puckered lips. We pecked. He smiled. "I'm glad you could come, Tay-Bae."

"Me too."

The elevator doors opened and we got on. After he pressed the seventh floor, I leaned on the mirror. He stood in front of me and his eyes studied my eyes. I did not waiver, because I wanted to read his mind as well. When the elevator opened, I held my arm in the door so he could pull my bag out.

He pointed to the left, saying, "We're this way. Room 705."

I walked ahead of him and he commented, "I can't believe we're here."

"Me either."

When we got inside of the room, I went straight over to open the blinds. He followed and sat at the small table near the window. I sat down across from him. He reached out for my hand. I willingly offered both.

"How did we get here?"

"I dunno." I hung my head and repeated, "I dunno."

He laughed. "Me either. I mean . . ." He stopped and shook his head. "Never mind."

I urged him to finish. "What? Tell me."

"I didn't foresee this."

Knowing that I'd fantasized about this for months, I decided not to say anything. He continued, "I can't believe how easily my feelings have resurfaced."

I nodded. "I know."

"It's been really hard to keep my mind on anything else."

I smiled. "Me too."

"I look at my girlfriend and . . ." I cringed and took a deep breath, as he continued. "I wonder if she knows what's going through my mind." He chuckled. "Tay-Bae, this shit is crazy."

"I know," I said quietly.

"It's like this just snuck up on me. I never expected to be here."

I looked at him and asked for the fifteenth time. "Why didn't you bring her to the reunion?"

"She didn't want to come."

"I never knew I'd feel like that when I saw you again either." I sighed and tried to explain my actions. "I mean, I always knew that our breakup was a mistake, but I never knew that I'd still want to be with you after I saw you."

"I know. Me either." He paused. "Now, I feel pressured to make a decision," he added.

With a sympathetic expression, I said, "Look Scooter, it's still early. You don't have to make a decision today. We have to make sure this isn't infatuation between us. You know?" He nodded. I continued, "Let's not make this heavy. When it gets heavy, then you make a decision. Today, let's just kick it."

I grabbed the City Guide from the table to see what there was to do in Stamford. It didn't appear there were any clubs that I wanted to go to. In pursuit of places to just kick it, I suggested a pub in what appeared to be a busy strip. Scooter was never hard to please. He was mostly down for whatever I was down for. And thankfully, that hadn't changed. Scooter gazed at me as I bent over and flipped through my bag as if I hadn't already decided what I should wear.

Peeping over my shoulder, I asked, "Do you want to get ready first?"

Snapping out of his daydream, he said, "Oh, yeah. It doesn't matter."

Scooter took all of ten minutes to throw on a pair of jeans and a Polo shirt. When he came out, my purple lace panties lay on the white comforter. My eyes followed his as he fantasized me with them on. I sashayed past him and picked them up as I headed for the bathroom. After I showered, slipped on my top and, of course, I walked out to grab my jeans. Tiptoeing bashfully past the bed, I said, "Oh, I forgot these."

He licked his lips and gave me a lustful expression, as I rushed back to the bathroom to slip them on. After I made up my face, I was ready to just kick it. I stood at the bottom of the bed and let Scooter admire me before asking, "Are you ready, baby?"

We left the room and headed into town, a town that Scooter claimed he was familiar with, but didn't know where anything was. So, I asked the hotel receptionist how to get to the pub. She suggested we try a Mediterranean bistro not too far away, so we did. I was shocked when we pulled up to the hole in the wall. Scooter and I looked at each other and began to laugh. We decided to just go in, because nothing else in this town looked plush either. The moment we stepped in, Arabian music was playing and we bobbed our heads in agreement. We were seated at a nice cozy table for two. When the bartender came to take our drink orders, I ordered a Royal Red Apple Martini and Scooter had a glass of wine. Once our drinks came, we heard loud drums and belly dancers filled the room. They jingled and twirled their little hips, rippled and snaked their bellies as Scooter and I stared in awe. Scooter joked that he bet I could do it, too. Why was he so supportive?

When they recruited people to dance on stage, I went up there. High on life and high on the possibility of love, I did my own booty-shaking version. If I could have controlled my giggles, I probably would have been a lot better at it. When I returned to the table, Scooter was standing up, clapping.

"Tay, you looked like you knew what you were doing up there."

"You're just trying to flatter me."

We laughed it off and finally our food arrived. I was with my Arabian prince on an Arabian night and all we needed was a magic carpet to take us away from reality. As we gazed into each other's eyes, we chatted about our expectations, our inhibitions, and our dreams.

By the time we got back to the room, his complaints about Akua had increased. The underlying tone of their relationship was comfort. Finally, I asked, "So, is it enough to be just comfortable in a relationship?"

"What's the other option?"

"Love."

He put his arm around my shoulder and leaned his head into me. "Like I said, that's why I'm here. I need to see if this is love."

I smiled and turned to give him a kiss. "Me too."

We dozed off and I awoke to my phone buzzing on the nightstand. I rubbed my eyes and looked at the clock. 10:33 A.M. I was in the bed alone. Scooter was gone. It was a degrading feeling to fall asleep with a man only to awake to a cold bed. I grabbed my phone, another message from Courtney.

Did I really want to read something that would make me feel worse?

WHATCHU DOIN.

I responded. WHAT THE HELL DO YOU THINK. I'M ASLEEP.

She responded. ARE YOU ENJOYING YOURSELF?

I wrote back. YES.

Scooter called and interrupted our line of communication. The jealous side of me answered in an irritated tone. "Yes, Scooter?"

"Hey, I'm on my way back. You know she . . ."

Before he finished, I said, "Yeah, I know."

I guess he'd rocked his princess to sleep and was on his way back to me.

"I'll be there in twenty minutes."

"Okay."

18

SCOOTER

I woke up at six o'clock this morning and drove recklessly to New Haven. I had to be tucked in the bed and snoring by the time Akua got home at seven-thirty.

Why did I think I'd be able to sleep? Last night confirmed my feelings. Taylor is the girl I'd searched for. We had no complicated decisions to make if we were going to be together. She was willing to go where I went. She wasn't power hungry. She grew up watching the example of a good wife. Still, in a sense, she was independent and feisty, but she knew just when and how often to use it.

As I was scrutinizing the Taylor versus Akua scorecard in my mind, I heard the front door open. My heart beat on the bed. I buried my head in the pillow. Please don't wake me up. Just leave me alone.

She walked in the bedroom. "Good morning, baby."

I didn't respond.

"Did you go out last night?" she asked.

Still, I played possum.

"I know you hear me talking to you."

I was afraid that my lack of sleep would be evident if I faced her. She continued, "I'm really proud of you. There are no dishes in the sink. No beer cans on the table."

She clapped. "Finally, you're learning."

She talked as if she knew I was listening. "I had a great night last night."

Oh no! Please don't say it! She said, "I'm not even tired."

It was just my luck. If I had to slip a sleeping pill in her drink, I was going to do it. She sat beside me on the bed and tried tickling me. "Wake up. Let's go to breakfast."

No! Go to sleep! "Wake up, sleepyhead."

I tossed around like I was irritated. "Damn, Akua. I'm tired."

"Tired? I've been on my feet for twelve hours and you're the tired one?"

I snapped, "Yes, I'm tired."

"Well I had coffee an hour ago, so I'm pumped up. C'mon baby, we can go eat and sleep all day long."

If I didn't go eat with her, there would be no way to explain I was going golfing in an hour or so. I sat up in the bed, rubbed my eyes like I'd been asleep all night. I fake yawned. "Where do you want to go?"

"We can go to the coffee shop across from the hospital."

"You don't need any more coffee," I complained.

"Boy, I want food."

I staggered in the bathroom and brushed my teeth. After I threw on a sweat suit, we headed out of the house. We didn't talk the entire walk to the coffee shop. All I could think of was when I could get back to Taylor.

During breakfast, she shared her hospital stories. Until Taylor and I began to talk, I forgot how good it felt to not have to talk about the hospital when I wasn't in the hospital. I laughed on cue and asked questions when I found it appropriate, but I really couldn't give a shit.

Finally, she began to yawn. As I noticed fatigue creeping up on her, I decided to ramble off my plans for the day. "Yeah, I'm going down to the city to hook up with my boy. We're going to play golf."

"How did you know I didn't want to do anything before I went to work this evening?"

"I just assumed."

She rolled her eyes. "You should never assume. When will you be home?"

My mouth hung open. "Ah . . . I guess sometime tonight."

She pouted. "I was hoping you could bring me lunch."

"That ain't happening."

"You can't sacrifice."

"No, I'm hanging out with D and I haven't seen him in a while and I don't want to rush back."

She rolled her eyes. "Pay the check."

I pushed back from the table and walked to the register. She followed. "You've really been smelling yourself lately."

"You're trippin," I said, shaking my head.

"Look at the pot calling the black."

We laughed as she struggled with the metaphor. When I tried to clean it up, she bumped into me. "You know what I'm saying."

When we got back to the apartment, she took a shower and I lay impatiently in the bed. Finally, she came out and climbed in to join me wearing her birthday suit. She wrapped her arms around my waist and kissed my back. "I want to do it."

Okay, I didn't anticipate her having so much energy this morning. She was really messing up my plans. She tickled the hair on my stomach. Then, she reached down and began stroking me.

I turned to face her, placing my right leg in between her legs. We kissed and I slid inside. Her top leg clamped on to me and we made lazy love. When we were done, she was the dude, passed out. I was the woman, pondering the future of our relationship. I climbed from her grip and went into the living room to call Taylor.

Just to cover my ass, I decided to take Taylor golfing. I picked up a case of beer on my way back to Stamford. When I got to town, I stopped at Starbucks and grabbed a breakfast sandwich and coffee for her. As I stood outside of the hotel room, tapping on the door for nearly five minutes, I dialed Taylor.

Running water was in the background when she finally answered. She came to the door wearing the skimpy white hotel towel and stormed away. Water rolled down her slim, shapely legs. Though I'd sensed some frustration on the other end when I spoke to her, her non-greeting perplexed me. I leaned on the rim of the bathroom door, holding her coffee in hand.

"Good morning to you, too."

She started brushing her teeth and rolled her eyes. I sat the cup down and stood behind her, wrapping my arms around her waist. "Taylor, what's wrong?"

"Nothing."

She rinsed her mouth and backed away from me. Following her into the room, I said, "Here, baby, I got you some coffee."

As she stepped into her panties, she smirked. "Thanks."

I sat on the bed and hung my head. After nearly ten minutes of one-word answers, I was frustrated. Finally, she was dressed and ready to go. When I told her our plans for the day, she shrugged. "That's cool. It's whatever."

The perfect words came to mind when we stood to leave. I said, "Taylor, you make me happy." I grabbed her head and looked into her eyes. "I had such a good time with you last night. Now, I remember why I was so in love with you."

Jackpot! A huge smile spread across her face and I knew that she just needed to know that all of the sneaking around was not in vain. She just needed me to reaffirm what we were doing and why we were doing it. "I'm really happy we're together again."

"I am, too, Scooter," she said, nodding.

We headed out to the golf course. Once we were on the cart, I pulled two cans of beer out of the cooler and handed one to her. She joked, "I hope you're not going to drink and drive."

I laughed harder than necessary. It was her clever way of

finding joy in the smallest things that made her special and humored me so. As we talked and drank and Taylor made an earnest attempt to play golf, I felt free again and I wished I was free to be her man. I was attracted to everything about her. How had I convinced myself that I was really over Taylor J? She was the girl that you could never forget and damn if I let this slip away again.

19

TAYLOR

Again, I woke up to an empty bed. This is not my style. I am nobody's bench warmer. I exhaled and reminded myself. "I'm a starter!"

I called Courtney just for some girl talk to get my mind off of the lowly pit I've fallen into. "Oh, girl."

I laughed at her urban impression of saying she had some drama to share. "What?"

"Why did Rachael go away for the weekend with this dude? She had me on the other line cracking up."

"What happened?"

She laughed. "She thought that he spent the money for a nice vacation. She gets there, gives him some because the room was nice and she thought he was really considerate . . ."

I laughed, before she finished, "Girl, why was it a time-share visit? He needed her income to get the fifty dollar deal."

"That is busted."

"She said she almost killed that cheap bastard. She was so mad, talking about 'It's a shame you can't take poom-poom back because she wants a refund.'"

"I know that's real."

As she gave the details of Rachael's weekend, I flipped back and forth whether Scooter was worth pursuing or not. My heart fluttered. Though I felt I needed to end this now, Rachael's story discouraged me. Why did Scooter have to be a good guy? It would be easy to resist if I didn't think he'd make a great husband and father one day. Shit! He was a great boyfriend.

As Courtney talked, I began to gather my belongings. I was trapped somewhere midway between common sense and discouragement. It's not like men like Scooter are on every street corner. I sighed. "You're crazy."

She giggled. "I know." She added, "But y'all love to call me with all the crazy stories . . ." That was my invitation into my drama. She said, "So, your turn . . ."

I sighed and repeated what I'd told myself all morning. I yelled, "I'm a starter. I can't do second string!"

Courtney laughed. "You ain't lying. I was wondering when you were going to snap out of it!"

I continued the pep rally. "I'm too cool for this shit. How am I going to wait until I'm nearly twenty-nine years old to play second fiddle?"

She sucked her teeth. "I know that's real. You got too much going for yourself than to settle for that. I'd rather be alone before I sit around and wait for somebody to figure out what they want to do with their woman. Especially when the other woman doesn't know about me. Whatever."

"Uh-huh," I huffed.

She ranted. "I'm Queen B. I am nobody's Wanna B."

She was killing me softly. I said, "Yup."

Was this empty feeling worth it? I shook my head. Courtney continued, "So what made you come to your senses?"

"Well, waking up to an empty bed for the last two days."

"I feel like this, I would definitely be Scooter's friend, but damn if I'd be flying up to visit him on the regular. Nor would I stop dating." She paused. "Cause, I know you."

I laughed. "What are you trying to say?"

"I'm saying that you need to multitask. Don't sit there and let Scooter drag you along. What makes you think he can just leave his girlfriend like that? And if he can, what makes you think he's who you want to be with?"

Just as her convincing argument began to seep in, Scooter put his key in the hotel room door. When he stepped in the room, Courtney's voice began to sound like the adults on the *Muppet Babies*, "Wonk, wonk, wonk."

His presence casts a stupid spell on me. The sincerity in his eyes erased the obvious. I wasn't letting this opportunity go, just as I wasn't going to drop the beautiful purple orchids he handed me on the floor.

"Tell Courtney I said, hi."

I sighed. "Courtney, Scooter said—"

Before I finished, she interrupted me. "Yeah, yeah, tell him I said, hi, too."

We got off the phone and I took another look at him. He was dressed in charcoal slacks, a cream dress shirt and a pink, blue, and brown plaid tie. Although I admired the vision, I frowned. "Why are you so dressed up?"

He snickered and sat down beside me, wrapping his arm around me. "It's Sunday morning."

"Okay. You didn't tell me that we were going to church."

He sighed and lay back on the bed and put his hands behind his head. He looked ashamed, as he said, "We're not. Church was my ticket out of the house this morning."

I looked at him stretched out on the bed. Courtney's voice filled my head. Uncertainty distanced us. I turned to face the television and laid the flowers on my lap. I huffed. He tugged at my arms.

"What's wrong?"

"I know this is early, but this is hard."

He sat up. "I know, but it won't be long. These last few days have made me really think about what I want."

"What is that?" I asked, sullenly.

He kissed my cheek and I turned my face. "I want to be happy."

"And what's going to make you happy?"

"I don't know, but I'm really convinced that Akua is not the one for me."

I prayed that he would tell me I was the one, but he said, "I love her, but the issues with her family, her controlling nature. It's all beginning to take a toll on me. And you . . ." He sighed. "It seems like I wouldn't have those issues with you."

I said, "I'm not perfect either . . ."

"I know, but we have a common upbringing."

"And . . ."

He smirked. "Common pasts help with future hurdles."

"You're right," I said, smiling.

He came in and rearranged the clutter in my mind. It was only a matter of time and a few days of emptiness would not kill me. He leaned in for a kiss. I obliged. We kissed and suddenly I believed. I believed he was my soul mate. I believed that it would all work out. I simply believed in love.

When he dropped me off at the airport, I was even more assured. He sat my bag on the sidewalk and we stood face to face. He held my hand and kissed my cheek. "I'm going to miss you." He kissed my lips, adding, "I'm glad you came."

"I'm glad I came, too."

He smiled and rubbed his hand down the side of my face. "Taylor Jabowski."

I smiled and he kissed me again. Then, a fat police officer on a motorcycle sped toward us. He pointed two fingers at us, then, pointed over his shoulder, demonstrating that we should move it. Scooter and I laughed. He kissed my cheek. "You would think we were at Dulles. He's tripping about this empty-ass airport."

"I know. Right?"

I released my grip. Our hands slid apart until there was nothing connecting us except fingertips. Then, air. He waved. "Call me when you get home."

He jumped into his car and pulled off. I stood there waving at his license plate. The skycap smiled at me when I turned to face him. "What city?"

"DC."

He typed on the keyboard and asked, "Your ID?"

I fumbled for my ID, and he took the opportunity to console me. "A little distance is good for the heart."

As I handed him my ID, I said, "I'm okay."

He proceeded to check me in.

Finally, he handed me a boarding pass, and I gave him a few dollars. My phone vibrated as soon as I walked into the airport. I looked at the message. I MISS U ALREADY. HAVE A SAFE TRIP.

20

SCOOTER

Why did I think spending a weekend with Taylor would help me figure this whole fiasco out? It made it worse. I didn't even want to see Akua. The big question now is how can I tell her that we're not meant to be?

I walked into the house without going into the bedroom to see if she was awake. I sat on the couch and dropped my head between my legs. She walked in from the bedroom. "How was church?"

"It was cool."

My eyes wandered around the room. How could I stare her in the face, knowing I eventually planned to hurt her? She asked if I'd eaten lunch. I took a deep breath. "Nah."

"Do you want to eat?"

Her presence was irritating me for no reason. I snapped, "No."

"What the hell is wrong with you, man?"

"I'm just tired."

"I don't know why."

Before I responded, I checked myself. *Scooter, chill out.* I flicked the television on to distract our conversation.

She fumbled in the kitchen. "I hope you don't plan to watch football all day."

"Why aren't you sleep?"

She walked out of the kitchen with a sandwich on a paper plate and a beer. "I'm not tired. Plus, I don't have to work tonight."

My neck snapped in her direction. "You don't?"

"No, my two weeks are up. I'm back on my regular schedule."

Shit! How am I supposed to talk to Taylor? I'd been so wrapped up in my new relationship that I neglected to figure out when I could escape from my current one. Trying to shake my shock, I nodded. "Oh, I forgot."

She plopped on the couch beside me. I wanted to scoot down. She put her feet on the couch, swung them around, and tucked them under my leg. Her toes made me cringe. She spoke to my profile. "So, do we have to watch this all day or can we go to the movies or something?"

With my eyes glued to the television, I said, "You can do what you want."

She shoved her foot into my leg. "Nigga, I know I can do what I want. What are we doing tonight?"

My hope was to piss her off to the point she wanted to go out without me. I nodded toward the television. "This is what I'm doing today."

She sucked her teeth. "Well, I guess this is what we're doing."

No! Take your ass out. She mumbled under her breath, "I've been working for two weeks straight and I have to watch football on my day off."

Pissed that my strategy didn't work, I ignored her grumbling. "You ain't shit," she huffed.

"I know. You tell me every day."

If I am so bad, why did she want to be up under me all day? Maybe she should go find a man that she thought was the shit. She stabbed her big toe into my thigh. "You're a smart-ass."

"So are you."

"You make me sick."

After sitting through an entire football game, it became clear that Akua would be latched to my hip for the day. I pretended I wanted to run out to get pizza for dinner. Wouldn't you guess it? She wanted to ride too. I searched for every possible reason why it made more sense for me to go alone. As we walked out of the house together, it was obvious I needed to get swifter with stealth techniques.

It never dawned on me how much we did together until I couldn't get away. We stretched out on our living room floor, separated by a box of pizza. How did I manage to take this relationship so far? It would be so much easier if we didn't live together. After a few beers, she was as intoxicated as I was. I asked, "Do you think we'd stay friends if we ever broke up?"

Without second guessing the origin of my question, she responded confidently, "Hell no!"

"Why?"

"After all the flack I get from my family for your ass, we better not break up."

"I'm just curious."

"Don't be." She joked. "I'll cut your ass with a scalpel."

She chuckled like she could imagine it. I winced, because I could too. She finished chewing her food. "I'm just playing. If you want me to leave, just let me know."

I shoved the pizza box into her. "Oh, so it's like that? You can just let it go like that?"

"I can't imagine my life without you, but I would never want to be with someone who doesn't want to be with me. If you're ever unhappy, don't do me any favors. Just tell me."

I wished I could explain to her what was going on inside of me. Instead, I gave her a high five and said, "Deal."

As if it finally hit her, she asked, "Are you trying to break up with me?"

"Nah," I lied.

21

TAYLOR

I called Scooter until I was too tired to continue. Finally, my home phone rang shortly after ten. I popped up. I picked up and sang, "Hello."

My mother cleared her throat. "Taylor."

Since it wasn't Saturday morning, I was a little off. I stuttered, "Hey . . . Ma. What's up?"

"How was your trip?"

Was I that excited? Hell, I didn't remember telling her about my trip. "I . . . uh . . . um . . ."

Then, I summarized the weekend. "Well, it was cool. I stayed in the Westin. He stayed at his place."

"Aw! Did he discuss the relationship?" she cooed.

"Well, we're just kicking it."

The empty feeling inside of me confirmed that I was lying to myself. She smacked her lips. "What is that supposed to mean, Taylor?"

I huffed, because I didn't know. "Ma, we aren't tripping. We're taking it slow."

"The last I checked, you didn't have a lot of time."

That comment was my cue to get off of the phone. I sighed. "All right, Mother, I'll talk to you later."

"We're still praying for you. Okay?"

"Okay."

I tossed and turned. Feelings of regret accumulated in my stomach. I went to the bathroom a million times throughout the night. I picked the phone up off the receiver and prayed there was no dial tone, hoping that could explain why my phone had not rung. Scooter promised me so much over the weekend. Maybe it was too good to be true. Coming to that conclusion didn't stop my body from popping up every hour, checking the caller ID.

My heart ached like it was broken. What's up with that? We spent one weekend together and I'm tripping. *Shake it off, Taylor.* I rolled back and forth in my bed trying to squash my feelings.

By the time the sun came up, I'd concluded that I could not be anyone's backup plan. So what if he's the only man I've ever loved. I'm too cool for this shit.

My phone rang while I was in the shower. When I checked my caller ID, it was Scooter. The message light blinked. I didn't want to hear a damn thing he had to say.

Before I left for work, I collected all of the business cards I'd accumulated at the CBC. My ego convinced me that I was in control of my situation, but my body knew better. If I planned to deal with Scooter, I needed a distraction.

On my way to work, I called Courtney. "Girl, dudes are no good. Why didn't I hear from Scooter until this morning?"

"Did you have sex with him?" she grunted.

"No."

"Damn. That's pretty bad. At least we could say he only wanted your poom-poom."

"Court, it's not funny."

"Why are you tripping? You know he has a girlfriend."

I huffed. She didn't share what we shared this weekend. He is not happy with his girlfriend. It's only a matter of time before it's over. Instead of explaining what we discussed, I threw in the towel. "You're right."

"Taylor, I'm telling you girl. Don't get in too deep. We're too old to play games like this."

Anything worth having is worth fighting for. As I fed myself affirmations, I sighed.

Courtney sighed, too. "Taylor, I just don't want you to get hurt."

"I *always* get out before I get hurt."

She laughed. "Yeah, okay."

"Do you really think I'll stick around if the ball is not in my court?"

"Do you think the ball is in your court now? If he can't call you when you want to hear from him," she argued, "the ball is not in your court."

Did I call her for advice? Sometimes you just want people to listen. My head began to pound. "All right then Courtney. I'm almost at work."

"I just don't want you to get hurt," she warned.

"I won't."

"You promise."

"Uh-huh."

How could I promise something that was clearly out of my control?

When I got settled at work, I paged Scooter. He called back almost immediately. Sounding out of breath, he said, "Taylor, I'm so sorry."

"For what?"

"You know. I wanted to call you back last night, but she wouldn't leave me alone." He chuckled. "I felt like she knew something."

"And how did that make you feel?"

"It didn't feel good, but I know what I want."

"Do you really?"

He cleared his throat. "Yeah, I want to be with you."

* * *

I tried to bury Scooter's promise in the back of my mind when I flipped through my new collection of business cards, leaving the same message for everyone. "Hi. This is Taylor Jabowski. We met at CBC. Hopefully you remember me. If so, call me at . . ."

To my surprise, no one returned my call. I guess people had staked their claim by now. When I got in for the evening, Steven returned my call. I racked my brain. I know I called him, but he didn't ring a bell. I chuckled. "Hey, Steven."

"I was hoping you'd call, since you refused to give me your number."

"Yeah, I like to control the dating game," I joked. "Don't call me. I'll call you."

"So, it's like that, huh?"

"Not really. I'm just playing."

We chatted for a while. He seemed pretty interesting. I found some of his jokes funny. But I was more interested in how he looked. I usually toss the ugly cards, so I assumed he was decent. Scooter began clicking into the line around seven. I decided to make him wait, since I had had to wait.

When I looked up and realized that Steven had exceeded my thirty minute first phone call limit by an hour, I rushed off the phone. As we were saying our good-byes, I asked. "Are you going to send me a picture?"

"Yeah, what's your e-mail address? Can I get a picture of you?"

"Sure, what's your e-mail address?"

He spelled it out, "O V E R D A T H O at yahoo dot com."

"What does that mean?"

"It doesn't mean anything."

When we got off the phone, I decided to give Scooter a taste of his own medicine. Let him worry about me tonight. My plan backfired when I woke up and there were no new calls on my caller ID. My mind reverted back to the weekend. Maybe it was just my imagination running away from me. I thought we'd made a connection.

He called before I got to work and explained that Akua is no longer on nights, which is going to cut our communication by eighty percent. I wasn't down for that. I shooed him off the phone, and logged on to e-mail Steven my picture.

When I hit the send button, I was prompted to save the address in my address book. As I began to change the default alias to something I could actually remember, it registered, "Over Dat Ho!"

That's serious. In the hour and a half conversation, he said very little about his ex-wife. If he felt the need to make that his e-mail address, he was bitter. I called Courtney.

When I described what I thought his e-mail was stating, Courtney laughed. "Oh yeah. He's bitter as shit."

"Court, you think?"

She laughed harder. "You don't think? That's funny as hell."

"He seemed cool, though."

"He might be cool . . . bitter cool," she said, still laughing.

"Maybe it doesn't mean that."

Courtney's amusement subsided. "Maybe it doesn't. I would damn sure ask him about it, though. It's one thing to create an ignorant-ass e-mail address like that, but another to actually give it out."

"I know. That is the crazy part."

Steven called around five o'clock. Knee-deep in work, I asked him to call back around eight. At 8:07, my cell phone rang.

Ten minutes into the conversation, I got enough nerve to ask about the e-mail address. He chuckled.

I looked at the receiver and frowned. "Well, are you going to tell me what it means?"

He chuckled again. "What do you think it means?"

"Um. I think it means over that ho."

"You're good."

Was something funny? Did he not know that sounded bitter? Just for confirmation, I asked again, "Is that what it means?"

"Yeah. That's what it means."

I thought about hanging up, but figured I'd get to the bottom of it. "So, are you really over her?"

He growled, "Yeah, I'm over that bitch."

I mouthed, "bitch?" and looked at the receiver again.

Without me prying, he began to rant. "Yeah, she was one of those independent heifers. You know the type."

I put my hand to my chest. *Like me.* He continued. "You know a hard-working brother like me wasn't good enough." He snickered. "I wasn't driving a Benz. I wasn't making six figures. I don't have good credit."

I mugged at the phone. Who the hell does he think gives a damn how hard he works if he has bad credit? We could have ended the phone call with that statement, but I figured I'd let him finish.

He continued, "You know how y'all do. She just wanted to get married and change me." He paused. "Why do women do that?"

"I don't know. I've never been married."

"Yeah, she wanted me to look for another job. She wanted me to go back to school. She wanted everything that I wasn't."

"Wow."

"Yeah I hope you're not like that." He sighed. "My mama always said stay away from y'all overly independent women."

Well, I prayed that he took her advice, because I had plans to stay away from him. When I didn't respond, he joked. "I'm just playing with you. But that bitch," he spat out with emphasis, "had the audacity to say she never loved me."

Just to give him ammunition, I said, "Are you serious?"

Sounding as if he was angry with me, he snapped, "Hell yeah, I'm serious. She said that I wasn't man enough for her. See, y'all independent women judge a man by the money he makes. If he ain't making what you make, you figure you can do without him."

"That's not true."

Why did I say that? He ranted for another thirty minutes about why it was true. I just prayed for the right opportunity to get off the phone with the lunatic. He had issues that I was not willing to help resolve. The moment his hysteria subsided, I yawned. "Whew, I have a long day tomorrow."

His gentle twin returned. "Okay. Well it was good talking to you."

Talking to me? I was under the impression that he was cursing all women like me. Anyway, I lied, "Yeah, it was good speaking with you, too."

"Did we make a date for this weekend?"

I stuttered, "Um. I don't think so."

"Well, I'll talk to you tomorrow. We'll set something up then."

Steven, speed on. Knowing I'd never talk to this lunatic again, I lied, "Yeah, we'll talk tomorrow."

22

SCOOTER

When I should be studying, I'm plotting how I can spend time talking to Taylor. I feel her getting annoyed with the whole situation, but my feelings haven't changed. I want to explore the possibilities of us. The only thing preventing it is my pity. When I look at Akua, my conscience bothers me. How could I do this?

I walk through the hospital in a daze, wondering when is the appropriate time. Where is the appropriate place? What are the appropriate words? When she talks about our future, I change topics. She turned the radio up to drown the silence as we drove home from work. She folded her arms over her chest. Did she notice a change in me?

I prayed every time she opened her mouth that she'd ask me what was bothering me. Then, I could segue into explaining my unhappiness. Her arrogance wouldn't let her mind wander into insecure territory. I pulled up to the building, and said, "I need to go to the library. I'll be back."

"Okay, bring me something good when you come back."

"Okay."

She kissed my cheek and got out. When she opened the car door, I felt the fresh air seep in the car. Before I drove off, I hung my head.

As I yearned to hear Taylor's voice, I accepted it was never

love between Akua and me. I called my mother. "Hey, Ma,"
I greeted her.

"Hey, Scooter. How you doing baby?"

I sighed. "Stressed."

"Oh, baby. It'll be okay."

"Yeah. I need a break. Can you do me a favor?"

"What?"

"Act like you need me to come home next weekend. I'm
off and Akua's not. You know how she gets all upset when I
come home."

"Boy, you have more stuff with you." She sighed. "What
do you want me to say?"

"Say that Pop-Pop isn't doing well and you want me to
come see him."

"Lawd, now you trying to kill my father."

"Nah, just call the house and ask to speak to me."

Pretending that she wasn't on board, she grunted, "Uh-
huh."

"When she says I'm not there, ask her if I said anything
about coming home."

"When do you want me to do this?"

"Now." She sighed, and I said, "You know I love you,
right."

"All right boy. I don't know why you want to make me a
part of your dirt."

I chuckled. "It's not dirt, Ma. I just want to come see you."

"I'm not a fool. You want to see someone more than me.
The question is who."

"Only you, Ma."

"Good-bye, boy."

That was her way of agreeing. Taylor was the next phone
call. She answered. "Hey, Scootie."

"I miss you, Tay-Bae."

"I miss you, too."

"I got used to having you put me to sleep at night. It's
killing me not to talk to you at night."

"So, what are you going to do about that?

"I'm going to figure out what to tell her real soon."

"What's real soon?"

"No more than two weeks."

"I hope so. I don't know how long I can be the other woman."

"You're not the other woman."

"I feel like the other woman," she whined.

When I walked in the house, Akua said, "Are you supposed to be going home next weekend?"

"I dunno. My mother asked me something about it. Why?"

"She called a little while ago asking if you were coming home."

I was grinning on the inside. "I might go. She said my grandfather wasn't doing well."

"Yeah, that's what she said."

My mother helped me obtain my get-out-of-jail-free card. In nine more days I would see my Tay-Bae three days straight with no interruptions.

23

TAYLOR

My feelings for Scooter were a lot deeper than I'd antici-
pated. Being with him consumed me. As I sat at my
desk, deciphering an escape plan, my cell phone rang.

A foreign voice struggled with English dialect on the other
end. "Is this Taylor?"

Feeling rather cautious, I wrote down the number and
said. "Yes. May I ask who I'm speaking with?"

"Randall. I got the message you leave at subway station."

Not in the mood for games, I snapped, "What?"

"I see you picture. You pretty."

I frowned and tried to imagine who'd want to play games
with me in the middle of the day. Trying not to draw attention to myself, I whispered, "Who the hell is this?"

"Randall. I got you message."

It was not the time or day to mess with me. Still whisper-
ing, I said, "Don't play with me, I didn't leave you a message."

I slammed the phone shut. Just as I got back to writing down
a note, the phone rang again. I sucked my teeth. "Hello."

Another foreigner, a different number. "I would like to
speak to Tyler."

I sighed. "Do you mean Taylor?"

He spelled it. "T-A-Y-L-O-R. Tyler."

"This is Taylor. Can I help you?"

"I'm calling to help you."

Anxiety boiled inside of me. I closed my eyes and prayed this was a silly prank. "Who is this?"

"Jean Claude. I got the message you leave at the subway station."

I hung up. The two calls had to be connected. On a separate sheet of paper, I wrote down both names and numbers.

Blocking my number, I dialed the first number. A receptionist answered. "Pepsi. How may I direct your call?"

I shrugged my shoulders and looked around as if someone were watching through my window. "Um, I'm looking for Randall."

"Do you have an extension?"

I huffed. "You know what. Never mind."

I put my phone on silent, left it in my office and went into the library to finish some reading. When I returned, the voice mail light blinked on my cell phone. Seven messages, all from different guys talking about some sign. One claimed I left a sign at his apartment complex. Another claimed it was CVS. Another claimed it was at the Greenbelt Metro station. Another said it was at Union Station. These weren't connected. There was obviously a sign posted with my information on it. Why was I the brunt of someone's cruel joke? My eyes watered as I listened to the messages on my cell phone. What have I ever done to anyone? Who would know all this information about me?

My phone rang and startled me. Another strange number. Another strange man.

I called Courtney. My voice trembled as I told her about the calls. We didn't know who would do something like this. She kidded. "Maybe it's KuKu."

"Courtney. Now is not the time for Akua jokes."

"Shit, I'ain joking. She's the only person that would want to hurt you." She laughed. "You said they're all foreigners. They're probably her cousins."

I can count on Courtney to add some comic relief to the worst situation. I chuckled. "I don't know. This shit is crazy."

My cell phone rang. I whined, "Court. It's another unknown number."

"Answer it! Answer it! Ask him where he got the number from."

I picked up. "Hello."

Finally an accent that I understood filtered through the phone. "Hello, can I please speak to Taylor?"

"Yes, may I ask who's speaking?"

"My name is Leonard. I saw the sign you posted."

His humble tone said that he sincerely wanted to speak to Taylor. I sighed. "Leonard, where did you see this sign and what did it say?"

"It was in my apartment complex."

"Where do you live?"

"In Glen Arden Apartments."

I mumbled, "Oh my God."

Courtney yelled in my other ear, "What did he say?"

Holding one phone with my neck and shoulder, I massaged my temples. "Leonard, I didn't put that sign up. Can you please tell me what it said?"

"I figured you were too pretty to do that, but I figured I'd call anyway. The sign says that you're looking for a monogamous relationship with a good man. It says only serious inquiries. It has all your numbers on there."

Again, I mumbled, "Oh my God."

Courtney was on the other end. "What did he say?" As if I was going to answer, she shouted, "Taylor! Taylor!"

Who would be so cruel?

"And there was a picture of you," Leonard said.

I shouted. "A picture?"

Courtney shouted, "What?" Just as he began to describe the outfit I was wearing in the picture, Courtney solved the case. "It was Over Dat Ho!"

He continued, "It looks like you're on a boat or something."

It was the same picture I'd e-mailed to Steven. I dropped my forehead into the palm of my hand. *How did I take such a simple thing for granted?* I sighed. "Leonard. Thank you. If you see any more signs, can you please take them down?"

He agreed. When I hung up the phone, I returned to Courtney's ranting on the other end.

As if I was supposed to be relaying each sentence to her, she snapped, "Did you hear me calling you? What did he say?"

The whole thing was too far-fetched to believe. I shook my head before I spoke. She impatiently shouted, "What did he say?"

"Girl, that bastard posted up signs with my picture and all my numbers."

"Oh my God."

"I don't believe this shit." My eyes flooded.

"I know. This shit is spooky."

"I know. I'm scared."

"Does he know your address?"

"No. Thank God."

I plugged my phone number into Google to see if my address would come up. It appeared to be safe from that angle. I searched my name. Only public court files appeared. I talked her through my searches. When I was done, I said, "I couldn't find anything that would lead to my house."

"Good thing we were able to remove our info from Zaba Search.com."

I huffed. "You ain't lying."

She searched and came to the same conclusion. "I can't find anything, but you never know."

She logged on to the Maryland Judiciary Case Search to check his record. She hissed, "This shit is so crazy." She mumbled, "I'll be damned."

"What? What do you see?"

"Why have two other women charged that lunatic with

harassment?" She paused. "Girl. It's a damn good thing you didn't go out with him."

"Tell me about it."

"One woman charged him with stalking her. The other stated he'd threatened her numerous times. Both have restraining orders against him." My breath got shorter and shorter as she read the files.

"I'm scared," I whined.

"You can stay with us until this dies down."

There was no one for me to call for help. The guy I'm claiming as my man is too far away. I felt helpless and lonely. Tears began to roll down my face. I sniffed. "Okay, I'll come to your house after work."

24

SCOOTER

As Taylor sniffed in my ear, I felt I couldn't cheat her any longer. I'd been out of the house longer than expected and I opted to deal with the punishment. I turned my car off and leaned back in the seat, listening to my damsel in distress and all I could offer were verbal condolences. She deserved more. She was worth more.

An obligation to Taylor loomed over my head as I crept into the apartment. The light from the bedroom guided my steps to confession. I stood in the doorway and studied her intensity as she read. For fear of not knowing how to began, I asked, "What are you doing?"

She looked up from the medical book. "What you should be doing."

Her sly comment confirmed my decision. As she dropped her head and returned to studying, she said, "So where the hell you been?"

My hand grasped the doorknob. I took a deep breath and said, "We need to talk."

"Not tonight." She twirled her neck. "Some of us are actually passionate about what we do. I have to study. We can talk tomorrow."

Waving me away, she flung her hand impatiently. As I half

turned out of the bedroom, my heart skipped a beat. *It will never be the right time*. Standing several feet away from her, I blurted out, "Akua, I don't know about us anymore."

She looked up from her book and squinted. "What did you say?"

"I'm not sure about us anymore."

Maybe I was thinking these words and not speaking. She frowned. "You what?"

"I don't know if I want to be in this relationship anymore."

Her face froze. She twirled her eyes in her head. Her mouth twitched. Her nose flared. She massaged her neck. The metamorphosis occurring in her expressions scared me. As I waited for the words to penetrate, my eyes demanded, say something.

Finally, like I'd startled her, she screamed, "Ahhhhhhhhhhh!!!"

The 8 X 10 inch picture of us on the nightstand flew across the room, barely missing my head. The sound of it hitting the door and glass shattering caused me to jump into the hallway. She hopped off of the bed and ran after me. She swung wildly in the air. As I tried to grab her arms, I noticed blood gushing from her feet.

"Akua, baby. Wait. Baby."

As she smacked me in the face, she yelled, "Don't friggin' 'baby' me."

Simultaneously blocking her blows and attempting to restrain her, I spoke softly, "Shhh. Calm down. You're bleeding."

She squirmed away from me. "I knew it. I knew it."

"Akua, you're bleeding. Wait."

She hit me and yelled, "How could you do this to me? Why?"

I promised myself that I would never hurt anyone like Taylor did me when we were younger. I never wanted to inflict this type of pain on anyone. I hung my head and let her wail on me until she got tired. By the time the struggle ended, it looked like a massacre had occurred on our beige carpet. She wept.

All I could say was, "Your feet, Ku. We have to take you to the hospital."

She rocked on the floor, holding her foot in her hand. Blood poured through her fingers and she cried. "Don't take me to the hospital. Don't touch me. I hate you!"

I sniffed back my tears. "I know you hate me. I'm sorry. Please, let me take you to the hospital." I grabbed a towel. "Let me wrap your feet up."

"Get off of me. You don't know what you're doing."

I struggled to wrap her feet. With her adrenaline level elevated, she couldn't feel the pain of the multiple deep cuts in her feet. I winced. How could I do this to her? I sighed. "If you don't want me to take you, can I call the ambulance?"

She whimpered, "No, don't call the ambulance. I don't want to go to the hospital like this."

"I know, but you have to go."

When I attempted to stand, she dug her fingers into my biceps. "I should spit on you."

My sympathetic expression transformed. "Akua, I know you're upset and all." I demanded, "Don't spit on me."

As much as it hurt me to hurt her, I would have fought her over spitting on me. Her eyes lowered and she wept. Was she crying because she loved me or because she wasn't in control of the situation? As blood continued to splatter from her feet, I decided to call the ambulance.

Following an ambulance was definitely not how I expected to spend my evening. I'd hoped we could talk about where we went wrong and how we could move on as friends. This was clearly not how it had played out in my mind.

Luckily, Akua went in there announcing that she was a resident at the hospital. Her arrogance got us in and out. Both of her feet were bandaged and she was to stay off of her feet for three days. As she rolled out in a wheelchair, I thought about not being able to visit Taylor this weekend. I tried to fight the selfish thought.

Akua was cordial up until the nurse closed the passenger side door. When I sat in the car, she rolled her eyes. "I hate you."

"I know. I hoped that we could settle this peacefully."

"You're an asshole."

"C'mon Ku. You're avoiding the situation. Let me explain."

"You said that you didn't want to be in this relationship anymore. You don't have to say anything else."

I felt compelled to explain. I took a deep breath. "Ku, let me tell you why."

"Just shut the hell up. You're going to lie anyway."

How could she not want to know? I dropped my head. Maybe if she understood why I needed to leave, she would be better for the next man. Suddenly, my head pounded. *The next man*? Was I prepared to see her parading around New Haven with a new man? But, I was even less prepared to make a lifelong commitment to her inflated ego. "I'm not going to lie."

She huffed. "What do you want from me? If you have something you want to say, just say it."

"I love you."

"You don't love me."

"I just don't think we're compatible."

"Stop the bullshit. Who is she?"

We pulled up to the house. Before I could get around to her side, she hobbled out. I tried to grab her arm. "Slow down."

"Who are you fucking?" she yelled.

"I'm not fucking anyone, but I do have strong feelings for someone."

I waited for her to swing. Instead, she looked to be amazed

at the words coming from my mouth. I hung my head. "I'm sorry."

She plopped on the couch. For the first time since I said I wasn't happy, her sensitive side finally appeared. She wept. "Why are you doing this to me?"

I sat beside her and put my arm around her. "I'm sorry. You deserve someone else."

"No, I deserve you. I have molded you into the man I want you to be and you're going to go off and share that with someone else."

I sighed. "That's the problem. I don't want to be molded. I want to be me. And sometimes I feel like I'm on pins and needles with you."

Her eyes softened. "I can change."

I sat speechless. Finally, I conjured up something. "That's just it. I don't think you need to change when it's someone you want to be with."

"What are you saying?"

"When it's right, you don't have to make any personality adjustments."

"Your bitch. Who is she?" She shook me vigourously. "Who is she?"

"You don't know her. She's in Maryland."

She pushed my shoulder. "You're going to leave me for a bitch in Maryland."

"Taylor. Remember I told you about Taylor."

She banged me again. "I hate you. I hope you die."

"Akua, I don't want us to hate each other."

She hit me again. "Too late. I already hate you." She huffed, "Don't say shit else to me. I mean it."

"Akua . . ."

She screamed, "Don't fucking talk to me!"

She waddled in the bedroom and yelled, "I hate you."

I slumped down on the couch. Could I really expect her to want to hold a conversation with me?

25

DEVIN

After my condo contract was approved and I was actually given a closing date, it was time to explain to my ex-wife our new schedule. I opted to tell Nicole first. When I picked her up from school, I took her to Cold Stone Creamery. She can handle any kind of news when she's eating Sweet Cream mixed with Snickers and caramel.

When she came out of the building, she ran to me. "Daddy!"

I stooped down for her to kiss my cheek. She rambled on about her day. She is such the opposite of Jennifer and me. She speaks with so much drama. Where did she get so much personality? When she took a quick breath in between stories, I cut in. "Baby, guess where we're going?"

She used my arm as a bungie cord and jumped up and down. "Tell me, Daddy. Tell me."

"Cold Stone."

"Yea! I can get um . . ." She said, "Ah . . ."

I completed her thought. "Sweet cream with Snickers."

She scrunched her nose. "No, I don't eat that anymore."

"When'd you stop eating that?"

She poked her tongue into her jaw. "Um . . . Daddy, I haven't had that since before I went back to school."

"So, you stopped eating it two months ago?" Her concept of time made me chuckle. "So what do you eat now?"

She put her index finger to her cheek. "Um, coffee ice cream and um . . ." She slowed down. "Can we call Mommy? I can't remember."

I handed her my cell phone, while we stood outside of Cold Stone. Her eyes batted when Jennifer picked up the phone. "Hi, Mommy. What are you doing?" She giggled. "Getting ice cream with Daddy."

She shrugged her shoulders and looked at me. "I don't know. Because he loves me."

I nodded approvingly. Then with confidence, she said, "He brings me here because he loves me."

She giggled. I pinched her cheek. She rambled for a moment, "I called you because what is the ice cream that Aaron always brings me."

Suddenly, I found myself not wanting to buy her what Aaron brought her. She blew a kiss over the phone. "Bye, Mommy. I'll see you tomorrow."

I opened the door and asked, "So what kind do you get now?"

"Cake batter and heaf candy."

I corrected her, saying, "It's Heath."

"Aaron gets it for me."

I took a deep breath and decided not to steal her joy. Why should it upset me that because Aaron loves Jennifer so much, he also loves Nicole?

"Are you okay, Daddy?"

I messed her hair. "Yes, Nicole."

"You look sad."

Damn. Did women's intuition start this early? "I'm okay. Just trying to decide what I want."

She ignored my façade. "Daddy, do you like Aaron?"

"Do you?"

With a timid expression, she nodded.

"What's wrong?"

She pouted. "I don't want you to be sad."

"I'm not sad, baby."

"Will you ever get a girlfriend?"

I chuckled and ordered our ice cream. After I paid, we stood at the counter to eat. Finally, I answered, "I'll get a girlfriend when you turn eighteen."

She started to count on her fingers. When she realized it was too much, she frowned. "Daddy, you'll be an old man when I'm eighteen."

"No, I won't."

"Yes you will." She sighed. "I don't want you to be by yourself."

"I'm okay, Nicole. Trust me. You make me happier than any girlfriend."

"Mommy said you're lonely. That's why you're mean to Aaron."

"Mommy's just hatin'."

She giggled. "Yeah, she's just hatin'."

"Don't tell her what I said though."

Just as Jennifer's sneaky comments come back to me, I knew for sure this one would get back to her. After our quick diversion, I got back to the purpose of the ice cream.

"Remember I told you that I was looking for a house in DC?"

She nodded.

"Since I'll be there two weeks a month, we're going to have to change our schedule. You won't be with me three days a week. Instead you'll be with me for one week. Then, your mother for a week. Back and forth like that. How does that sound?"

"Okay, I guess."

"Don't tell your mother. Let me tell her."

She nodded and asked, "Do you want to call her now?

"No, I'm going to take her to dinner tomorrow."

"You like Mommy, don't you?"

How could I not like Jennifer? Every time Nicole says something clever, if nothing more, I appreciated her. I nodded. "Yes, I like your mother."

Her eyes squinted and she folded her body like someone tickled under her arm. "I knew it."

"Yep, you knew it."

Adrianna picked Nicole up from school, so Jennifer and I could meet at the Shark Bar. When she came rushing in, I was sitting at the bar sipping Grey Goose. She stepped up to me, "Okay, Devin. What's up?"

I turned toward her. When her hair was pulled off of her face, she looked stunning. She'd lost almost fifteen pounds as she planned for her upcoming wedding. I looked her up and down. She returned the gaze through her Burberry glasses. She smirked as if her analysis of me didn't bring her as much satisfaction. I smiled. "Hey, Jay."

She sat on the stool beside me. "What are you up to? You only call me Jay when you're up to something."

"I guess you know me."

She did an impatient eyelid flutter. "I guess." She leaned her elbows on the bar. "So, what's up?"

"Would you like a drink? Our table will be ready in a minute. I did ask you to dinner, right?"

"Yeah, and . . ."

"Why are you looking at your watch?"

"Well, I was hoping we'd be out of here by eight."

I nodded. "We should be. Now, do you want a drink?"

"Shiraz."

We were two drinks in by the time we sat at the table. I asked miscellaneous questions about the wedding and about her job. Finally, she leaned toward me. "Devin, I can count the number of times you've asked me out to dinner since our divorce and—"

"And."

She shrugged her shoulders. "And I'm curious what you want."

"Can't I just want to take you to dinner for general purposes?"

"Not anymore." She shook her head. "Devin, this just brings back those feelings I don't want to remember. Until I met Aaron, every time you asked me to dinner, I prayed that you were tired of being out here and you wanted to reconcile. And it was never that. It was always about something you could have said over the phone."

Her confession shocked me. I squinted. "Jay, I'm sorry. Forgive me for wanting to just have parental conversations with you over dinner."

"It's cool." She joked. "I'm over your ass now."

We laughed. It has been years since we'd found each other funny and it actually felt good. She laughed harder. "Devin, you're old news."

"Okay, I see how it is."

"So what parental issue would you like to discuss Mr. Patterson?"

"Well, Mrs. Patterson—"

"In ten months, you won't be able to call me that."

Before I realized it, I said. "Jay, you'll always be Mrs. Patterson to me."

"You've always been a dreamer."

As we enjoyed each other's company, I was apprehensive to tell her my plans. "You know I opened a Legislative Division of Patterson & Patterson in DC. Right?"

"Yes," she answered.

"I've been doing more consulting than initially planned."

"Devin, don't tell me you're moving to DC."

"I'm going to be back and forth. I still have a business to run and a daughter to raise."

That seemed to alleviate the stress forming in her face. She sighed. "What are your plans, Devin?"

"I plan to be here two weeks out of the month. We'll swap weeks, instead of days."

"Devin, I don't know if that's healthy."

"You didn't think swapping days was healthy." I paused

for her to reflect on our achievement. "We've managed to raise an intelligent, outgoing, respectful little girl."

"Nikki's not going to take this well."

"We've talked about it."

"Do you really think she understands how long being away from someone you love is? When you go on business trips for a week, I have to hear her whine about when you're coming to get her."

Wishing my ambition didn't interfere with Nicole's happiness, I dropped my head. "I know Jennifer. I know. I'm sorry."

"Devin, I wish I could say I understand, but I don't."

How could she part her lips to tell me that she didn't understand? Did she understand that she confessed to trapping me? Did she understand that I sacrificed my dreams to live in New York and be close to my daughter? Why was she trying to ridicule me?

"I'm not asking you to understand. I'm just telling you what I plan to do."

"So, Nicole is just secondary to what Devin wants."

I poured more Shiraz in her glass. "Jennifer, don't try to make me feel bad. You act like . . ." I sighed. "Whatever."

She sipped her drink. "Devin, you know, this is not about me. You're not inconveniencing me by being in DC. You're hurting your daughter."

I swallowed more Grey Goose to soothe the pain. How could she question my loyalty to my baby? My rising temperature and the burn going down my throat made me want to explode. My teeth clenched together. My jaws pulsated. She rolled her eyes. I reached across the table and wrapped one hand around her throat. The ball of my thumb cut off her air passage. She gagged. Relentlessly, I choked. Her head banged against the wall.

I looked down to find that I was not gripping Jennifer's neck. Instead, my fingers were clamped tightly around my glass. Closing my eyes to erase the vision of strangling her, I swallowed. "Jennifer, that was a low blow."

"Oh well. This is a low move you're making."

If she were more into me instead of into marrying me, she would have listened to my dreams. This was no low move. This was a move for my daughter. I took a deep breath and finally asked what I always wondered, "Do you say things just to hurt me?"

She swallowed the last of her third glass of wine. Either her eyes watered or I'd missed her yawn. "Devin, I'm not trying to hurt you. I'm a mother and it hurts to see my child hurt."

"I'm a father. I would never intentionally hurt my daughter."

"Devin, I'm sorry. You're right."

Our food came. She looked down at her plate and mumbled, "Why do you get so defensive?"

"I'm not defensive."

"Whenever I question your judgment, you take it as an attack." She continued, "There's always this tension between us for no reason." She closed her eyes. "You've never forgiven me for intentionally getting pregnant. As much as you love Nicole, you still see me as the enemy."

"No, I don't."

"Yes, you do. You don't think I can tell you anything about being a parent because I asked for this. Right?"

"Nah, it's not like that."

Her voice got louder. "Devin, she's six years old. Let it go. Anything you missed out on because of what I did in bad judgment, it's gone." She stared into my eyes. "I'm sorry, Devin."

Why hadn't she been able to apologize to me before? I dropped my head for knowing how much I held her accountable for.

"You'll never move on until you let go."

I frowned. "Let go?"

"Yes. Let go of your anger."

"Anger?"

"Yes. You're angry." Obviously inebriated, she giggled. "You hate me."

"I don't hate you."

"Yes, you do. But, you're a great guy."

"What?"

"You could have just run away from us, but you stayed, despite hating me."

Trying to prove it to myself and to her, I shook my head. "I do not hate you, girl."

We hadn't shared a moment like this since months after Nicole was born. Suddenly, I found something lifting off of my heart. Maybe all I ever wanted from her was an apology and for her to acknowledge how I rearranged my entire life to adapt to her sneaky trap. More than that, I forgave myself for believing in her. The girl across the table was the one I fell for. "Maybe I did hate you."

We laughed. She shook her head. "That hate is only pulling you down. I love you, Devin. You deserve to be happy." She sighed. "You won't be happy until you forgive me."

"I forgive you, Jay. I forgive you."

26

SCOOTER

If I could take her pain away, I would do it in a heartbeat. She lay in the bed we shared, watching our relationship crumble to pieces. Each time I stepped into the bedroom, she'd throw something or curse at me. After forty-eight hours straight of this, it began to sound like background music. As the weekend approached, my heart was in limbo. Should I stay and doctor her and deal with her verbal abuse or should I go and solidify the relationship I want to be in?

When I sat on the edge of the bed, she moved her leg over. I stared at the wall and took a deep breath. She snapped, "Why the fuck are you in here?"

"Maybe because I care."

"You don't care about me. I swear, I hope you die."

Her words were so brutal. I rubbed my eyes. "Yo, it doesn't have to be like this. We were friends first."

"What makes you think I want to be your friend?"

Decisions needed to be made. As long as she could avoid talking to me by talking at me, we could not come to a resolution.

"We have to discuss what we're going to do."

"I can't even walk and you want to know what I'm going to do. I'm not going anywhere. If you want to leave, you can go."

"Okay. I'll do that."

"When are you leaving?"

"I don't know."

"You have to continue to pay your half of the rent." She sucked her teeth. "We're going to have to replace the carpet."

As she ran down the additional money I needed to resolve the relationship, I began to reconsider. *It's cheaper to keep her.* How was I to finagle this whole situation on my resident salary?

My search for freedom began to feel like entrapment. I touched her thigh. "Akua, you don't think you can find a roommate?"

"You find a damn roommate! You think I'm going to make this easy for you."

"You're right." I paused. "I'm going to Maryland to see my family this weekend."

"Are you calling that bitch your family?"

"You know my grandfather is sick."

She winced and I jumped because I thought I bumped into her foot. After throwing a highlighter at me, she shouted. "You think I'm stupid. Your grandfather has been sick forever and you haven't gone to see him." She panted. "Is your mother in on this?"

"My mother doesn't know anything about what's going on."

It all began to register, as she shook her head suspiciously. "I thought that phone call was strange. Your mother never talks to me that long."

"She doesn't know anything. I really want to just keep this between us until it's all settled."

"Go to hell! It is settled. I'll tell whoever I want!"

I stood up and looked at her sitting helpless and full of rage. I pleaded, "Akua, please."

She put her middle finger up and dropped her eyes back to the book like I wasn't even standing there. I walked into the hall and heard her dialing a phone number. Akua's voice trickled from the room. My antenna stood up wondering if she had called my mother back. Her thick accent made me assume she was speaking to someone in her family. Then, I heard her say, "Daddy, I want to come home. I'm off until Saturday. Can you come get me tonight?"

I mouthed. "Damn."

After I'd just asked her to keep it on the low until we settled everything, she called my worst enemy. My heart raced, as I prepared for confrontation. I walked back and stood in the doorway. Her trembling voice didn't match her composed appearance. "Daddy, I'm hurt. I cut my foot. I can't drive. Come get me."

I slouched on the door frame and shook my head. I mouthed. "I'll take you home."

She put up her middle finger and mouthed. "Go to hell."

She chuckled into the receiver. "You're right, Daddy. He is a no-good man."

I grabbed my keys from the nightstand and stormed out of the room. It was time to make my phone call, plus I didn't want to be around when her parents got here and saw the mess I'd created.

She said, "What time will you be here? If you leave now, you can be here in an hour and a half."

Driving from New York could take a little shy of that, so I decided to get out now and stay out for the next three hours. Damn if I wanted to face a man whose daughter I just crushed. With my hand on the door, I concluded that we had declared war.

27

TAYLOR

By week's end, the phone calls had stopped and my life was back to normal. I could hear Scooter's car running, as he kept telling me about the surprise he had for me. I rambled off some special items I needed.

"Is it a laptop?"

He chuckled. "Tay-Bae. Just wait."

"Um, is it the Louis Vutton I showed you?"

He snickered. "It's a surprise."

It reminded me of when we were young. Scooter was always full of surprises. He changed topics. "So, are we going to have a long-distance relationship or are you going to move to New Haven?"

Whatever, I'd been around and Scooter was definitely a rare catch. "No, I'll move to New Haven."

"Would you really?"

"As soon as you handle your business, I'll move."

"So, what are you going to do when you get here?"

I smiled because I'd already sorted this out in my mind. "There are enough firms in Connecticut. I can get a job. That's nothing."

"Wow. You got it all figured out. Huh?"

Not to sound too excited, I chuckled. "Nah, just a few thoughts."

"So, what about your house?"

"Rent it out."

"You are such a risk taker."

"Life is short. You might be my baby daddy."

"You ain't lying."

I looked at the time. He'd long passed his curfew. A piece of me wanted to ask if Kuku was working, but I decided not to. When I heard his car start, I knew I had five minutes before he was gone.

"I miss you, Scooter."

"I miss you, too."

"I can't wait to see you."

Instead of the synonymous response, he said, "I'm glad you've already figured out whether or not you'd move here. That makes my decision easier."

"I thought you said your decision was going to be easy anyway."

"It's easy and hard at the same time."

I held my chest. If Kuku was as anal as he claimed, why was this hard? I'm his ideal. She is his might-as-well. We have a connection. They just have an agreement. Isn't there a difference? Shouldn't it be easy to decide?

While my mind mulled over his options, he said. "I never wanted to hurt anybody."

Man up, Scooter. "I never wanted to end up with the wrong person. At our age, if you hang in there just because you don't want to hurt someone, you'll find yourself in divorce court five years from now," I said.

He gasped. "I feel you, Tay-Bae."

His engine stopped running. Trying to take control, I initiated our good-byes. "Okay, I need to get this place in order for my company this weekend."

"Now?"

"Yes, now."

"I want to talk to you."

I could no longer pretend this wasn't strange. "Aren't you home?"

He snickered. "Yes."

"Where's your roommate?"

He huffed. "I don't know."

Refusing to be his entertainment while his roommate was away, I told him I had to go. He asked questions to keep me going, but I finally hung up. *Stay in control Tay. You're ahead of the game.*

28

TAYLOR

Scooter knocked on the door around eight o'clock. Our reservation at the Melting Pot in Annapolis was at eight forty-five. When he walked in, I looked behind him and in his hands. Where was my surprise? His duffle bag hung on his shoulder. Okay, maybe it's in there. As I inspected him for my gift, he reached out for a hug. His entire weight collapsed on my shoulders. I kissed his cheek. He pulled my head into his chest and stroked my hair. "Tay-Bae."

Since it appeared he wanted to extend the length of our embrace, I leaned into him patiently. He sighed. I mumbled, "You okay, baby?"

Finally, he let me go. "Yeah, I'm good. Especially, now."

Although I really was more interested in seeing my surprise, I blushed. "I'm happy to see you, too."

He dropped his bag and fell onto the couch. I sat beside him. "What time did you leave Connecticut?"

"Ah, around four."

"You must have been flying."

"Just escaping the drama."

I was curious what he meant, but I refrained from asking. I rubbed his leg. He wrapped his arm around me and kissed the side of my forehead. I curled my legs up on the couch. He reached over and rubbed my thigh. Without apprehension, he said, "I love you, Tay."

"Uh, I love you, too."

"I'm glad we have a second chance."

"Me too."

He said, "What time is dinner?"

"Eight forty-five."

He checked his watch. And I looked too. No man of mine should be walking around with a stainless steel Adidas digital watch. A nice watch is a prerequisite. Well, Scooter was the exception and not the rule. Still, I asked, "Is that the only watch you have?"

"Yeah, why?"

"I'm just curious."

Obviously not as superficial as me, he glanced down at the scratched face and shrugged. I chuckled. He looked again. "What?"

"Nothing."

He grabbed my wrist and examined my watch. "What kind of watch is that?"

"Michele CSX."

"I guess that's some designer, huh?"

I nodded. He stood up. "Let me go wash my face and get ready to go."

He grabbed his bag and headed upstairs. Still, no mention of my surprise.

When we got to the restaurant, I'd given up on my surprise. The waiter came to explain the menu and the cooking procedure. Our first selection was a cheese fondue. We agreed on the type of cheese. Then, the waiter asked for our drink order. Just as I was about to blurt out the ingredients for a Royal Red Apple martini, Scooter said, "Give me a bottle of your best champagne."

No. I don't drink champagne. I'm a martini girl. The waiter raised his eyebrows, "Celebrating something tonight?"

"Just being together," Scooter said.

The steam from the fondue pot began to rise between us. With clouded vision, we blushed. The two of us sitting here together, realizing all the dreams we shared as teenagers. We'd come full-circle only to realize where we wanted to be.

The waiter mixed up the cheese before pouring our champagne. He looked at Scooter, "Do you guys want the cheese to be spicy?"

He nodded. I smiled, because it was a pleasure to be with someone who knew my tastebuds. Finally, he poured the champagne. When the bubbly settled in our flute glasses, Scooter raised his up. I returned the gesture. "Let's toast."

I nodded. "To us."

"Yes, to us."

As I tilted the glass to my lips, he said, "I broke up with my girlfriend."

I sat my glass down. I said, nearly choking on my words, "You did what?"

"I told Akua that I wanted to end our relationship."

Though I'd fantasized about this moment, fear consumed me. Did he leave her for me? Oh shit! This was real. He really did love me like no one else. *Okay, Taylor, say something.*

Nothing of substance would exit my lips, as I repeated, "You did what?"

He laughed. "Tay, we've been talking about this for weeks."

Exactly. Weeks. The conflict occurring inside of me made me wonder if this was what I really wanted. Did I really want a man who could walk out on his girl in weeks?

"After the day you got those phone calls, I knew I had to decide. I didn't want you out here anymore. I wanted to make you happy."

Should a tear be welling in my eyes? Should I jump up and down? Suddenly, Akua was more than this other woman. She was a person whose man rolled out on her for me. As my mouth hung open, he dipped a piece of bread into the fondue and extended the fondue fork for me to taste.

"Don't look so shocked."

I chomped down on the fork. My thoughts flowed rapidly. "I'm not shocked. I just want to make sure we both know what we're getting into."

"For me, it's more of what I'm getting out of. You were just my wake-up call. I was complacent until I found what I was always looking for."

"For me, I guess I've waited so long to be with you again that I'm actually scared. It's been a long time since I've been on the same accord with someone. You know?"

He dipped an apple into the pot and handed the fork to me. "Don't be scared, Tay. We're going to take this one step at a time. I feel like if we're going to do this, we have to do it right. My heart can't be in two places at once. I know you told me to take my time, but you know I'm a one-woman man."

"That's why you can't be replaced."

"I hope you're not trying to replace me just yet."

I smirked. "I learned my lesson."

"I hope so." He sighed. "My fear is that I could end up alone."

I wanted to promise him that he wouldn't, but you never can foresee the end in the beginning. Instead, I smiled. "I understand. This is very scary. So, how are you going to manage your living arrangement?"

He blew air out of his nose. I raised my eyebrows and twitched my eyes, demanding he dispel his evacuation plan.

"That's the thing."

"What thing?"

"Our lease isn't up until March. She still wants me to pay half of the rent and utilities until the lease is up."

I nodded. "Understandably so . . ."

"Yeah, but I can't afford that and my own place and trips back and forth to see you."

Just as I was about to offer some financial help, I retracted.

Taylor, you are too cool for that. If this is really what he wants, he'll figure it out. "So what are you saying?"

"Akua and I will be roommates until March. We have a two bedroom apartment."

I sipped some of the champagne. "So, are we supposed to be just friends until March or what?"

"That's not what I was hoping. I hoped we'd be a couple."

The server came with our meats and vegetables. He mixed our bouillon in the fondue pot. The fresh steam seeping between us distorted reality and my common sense went up in smoke.

"How can we be a couple if you live with her?"

"Every weekend that I'm off, I'll be here. On the other weekends, you can come to Stamford."

It seemed reasonable enough. By golly, I'd waited nine years. What's four months? If I miss this boat, it's almost guaranteed I'll hit the big three-oh as a damn spinster. Scooter and I were already past the fluff. Anyone else, it would take a year or two to get to this point. This is clutch time. He was the shortest distance between here and my destiny. As I rationalized this irrational relationship proposal, Scooter took the cooked meat from the pot and put some on my plate. I looked at the guy who'd always taken care of me and my unstable brain said, "Whatever, man."

He lifted his glass again. "Whatever."

"Whatever. Whatever."

He said. "Whatever. Wherever. Whenever."

I stared at the ceiling, searching for another spin on whatever. Finally, I giggled. "What the fuck ever."

We giggled. Our eyes glazed over as we stared through a cloud into the eyes of our future. It was whatever.

When we walked into the house, Scooter took my hand and began to dance with me. No music played, but we were on beat, gliding to the possibilities. We two-stepped to the entertainment center, he picked up a remote. "Is this for your stereo?"

I shook my head and grabbed the remote for my stereo. Then, I fiddled with my iPod to get to my slow jam playlist. Old-school slow jams came through the speakers. Scooter kissed on my neck. I rubbed the back of his head. His forehead tilted into mine. He stared into my eyes. "It's funny how you can love someone your whole life."

"I know. It's funny."

"I'm glad we're here."

"I am too."

His tongue plunged into my mouth. I pulled his shirt from his pants and my hands explored his body. Intense kisses mixed with soft pecks united us. Removing his lips momentarily to lift my sweater over my head, he said, "I love you, Tay."

Muffled by his mouth, I replied, "I love you, too."

After practically ripping our clothes off, he backed into my recliner. His astute soldier saluted me. My eyelids fluttered as I basked in his physique. He gestured for me to come closer as he quickly put on a condom. My legs straddled the chair and I lowered myself onto him. Each thrust transmitted tiny shocks to my heart. I leaned my breast into his mouth. He tantalized my nipples with sensual tongue flickering. I moaned. He groaned. As his body absorbed mine, I came to peace with the skewed love triangle that my extended degrees of single life forced me into.

My head collapsed on his shoulder. His arms slouched around my back, as we panted. This is who I'd waited nine years for. This is where I want to be. His deep breaths of gratitude told me he was elated that I convinced him this was right. He deserved me and I damn sure deserved him.

He kissed my shoulders. "Tay-Bae, let's go upstairs."

When we got into my room, remnants of the night we shared when he was Akua's man lingered. As an afterthought, I asked, "Are you happy with your decision?"

"What do you think?"

I shrugged my shoulders. "I don't know. That's why I'm asking."

He nodded. My stomach proceeded to sink, similar to the feeling of being nanoseconds from a collision. "Are you sure?" I asked.

He hugged me. "Yes, Tay-Bae. I'm happy we're together."

Just like that. In a few days shy of a month, I stole him from the girl he thought he'd marry. I felt nauseous. Was it my fear of commitment or his lack of it stuffing me with these emotions?

29

TAYLOR

I sped down Route 50, rushing to work. It was as if my brain wasn't in control of my motor skills. I whispered, "Slow down Taylor." Still, I drove recklessly. I ducked in and out of lanes, tailgating and intimidating. My aggressiveness landed me behind some people on a scenic morning drive. I inched up behind them, flicking my lights. Suddenly, they stopped. Kaboom! My car slammed into their car. We were engulfed in flames. I banged on my window. *Get me out of here! Somebody help me!*

My phone rang and rescued me from my tragic dream. I wasn't surprised to see Yale Medical Center flash across the caller ID. I picked up and said, "Hey Scooter."

He squirmed beside me. My heart dropped. If he is here, who the hell is this calling me at six o'clock in the morning? As I answered my own question, my mouth hung open.

Pain trembled in her voice. With her strong accent she spoke softly, "Good morning, my sister."

The emphasis she placed on the word sister struck my conscience. My bottom lip dangled, as I struggled to ask, "Who is this?"

"I should be asking you. Who are you? What kind of person are you?"

My eyes shifted from side to side. "Who is this?"

"I am Scooter's girlfriend."

As if she didn't know him by that name, she imitated the juvenile way I'd said it when I answered. I stuttered. "Why are you calling me?"

"Taylor?" She paused, waiting for me to confirm my identity. I considered pretending it wasn't me, but decided to answer.

"Yes, this is Taylor."

"Taylor, you should know why I'm calling."

"How did you get my number?"

She sniffed. "I got it from his cell phone bill."

She sighed, and asked again, "What kind of person are you?"

Sitting up in my bed, rubbing her comatose man's back, I scrounged for the words to defend myself. She continued, "Why do you want my man?" She sniffed again. "I love him."

Finally, I said, "I love him, too."

I looked down at him praying he would wake up and help me.

"Why can't you find your own man to love?"

As I heard the desperation on the other end of a woman afraid to get back in the game, how could I explain to her that there were no good men to love out here? I hung my head as she scorned me.

"Why do you want my man? He says that he loves you, but he doesn't even know you. It's easy to love the woman that's not taking care of you. The same problems he tells you we have, you're going to have them eventually. You will be the same *bitch*"—she accentuated the word as if she were calling me one—"that he tells you I am."

My entire body was paralyzed. Her words made me want to tell him to forget we ever got involved, but my heart said we were meant to be. She was just a woman scorned. I begged her, "Akua, I'm so sorry. It wasn't supposed to be this way. I didn't know . . ."

As I attempted to explain the inexcusable, Scooter's head

popped up. Holding the phone loosely from my ear, my startled eyes told him Akua was on the phone. Pain rippled through his face. I stuttered, "I swear. I am so . . ."

She interrupted me. "I hope the two of you go to hell. But before you do, I pray that he hurts you ten times worse than he has hurt me. Have a great freaking day, bitch!"

She hung up the phone, and I dropped mine in my lap. The busy signal came through the receiver. I inhaled, before I spoke. I propped my head on my hand and looked at Scooter. "I can't do this."

"The hard part is over."

"Not when your girlfriend is calling my house."

He struggled onto his elbows. "Tay, you're my girlfriend."

"Scooter, I've never dealt with anything like this. I . . ."

He rested his head in my lap. "Neither have I. We'll just have to figure it out as we go along. But I know this is what I want."

Why wait until you're twenty-eight to have the other woman calling your house? I shook my head, disgusted with my situation, angry with the poor selection of men, and pissed with the nonchalant man beside me.

I kept replaying her words. Doubt plagued me, because I hadn't considered the negative things I was inheriting. "Are you sure you want to go through with this?"

He huffed. "Yes Taylor. She thinks I'm leaving for superficial reasons. I'm leaving because . . ." He took a deep breath. "You know why I'm leaving. We're going ahead with the schedule."

He was convinced. Was I to stop the plan now? I closed my eyes and sucked up some confidence.

30

SCOOTER

Taylor ordered take-out from IHOP. I eagerly accepted the responsibility of picking it up. Suppressing my eagerness to talk to Akua was suffocating me. What made her call? Never in a million years would I believe she'd abandon her pride like that for me. I stepped outside of Taylor's front door and immediately inhaled a cigarette before paging Akua. The frigid fall temperatures would not smother the bonfire blazing inside of me.

I smoked two more cigarettes on the ride to and from IHOP. Still, Akua had not called. Sitting outside of Taylor's house, I prayed she'd call. I stared at my phone, as the food sat in my passenger seat. *Please, Akua. Call me back.*

Finally, the phone rang. I took a deep breath and prepared for battle. I looked. *Taylor.* "Hey, what's up?"

"It's fine if you want to stay out there and talk to your little girlfriend, but bring me my food please."

"I'm on my way in now."

Before I got out of the car, I put my phone on silent. After a three-hundred-mile drive, damn if I'd let Taylor be angry with me too. She opened the door and stuck her arm out.

"Girl, stop playing. I'm coming in."

She smirked. "It's cool. I understand."

No female is that cool, and damn if I was falling into her

trap. I stepped in the house and hugged her, leaving my compassion for Akua outside. I stuffed my phone in my jacket and hung it up in the closet. Taylor's long legs and boy shorts gave me amnesia. In the kitchen, I wrapped my arms around her. She didn't reciprocate the gesture. Her arms hung to the side. She huffed. "Let me warm up the food."

"C'mon baby. Give me a hug."

She pushed me away. I grabbed her forearms. "Tay. Don't act like that. You know this is what I want."

I released my grip and sat at the table while she warmed the food. "Do you really think I'd go through all of this if I wasn't sure this is what I wanted?"

She shrugged her shoulders. "I don't know Scooter."

I dropped my head. "Tay, please don't act like this now."

After putting the time on the microwave, she turned to me with her hand on her hip. "Why?"

I shook my head. "You can't tell me you thought this was going to be drama-free."

As the revelation seeped into her, I watched her limbs relax. "You're right, Scooter. I think I'm primarily disappointed in myself. I would have never been a part of this a year ago."

I stood up and hugged her. She leaned her head on my shoulder. I said, "Baby, this is different. This isn't your average situation."

I tilted my forehead into hers. "We belong together."

"I know. That's the only reason I'm here."

I backed her up into the counter. My weight leaned into her. I pushed. We grinded, and I hoped to squash her insecurities. She mumbled, "We need to eat."

"We need to make love first."

She shook her head. I lifted her wife beater and pulled her shorts down. She stopped resisting. I raised her up on the counter. Her legs wrapped around my waist. As I pulled down my sweatpants, I looked into her eyes. "I'm where I want to be." I kissed her. "Okay?"

"Scooter, I'm just scared," she whined.

I slid into her and picked her up from the counter. In between slow strokes, I said, "Don't be scared, I won't hurt you."

She buried her head in my shoulders and winced.

I retracted slightly. "Am I hurting you?"

She moaned, "No, it feels like . . ."

I put my mouth over her mouth. Propped up on me, she twirled her hips aggressively. I stroked harder. Feeling the arch in her back curl in, out, and side to side rendered me helpless. I backed into the chair. She stopped moving when we sat down. We panted and inhaled each other. She cooed, "Don't hurt me."

"I won't."

I pushed her hips into me. After a few seconds, she returned to her seductive swerve. I kissed her breast. When all the nerves left one head en route to the other, I gasped, "Tay, I love you."

I lifted her up again and drove it in until we conked out. Akua was the furthest thing from both of our minds as we served each other breakfast.

31

DEVIN

The day after the closing, I stood in Danker Furniture and selected a living room display. "Give me all of it."

The young sales lady flirted. "I guess there's no Mrs. to dispute your selection."

"Nah, not at all."

"Really, you're quite handsome to be a free agent."

I nodded. "Thank you." Pointing to a bedroom display, I added, "Yeah, give me that too."

She laughed again. "I guess you know what you like."

"Pretty much."

Her gestures were inviting. I suppressed the desire to flirt. I knew I wanted nothing more from this girl than sex. I already had my roster of sex partners in the area. *Devin, keep it simple.* A part of me believed that the more women I had, the less I'd feel the need for true intimacy. Quantity can't replace quality.

While my nature and I tussled, she rested her elbows on a dining room chair. "You can select different upholstery for your chairs."

As she leaned onto the opposite leg, she caught my gaze. "Would you like me to come to your place and help with the decorating?"

Don't fall for that one Devin. Once a woman helps decorate the house, she thinks she owns the place. I shook my
head. "Nah, I'll pass."

She pulled out her card. "You're spending a lot of money
and I would hate for the furniture to get there and the space
isn't appropriate." She smiled. "Personally, I would prefer to
come out and see it first. Do you have an interior decorator?"

I chuckled. "Me."

"We offer it free of charge. I think it's a really good perk."

"Oh, okay. You're right. When can you come out?"

"Let's walk up here and look at my appointment book."

As we walked to the front of the store, I asked, "So, you're
no bootleg decorator are you?"

She laughed. "No, I went to school."

The shapely young lady looked no older than twenty-two.
I chuckled. "How old are you?"

"Take a guess."

I said, "Let me see, You're nineteen."

"Thank you. I like you."

"How old are you?"

She opened her appointment book and smirked. "I'm
thirty-four."

Shocked, I shouted, "Hell no!"

"Yes. I'm thirty-four. I'll show you my license."

Her cute factor exponentially increased. My eyes checked
her schedule, too. Poking her cheek with the back of her pen,
she said. "I can come out tomorrow."

"What time?"

"Anytime between twelve and three."

I flirted. "So what about this evening?"

Missing the invite, she shook her head. "Nah, I don't work
on Saturday nights."

"I'm just joking."

"Are you asking me out?"

"Actually, I am."

She chuckled. "Well, I will do that on a Saturday night."

"So, if you don't have a good time this evening, will you still come tomorrow to decorate my place?"

"Definitely. This is how I pay my bills."

I chuckled. "Good."

"So, what time?"

"Nine is good for me."

She laughed. "I mean for tomorrow's appointment. I gave you a three-hour window. Twelve through three."

"Two is good."

"So, you want to go out at nine tonight?" she asked.

I nodded. "Is that good for you?"

"Yeah."

We exchanged information and planned to meet at Rosa Mexicana. It took me fifteen minutes to explain the location of the restaurant in her home town.

She called me after I'd been in the restaurant for fifteen minutes, turning around each time the door opened.

"Hi, Devin. It's Jamise. I'm parking now. I'll be in there in a minute."

When she finally came in twenty minutes after that, she walked over to the bar. Though I was beginning to feel agitated, I smiled. "Hey, Jamise."

We exchanged a friendly hug. "I'm sorry. There's nowhere to park."

"Why didn't you valet?"

"Whatever. I'm not paying anyone to park my car for me."

"I would have paid for it."

After excusing myself, I walked up to the hostess to let her know that my date for the 9:00 reservation had arrived. She chuckled when she looked at the time. I nodded to acknowledge my irritation. She told me it would be a moment, but she would seat us as soon as possible.

I stepped back to the bar. Jamise had her compact open checking on her makeup.

"You look fine."

She closed it and looked at me. "Thanks."

"Would you like something to drink? Some wine or something?"

She smiled. "Ah, White Zinf."

I nodded. How do I always end up with White Zinfandel girls? Shortly after the bartender handed her the glass of wine, the hostess got my attention.

I tugged on Jamise's arm. "C'mon. Our table is ready."

She walked in front of me. Her tight jeans and fitted velvet blazer seemed to lessen my irritation. Physically, she was all in place. Her hair was pulled back into a fake ponytail that hung to the middle of her back. It swished from side to side with her seductive swagger. I pulled her chair out. She looked around and asked, "Can we get a booth?"

If your ass were on time, maybe we could have. Though it looked doubtful, I asked anyway. The hostess smiled. "I'm sorry, Mr. Patterson. This is all we have."

Once we sat down, she leaned in. "You know these low-rise jeans will have your ass all out. That's why I prefer booths."

Somebody tell me where are all the women with class? Trying to convince myself that she didn't say what I thought she said, I changed subjects. "So Jamise, how'd you become an interior decorator?"

"Well, I used to work at the Room Store. Then, I got a job with Ethan Allen." She shrugged her shoulders. "I took some classes."

"I see. So do you like it?"

"It's okay. I'm also an actress."

Am I in DC or New York? How is it that I attract the women seeking stardom wherever I go? I'm now convinced that it's me. She asked, "So, what do you do?"

"I'm an attorney slash political activist slash . . ."

I chuckled. She didn't. When the waiter came, I ordered guacamole. She frowned. "You eat that stuff?"

I nodded. Her nose curled up. "Ill."

"You should try it."

"I'm not eating anything that looks like that."

She perused the menu. Her expressions stated she found nothing appetizing. After I closed my menu, she still looked confused.

"Would you like me to make any suggestions?"

She shook her head and scrunched her face as the waiter brought the guacamole. "No, not if you eat that stuff." She chuckled. "I probably won't like what you suggest."

"You're probably right."

I looked at my watch and decided to give her five minutes longer. Then, I planned to be rude and order. She huffed. "I don't see anything I like."

Why me? I stared at her. *You're kidding, right?* "So, what do you want to do?"

She smirked. "I'll just have the . . . uh . . ."

"The filet mignon is good."

"Nah, I don't eat red meat."

My head drooped. I assumed she preferred chicken fingers or Buffalo wings. "Do you want to go somewhere else?" I asked.

"No." She pouted. "I'll get something."

I nibbled on my chips and guacamole and stared at the ceiling. I should have stayed my ass in the house and ordered pizza. More and more, I find myself on dates with beautiful women lacking substance. Next time, I'll just call some airhead that I've already been with.

Finally, she ordered a seafood dish. We continued our get-to-know. I asked, "What's your status? Single? Married and looking? Divorced?"

She chuckled. "Single. And you?"

"Divorced."

"Do you have kids?" I asked.

"Yep, two boys."

"Wow. How old are they?"

She smiled. "My boys are men. One is eighteen. The other is fourteen."

Damn! When did she get started? As I processed the calculation in my head, she asked, "And you?"

"Ah." I laughed. "Yeah. I have a little girl. She's six."

She nodded. I'd convinced her to order a margarita. After a few sips, she relaxed. Her artificial pose began to disintegrate. Suddenly, I found myself having dinner with a shell. Nothing hid beneath the surface. When the check came, I wanted to run out and leave her behind. Instead I did the gentlemanly thing and walked her to her car.

"Okay, Ms. Jamise. I'll talk to you soon."

"I'll see you tomorrow."

Shit! I forgot about the appointment. How could I shake a woman who has access to my credit card and address? I planned to wake up early and cancel my appointment. Then, go to another furniture store, and find an old, white interior decorator.

When I stepped into my empty condo, I thought about calling one of the fellas, just to hang out. Instead, I stretched out on the floor and turned on my flat screen. Before I knew it, I was flipping through the Match.com personals. My profile was hidden, because I wanted to control my selection. Though I'd never actually pursued anyone on the site, I enjoyed looking. Finally, I checked my e-mail. Ever since I'd given Taylor Jabowski's home girl my business card, I'd been praying that she'd e-mail me. Still, nothing. What was I thinking? I went to the Train Workers' Union's Web site and found her e-mail address. In the subject field, I wrote, "I love my people." After I pressed SEND, I kicked myself. One in the morning, on a Saturday night, I'm sending an e-mail just to say hey. Damn, Devin. Times have gotten rough.

32

TAYLOR

Scooter woke up and suggested we go to church. I tried to discourage him, but he insisted. We'd initially decided on 9:30 service. After we finished talking, it was after ten. We drove separate cars, so he could see his mother and be on the road by four.

We walked into church and immediately I felt jittery. Every one and his mama wanted to come and hug me. "Ooh Taylor, it's so good to see you."

"We don't see you anymore."

"Honey, is everything okay?"

Leave me alone! I smiled and nodded. Of course everyone remembered my mannerly high school sweetheart. One of the deacons even commended him for bringing me back to church. These people are funny. I grabbed Scooter's hand and strutted up to the pew right behind my mother. I tapped her and put my arm around her shoulder. "Surprise."

She turned around. "Oh baby, I'm so happy you're here."

She hugged Scooter. "Oh, Scooter. When did you come into town?"

I answered, "He came in last night."

It's a shame when you're lying in church. I didn't have much of a choice since I didn't mention him when we talked yesterday. Her watery eyes told me she didn't care, she was just happy to see me with him.

When service began, my father strutted into the pulpit. He looked down at his previously favorite daughter. He extended his hand toward me, without specifying what he was talking about. He said. "God is good."

The congregation rallied with him. Toni directed the choir in song. My father delivered an empowering message, and I was glad I came. Scooter held my hand when we stood to pray. His grip tightened as the prayer heightened. I peeped from the corner of my eye. The intensity in his face said that he really wanted our relationship to work.

When church was over, my mother invited us to her house. "Scooter has to get back and he has to . . ." I begged off.

He interrupted me. "Did you cook candied yams?"

"Of course. If I would have known you'd be in town, I would have made sauerkraut."

"You remember that?"

She nodded. "I sure do. I know all my children's favorite meals."

Okay, she'd taken this too far. I tried to finish. "He has a four-hour drive. Plus he has to go back to his mother's house."

"You can get on the road by five. Another hour won't hurt."

"You're right."

Just great, Scooter. She said, "I'll be there in a minute. Go on Taylor. Go in through the garage and start warming the food up."

"Okay."

As we left the church, I snapped, "Scooter, they are going to harass us if we go over there."

"Taylor, we don't have anything to hide."

I smirked. Did he or did he not still live with Kuku? He kissed my cheek. "I'll be over there in thirty minutes."

I huffed. "Okay."

When I pulled up to my parents' house, Toni's minivan was parked outside. Anxiety rushed through my veins. I contemplated just turning around. Instead, I opened the garage and entered the house.

When I stepped in, she sat in the family room. She was the only one there. Why aren't her kids here to distract us from talking?

"Hey Toni."

"Taylor."

It didn't sound like a greeting, but more like confrontation. This was dangerous. We're usually amongst a group and my mother acts as referee. I walked over to the stove and began peeping in pots. I turned to find her staring at me with her arms folded.

"We should talk."

"Talk?"

She shook her head. "It's like every time I say something to you, you get defensive."

"Maybe it's what you don't say to me, but find time to say to everyone else that makes me feel as if I need to defend myself."

I tilted my head and smirked. *Now answer that.*

She shifted her weight and sighed. "I don't know why you feel like I talk about you behind your back, because I . . ."

"Because what?"

I'd now shifted her into defensive mode. Her neck began to roll. "I don't talk about you to anybody. I don't know why people always say what I say and no one ever says what they say."

I smiled. "Who are *they*? Why don't you say who you're talking about? And what do they say?"

As if she was holding back tears, she took a few deep breaths. She and I hadn't talked alone in three years. Since the time she assumed I was a slut and married women shouldn't deal with people like me.

As I saw her about to get emotional, I got emotional. I thought about how it all went down. How we went totally wrong. We'd always had our jealousy issues, but the incident that tore us apart for good flashed through my mind. I took a deep breath. Three years ago, I was young and dumb. Toni called me over to her house. I remember the conversation like it was yesterday.

"Taylor, girl. Andre has this fine friend over here. He went to seminary school with him." She giggled. "Girl, his father has a big church in Atlanta and he's so fine."

"Girl, I am not coming over there. You know I don't mess with men in the ministry."

"Girl, this one is fine as they come. He seems cool too. Plus, I've told him all about you."

Two days prior, I'd found out that I passed the bar exam. I was in my apartment, having a celebratory happy hour alone. What could it hurt? I got in my car and rushed over to Toni's house. Often, I wish to God I could rewind those steps.

When I walked in, my weakness sat on her couch. He was neatly groomed. I blinked. Was I looking at the right person? I frowned. Minister? I shrugged my shoulders and they introduced me to Minister Jabari Mason. His brown eyes smiled at me through his black wire-framed glasses. We stood face to face. As his presence attempted to inhale my breath, I struggled to hold it. His baggy denim shorts and navy-and-white Polo shirt invoked amnesia in me. He does what again?

Toni confirmed. "This is Minister Jabari Mason."

Discounting all ministers was a bit narrow-minded of me. Never say never. I smiled. "Hi, Jabari."

When I extended my hand to connect with his, I noticed a stainless steel Movado with a round black face. While I admired his watch, he yanked my forearm and embraced me. "Down south, we give hugs."

Feeling slightly dizzy, I nodded. He laughed. "I'm an Atlanta boy."

I cracked a smile. When I walked in the kitchen to get more detail from Toni, she was smiling from ear to ear. "I think he's perfect for you."

"Whatever."

I'd been claiming celibate for nine months and the last thing I needed was someone that wanted to wait until marriage. My seasonal celibacy commitment was nearing its threshold. I was tired of holding out. At that moment, I was only as celibate as my options. And Mr. Jabari was too fine of an option.

Toni continued to convince me. "Girl, he is so your type. He knows the word, but that ain't the only thing he talks about. He's cool. He's fly. And you know Daddy's been praying that we all marry ministers."

I sucked my teeth, because we'd heard that all of our lives like that was the ideal thing to do. Anyway, as she made Jabari sound like the most ideal of my last resort, I began to even convince myself.

"Well he is fine."

For the next hour or so she and Andre played matchmaker. Finally, Jabari made it clear that he was interested in spending a few private moments with me. Toni lived across from a little park, so I suggested going for a walk. He popped out of his chair like I suggested a steak house. When we left the house, Toni was as excited as if this man asked for my hand in marriage. I gestured for her to calm down. We walked in circles and chatted about life and growing up as preachers' kids. We seemed to bond well. Finally, he suggested we chill on the playground. Seemed like a fun option. As we spun around and giggled like ten-year-olds, his spirituality and his sexuality must have gotten all mixed up. At nine o'clock on a Sunday evening, Mr. Minister practically attacked my horny ass on the neighborhood playground. He had a way with words and an even better way with his hands. And damn it, before I knew it we were discussing the ramifications of having sex. All I could rummage up in my mind to stop the fire-works flaming between us was to say, "I thought you were a minister."

In between swallowing my tongue, he nodded. "I am, but I'm a man too."

He gripped my bottom as we stumbled over and leaned up on the ladder to the sliding board. I swear my hands were not touching him. As if to put brakes on the progress of this train wreck, I gripped the sides of the ladder. The horny devil on my left shoulder said, "Damn Taylor, if he kisses like that, what will sex be like?"

He kissed my neck and the angel on my right shoulder said, "He ain't nothing but the devil. Get away from him."

He thrashed his tongue in my right ear and drowned the angel speaking in it. When my backed-up love started to come down, my horny ass asked, "Do you have condoms?"

He nodded and whipped one from his back pocket. In the heat of the moment, I decided not to ask why he kept con-doms handy. I was just happy he had one. His hands ex-plored parts of my body that had been ignored for months. My hips began to grind in unison with him. He reached his hands down my jeans. He leaned his forehead into mine. "Taylor, I don't do this all the time. I feel like there's some-thing special between us." He asked, "Do you?"

I agreed with the bullshit he was spitting, "Yeah, some-thing is special about you." In between moans, I added, "I just feel like you're different." I shook my head as he cupped my breast. "I've been celibate for eighteen months."

Nine months didn't sound as official. He quickly reached down and practically ripped my jeans open. He looked me in the eyes. "May I?"

Wasn't that so polite? I nodded. He parted the bridge that protected my flow. He felt the moistness. "Ooh . . . Taylor."

"Jabari, stop . . ."

"Why?"

"Because this isn't right."

I don't know how it became right, but before I realized it, my jeans were at my knees and my long limbs were bent over the sliding board. I took my plight from sensual celibacy in the most unsensual position. As my hands clung to the second to the last step on the kiddy ladder, he sent chills through me. My head bobbed back and forth. For those moments that he ministered to my body, I concluded that a man of God was all right with me. With the last stroke, he gasped, "Ah . . ."

And I said, "Shit!"

Guilt settled in as he wrapped his arms around my waist and rested his soggy face on my back. I rested my arms on the steps. And we stood, sack against saddle on the playground. I squirmed. I shifted. I huffed. He got the message as he backed away. He pulled up his shorts and assisted me with my jeans.

He followed my lowered eyes. I shook my head. "We shouldn't have done this."

"Why?"

I hung my head. "Because . . ."

He lifted my chin. "Look. This was different. I don't do this every day. We can't help it if we have chemistry."

He continued, "I know your people. I wouldn't have done this if I wasn't feeling you."

Of all the people to have a one-night stand, it would have to be a minister. Good thing the sky was clear, because I should have been struck by lightning.

"I just feel so bad."

"Me too."

He grabbed both of my hands and began to pray. Did he really think that it was okay to screw my brains out and immediately ask for forgiveness? As he asked for anointing to fight his temptations, I laughed to myself. This fool was crazy. But in the end, he wasn't the only fool.

When we got back to Toni's house, I immediately said my good-byes and darted to my car. Toni looked at me inquisitively, but I didn't offer an explanation. Obviously, Jabari did. He stayed up all night telling them how I jumped his bones on the playground and he had succumbed to the temptation of this worldly woman. Who do you think they believed? And my own sister began to refer to me as Delilah. She told my parents and everyone else in the church that I *made* the nice minister screw me on her neighborhood playground.

As Toni stood in my face wondering why I don't talk to her, I still wondered why. Why would my sister never discuss it with me? Why would the whole church have to think I was a whore? Why did she tell anyone who'd listen that I had sex on the first night with a good minister that she hooked me up with? Why didn't she care about my feelings? Why did my father have to call me and tell me if I wanted to be a whore, keep it out of his church?

As all the questions that plagued me trudged through my head, I huffed. The anger I felt when it first happened returned and my blood sugar began to rise. My right hand clamped tightly around a fork, as I stared into her eyes.

"I'm just saying."

"You're just saying what?"

The sound of the garage interrupted us. She stood up straight. "All I'm saying is that I'm not the only one that has something to say about your lifestyle."

"My lifestyle?"

"Your lifestyle."

My mother opened the door that led into the kitchen. An expression of uncertainty and joy sat on her face. She looked around to make sure nothing was broken. She smiled at me. Then, at Toni.

Toni ignored my mother's presence and said, "Let's go upstairs."

I ignored her and pretended to be preoccupied with helping my mother get dinner together.

My mother wasn't sure if we were getting along or not,

because she appeared on edge each time either of us breathed. Scooter was on his way and I wasn't prepared to heal the ugly wounds that had torn our sisterhood apart.

I walked out of the kitchen. Toni tagged along. I turned around and huffed. She was probably betting that I'd be anxious to settle our issues. Too little, too late to learn to love. I smirked and opened the bathroom door.

Toni grabbed my shoulders. I turned to see what she wanted. She obviously had a lot on her mind. As tears filled her eyes, I felt I should grant her the opportunity to say what was on her chest.

I looked at her as if to say, "Say what you have to say."

She stuck the tip of her chin into her black turtle neck. "Taylor, I was wrong."

I shrugged my shoulders. She had done and said so many cruel things about me, simply because I was single. As if it was my fault for not finding some guy who wanted to marry me by the time I was twenty-four. "Toni, I really, I . . ."

She touched my hand. "I have prayed about our relationship, and I want it to be better."

Her grown-up act scared me. Was I ready to abandon my bitterness toward her? I curled my lips because I wasn't sure. Her eyes watered. "How can I teach my kids how to love each other and I can't even get along with my sister?"

Our childhood played in her eyes. My parents never allowed us to go to bed angry. When we fought, they locked us in a room until we got it together. How had we grown so far apart? I blinked and returned to the present. She didn't understand the struggle. My struggle. In her eyes, single translated to wild. I was out of hand for the cards God dealt me.

"Taylor, I'm sorry."

"Taylor, say something. I miss you," she begged.

As I sat there searching for what I wanted to say, I wasn't sure. Why did I feel I couldn't forgive her, when I expected Scooter to forgive me? I stretched my arms out to hug her. As we embraced, she repeated, "I'm so sorry Taylor. I hope you can forgive me."

"Taylor, talk to me."

I chuckled. She laughed too. That was always how it was. She always got on me because I was the loquacious one, but she could never handle it when I wouldn't talk. Hoping my words changed my heart, I rolled my eyes. "All right, Toni, I forgive you. Now I have to pee."

She chuckled. "Thank you, Tay. Thank you."

I closed the door and sat on the toilet. A part of me was elated that the friction between us was partially settled, but doubt settled in me. Was she only interested in our relationship, because it appeared that I was in a relationship? I was baffled. Why now?

When I came from the bathroom, Scooter and my father walked in through the garage. I stepped into the kitchen. My father grabbed me. I leaned to wrap my arms around his large belly. "Hey, Daddy."

He kissed my cheek. "You sure looked beautiful in church today."

I smirked and Scooter nodded. "I agree Bishop."

We all laughed. Toni hugged Scooter. "I'm happy to see you again, brother."

We transferred into the family room while my mother got things together. Scooter and I sat next to each other on the couch. My father stood in front of us. We scooted apart to allow his three-hundred pounds in between. He rested his hand on my knee and took a deep breath. "My Taylor."

Somehow I think he thought Scooter could convert me into the devout Christian I was as a teenager. He rolled his neck over to Scooter. "Son, what are your plans for my daughter."

I leaned up to check Scooter's expression. He smiled. "Our plan is to be together."

My father frowned. Scooter said, "I plan to marry her."

Huh? Marry me? We just declared ourselves a couple. His

ex-girlfriend just called my house. My heart raced inside of me. My father chuckled and patted my knee, silently telling me a job well done.

Despite all of my accomplishments thus far, Toni and my mother looked like I'd finally had a notable achievement. Toni raised her thumb up. My mother winked. Excitement beamed on everyone's face. By golly, Taylor has found someone to marry her. I sat bewildered. What the hell was Scooter thinking?

33

SCOOTER

Taylor's jaw dropped when I told her father my intentions. I wished I'd been prepared for that question. Unconsciously, I said what I thought he wanted to hear. It's not like he could arrest me if I didn't follow through. As I envisioned my future with Taylor, I reluctantly turned my phone on. Still, Akua hadn't called. She hadn't texted me.

As I drove home to the unknown, I inhaled so much nicotine, it ain't even funny. In all of two months, I went from an upstanding recovering nicotine addict, in a stable relationship, to an addict in between relationships. Something has to give. I paged her again. By the time I reached the New Jersey Turnpike, she called back.

"What the fuck do you want?"

"Are you okay?"

"You don't give a fuck how I feel."

I huffed. "I do."

"I talked to your bitch yesterday."

"I know."

"I moved your shit to the other room."

"Ku, how are you doing?"

She retorted, "It doesn't matter."

"Are you already back on your feet?"

"I had to go to work."

"You could have gotten someone to cover for you."

"What should I do? Tell them that my boyfriend left me and I ran behind him and sliced my feet all up. I can't work."

"Ku, c'mon now. You don't have to get into all of that."

"Don't tell me what I need to get into. There's no telling what you been into this weekend."

I guess the thought was too much for her to bear, since the phone slammed in my ear. I closed my phone and turned up the music to drown the doubt floating through my head.

My dirty clothes were thrown in the corner of the second bedroom. Akua had dumped all my shit on the small twin bed. For hours, I aimlessly attempted to organize this mess I'd made. When hunger pains pierced through my side, I checked the time. 11:54 P.M. I'd been fumbling around the house for three hours and Akua still hadn't made her way home.

I called her on her cell phone. She didn't answer. I went into the kitchen to find something to eat. The refrigerator was empty. I swung cabinets open. *Nothing.* I returned to the same cabinets just to make sure. *Still nothing.* I stood there realizing how I ended up in a serious relationship. These types of things don't occur when a woman is in the house. Frustration forced me to dial Akua again. I began pacing the floor. She had to go to work in less than five hours. Where could she be?

I went into the bedroom to check the closet. Her stuff was still there. Why was there no food in the house? Every thing in New Haven had shut down. Shit! I was about to starve. Damn! I forgot to call Taylor when I walked in the house. I rushed into the bedroom to find my cell phone. Then, I heard Akua's key in the door. I rushed back to the living room. She limped in carrying a Styrofoam container. I stood in front of her like I had a right to inquire about her whereabouts. She sucked her teeth and brushed past me and stormed into the bedroom, taking her food with her. My stomach barked after the aroma lingering behind her. I knocked on the bedroom door.

"Hey, Ku."

She didn't answer, but I was determined to get her leftovers. I tried the door, but she'd locked it. "Where's all the food?"

It sounded as if she laughed. I sucked up my anger and asked again, "What happened to the food?"

This time she made her humor known. In between chuckles, she said, "It left when you left."

"C'mon. I'm starving."

I heard her hopping around and suddenly the door swung open. When she tossed the food container at me, I cradled it. Before I could thank her, she slammed the door. She mumbled, "Next time make sure your bitch feeds you before you come home."

I shrugged off her rude comment. Half of a grilled chicken breast and a small pile of mashed potatoes were inside. I rushed to the kitchen and gobbled down the food. Seconds passed and everything got hazy. I took deep breaths to revive myself. Suddenly, I began to feel nauseous. I ran to the bathroom. My head spun in circles as I kneeled by the toilet bowl, purging everything I'd just eaten. Maybe I'd eaten too fast. Too tired to investigate, I staggered into my room and closed my eyes. My mind called Taylor but my muscles were too weak to move. I knew she'd be upset but my eyelids lowered and lowered. I was out.

When loud music blasted throughout my apartment minutes later, I looked at the clock. 5:02 A.M. I lifted up to yell at her, but my head collapsed on the pillow. Despite the loud racket, I dozed off.

When my alarm clock rang in my ear, I pressed snooze. After my ten minute break, I looked up to find that it was after eight. Shit! I checked my alarm. It was set for 6:30. How did I sleep for an hour and a half with it buzzing in my ear? As I attempted to roll out of bed, my body was still sedated. When I finally found the shower, the water splashing in my face awoke my understanding. Akua intentionally tried to make me sick. I felt the same as I did when I'd taken Percocet after my tooth was extracted.

After I jumped out of the shower, I hunted for the painkillers. They weren't in the medicine cabinet where I'd last seen the bottle. I rushed into her bedroom and looked in the nightstand. As I stood there with the bottle in my hand, I couldn't believe she would stoop so low. Did she plan to do it or was it a last minute decision as I stood at her door begging for food. Whatever the case she was making my decision that much easier.

In the midst of my investigation, I remembered that I was almost two hours late for work. I rushed into my room. My pager buzzed on the desk. I didn't check it because I knew it was the hospital. I searched for clean scrubs. Everything was dirty. I went back into Akua's bedroom, hoping she'd inadvertently washed some of mine. Her scrubs were folded neatly at the top of the closet. I lifted each set and prayed I'd find a 2XL hidden in there somewhere. *Nothing.* I shook out my least soiled pair and sprayed some Febreze on them and left for work.

When I got to the hospital, I searched for Akua. Trying to suppress my anger, I calmly asked, "Did you put Percocet in the food I ate last night?"

She smirked. "Don't ask stupid questions."

"I know you did."

"Dr. Evans, I'm on my way to surgery. Can we discuss your issues later?"

I said, "Ku. That's some crazy stuff. Why did you stoop to that? I found them in your nightstand."

She glared at me. "Did you ever think I needed them for my pain?"

I looked down at her bandaged foot and walked in the other direction. Maybe all of this drama was what was making me sick.

34

TAYLOR

Why does it seem that most of Scooter's communication involves apologies? I looked at his text message: SORRY BABY. BY THE TIME I FINISHED MOVING THINGS INTO THE OTHER BEDROOM, IT WAS 2 LATE 2 CALL. WILL CALL U SOON. MISS U.

I huffed. How is it that when he is with me, I know he is sincere, but the second we part I question everything. As much as Akua's phone call upset me, it confirmed Scooter's honesty. Still, I was vexed.

Frustrated by my situation, I caught myself storming through the office with an attitude. I closed the door to my office just because I didn't want to be bothered. My voice mail light blinked. I listened to my message. I was delighted to find there were no stalkers, but irritated to see it was now 10:00 and I hadn't spoken to Scooter.

I opened Microsoft Outlook and noticed I had too much e-mail for a Monday morning. I looked at the subject to decide what I wanted to read first. The majority of the e-mail was work related. Then, "I Love My People" jumped out of the monitor. I love my people? Devin Patterson. Oh my goodness! The guy from the Congressional Black Caucus. I forgot about him.

I anxiously selected the message. He opened the message

reintroducing himself and explaining that he gave his card to Courtney. I recalled her telling me that, but I was all preoccupied with my new boyfriend that it fell on deaf ears. He proceeded to ask me about Katherine. Katherine wanted me to meet him. He's a union consultant. Okay, this was all too eerie.

Before responding, I went to find Katherine. I trapped her inside the break room. "Katherine, remember some months back. You were in that legislative meeting."

She frowned. "Yeah and that fine New York attorney was there that I tried to hook you up with."

"Do you know I met him? He just e-mailed me."

Her eyes danced in her head. "And . . ."

"I'm wondering how he put two and two together. Have you talked to him since?"

"No. I didn't exchange info with the man. I was trying to hook you up."

I kidded. "For the record, I'm taken now. You don't have to worry about hooking me up anymore."

Knowing she'd follow, I turned to leave. "Who's the lucky man?"

"Um. Remember I told you about Scooter?"

She nodded. I blushed. "Well."

A huge smile spread across her face. Then, she immediately frowned. "I thought you said he had a girlfriend."

"He left her."

"Taylor, you're lying."

As she began to ask more questions about my situation, insecurity stormed into the room. As Katherine examined me, I began to feel silly.

Despite the nonsense answers I gave, I realized that people want to marry you off at all cost. She was onboard with my drama the second I told her that Scooter felt like I was the one.

When I got back into my office, I read Devin Patterson's message again and decided to reply. A friendly message never hurt anyone. I told him that I, too, thought it was ironic that of all people at the caucus, we ran into one another when Katherine was so pressed to introduce us. I also mentioned how much I enjoyed dancing with him.

I called Courtney to tell her that Katherine was trying to hook me up with "I Love My People." As we began to giggle about the irony of the meeting, she said, "He seems like a smooth dude."

"Yeah, he seems cool."

Disregarding the fact that I was really now in a relationship, she joked. "You better holla."

My new message alert sounded. Devin Patterson. I laughed. "Girl, 'I Love My People' just responded."

"What did he say?"

I glanced at the message, skipping a few lines. In a nutshell, he wanted to hang out for drinks between now and Thursday. Courtney coaxed me to respond. I did and agreed to hang out tonight. When I pressed SEND, the new e-mail alert sounded simultaneously. Scooter. Oh yeah, I forgot I was pissed off with him. An American Greeting has been sent to you.

I opened the greeting card. His ability to express himself so eloquently is a quality that few men possess. As I sat full of anger, his words dismantled my frustration. It was a thank you card. He told me how special he felt to have me in his world and despite our troubles he thanks God every morning for our reunion. XOXO.

Courtney chatted in my ear as I gazed at the greeting card. This is why I had to go and take Kuku's man. How many men are so affectionate? Sorry Kuku. I'm in it to win it.

A new message from Devin popped up as I daydreamed about Scooter. He asked if I had a preference. I responded not really. He sent the agenda. He had tickets to a Wizards game and we'd eat at the DC Chophouse prior to the game. Wait! I thought we were just hanging out. Oh whatever. Dinner and a good game were always up my alley.

I left work early enough to change and get downtown by 6:00. As I ran around the house deciding what to wear, I took a deep breath. I have a man. And besides I had such a good time the night of the Black Party, Devin was a blur. I searched for an outfit that was not too sexy and not too conservative. If he wasn't as fine as Courtney and Katherine claimed he was I didn't want to be too provocative. Clothes were scattered all around my room. I checked the clock. I had forty-five minutes. When I turned on the shower, "Ring The Alarm" played on my cell phone. Shit! Trapped between my phone and the running water, I made the decision to call Scooter on my way to the restaurant.

I paged Scooter when I got in the car. He called right back. Excited about my outing, it slipped my mind that I was supposed to be mad. I picked up with the beat of the song ringing in my head. I sang, "I'll be damn if I see another chick on your arm."

He chuckled. "Hey baby."

"So, you come here, sex me up. Have your girl calling my house and stuff. You leave and I don't hear from you for twenty-four hours. What's up with that?"

"Tay, you know it's not like that. Right?"

"No, not really."

He chuckled, but sounded more like he wanted to cry. "When I got home yesterday, she had moved all of my shit in the other room, taken all the food out of the house. I was running around like a chicken with my head cut off. This morning, I got to work late, because she woke up blasting music. It took me an hour to get back to sleep." He huffed. "This shit is stressful."

Yada. Yada. Yada. A part of me sympathized with him. The other part of me understood Akua. She wanted him to suffer. I wanted to be there to help, but he needed to man-up and figure out how to take care of himself again.

As I entered the restaurant, I still chatted on the phone.

"Hey, baby, I'm going to dinner with Courtney. I'll call you when I get in."

"Okay, baby. Look forward to talking to you."

"I love you."

He coughed. "I love you, too. Talk to you later."

I looked around and saw Devin. Damn. They were right. He was fine. His short hair cut and groomed six o'clock shadow made me blush. I walked toward him. He was a militant brother. He wore a black blazer with a black T-shirt underneath that had a red-and-green American flag with WE BUILT THIS underneath.

I smiled and said. "I like your T-shirt."

He chuckled. "Déjà vu."

"Could it be that you just wear shirts that strike up conversation?"

"It's not intentional."

"So, you're trying to say that you don't wear these shirts to grab attention."

He raised his right hand. "I swear."

"That doesn't mean anything. You lie for a living, so you can do it with a straight face."

We laughed. He extended his hand. "Let's start again. Hi, Taylor. I'm Devin Patterson. It's good to meet you."

"Good to meet you, too."

"Katherine spoke highly of you. I thought you were white, though."

"Uh-huh. So, is that why you told Katherine you didn't want to meet me? You're prejudiced, huh?"

He chuckled. "Well, I know I don't look like it, but my mother is white. I don't have anything against white women, but I am more attracted to black women." Smiling, he added, "Especially black women from the Maryland/DC, area."

"Are you trying to flatter me?"

He chuckled. "Maybe just a little, but I think God sprinkled too much black beauty in this little area. It's crazy."

"You're funny."

"No. Actually, I'm very serious."

As we diverted to the women in The District being attractive, it dawned on me what he said initially. My forehead wrinkled. "Did you say your mother was white?"

"Yep."

I couldn't see it, but I guess he had no reason to lie. My eyes must have twitched back and forth, searching for the slightest inkling of biracial decent. Recognizing my confusion, he chuckled. "I know. I don't look like it, right?"

I smiled. He smiled. "It's okay. I know."

We were seated. After I browsed through the menu, I asked. "So do you live here or New York."

"Both."

I smirked. "Okay. That makes sense."

"You're funny. You know that, right?"

"If you say so. Why do you live in both places?"

"Well, I run two branches of the family law firm."

"And what firm is that?"

"Patterson and Patterson."

"I don't think I've ever heard of them."

"Well, we're just trying to make a presence in DC. This is primarily a personal venture for me. This branch is specially geared toward the legislative community. My New York branch is geared toward real estate, investments, and things of that sort."

"So, you're all over the place."

"Nope, I have plans."

The waiter came to take our order. I immediately returned to his plans. "So, what is your ultimate plan?"

"Ultimately, I'd like to be in the House of Congress."

I smirked. "One of them, huh?"

We laughed. His admiration for me seemed to be growing. I found him quite charming, too. I asked, "So besides the professional Devin, what's your story?"

"What do you want to know?"

"Whatever you want to tell me. Whatever you think defines you."

"Why don't you tell me your story and then I'll know what it is you're looking to hear."

Without hesitation, I said. "I love life. I have two sisters. I fall in the middle. My father is a pastor of a huge Baptist church. I grew up in Bowie, Maryland. No kids." I paused. Should I tell him about my man that was still living with his ex-girlfriend? Nah, I kept that to myself.

"Interesting."

"Interesting?"

He nodded. "Yes, interesting. I assumed that maybe your wedding band was in the shop for a cleaning or something."

I kidded. "So, do you usually take married women out to dinner?"

His flirtatious comment backfired. He chuckled. "Nah, actually, I don't. I was just messing with you. I knew you weren't married."

"Are you married?"

"Yep."

He smiled and reached in his back pocket for his wallet. He opened his wallet, and with pride he said, "Here's my wife. Isn't she beautiful?"

I peeped over at the picture and a beautiful little girl with a long, flowing pageboy smiled back at me. I smiled. "Is that your daughter? She is so beautiful."

She looked more biracial than Devin. He took a look at the pretty little girl dressed in all white and smiled proudly. "That's daddy's little girl. Her name is Nicole."

I admired the adoration twinkling in his eyes as he talked about Nicole. I sighed. "Aw." I reached for his wallet again. "She is so adorable." Trying to figure out the nationality of her mother, I commented, "Who does she look like?"

He tilted his head. "Me."

"I guess I see a little of you in her."

He laid the wallet on the bar. "A little?" He pointed. "She has my eyes." He stretched his eyes open. His long lashes reached out and invited me in to fantasize the possibilities of us. "My nose. My lips."

As he forced me to study his flawless features, I found myself grinning. So, I asked without being definitive, "And her mother?"

He smirked. "And her mother." He chuckled. "We are good parents." He paused. "She's an attorney. We went to Columbia together. We got married in our second year." He shook his head. "Big mistake."

I wasn't shocked that he got scooped up early, but I was curious what went wrong. My mind wandered. *He probably cheated.*

I asked, "What happened?"

"Are you sure you want to know?"

"Why not?"

"Well her mother . . ." He sighed. "My ex-wife was probably one of the sweetest people I'd ever met in my life." I frowned, prepared to hear how he screwed up. Acknowledging my thoughts, he clarified. "I mean, at that time. That's what I thought."

We chuckled. He continued. "At that time in my life, I was coming to grips with Devin, with accepting my mother, and with managing a long-distance relationship."

I frowned. He laughed. "It all relates. Give me a second."

I nodded slowly as if I wasn't sure he could combine all the variables.

"So, here I was twenty-three years old, madly in love with a beautiful young lady from Maryland and . . ."

I smiled, because I now understood his admiration for the women in the area. He smiled. "This young lady." He paused as if he should give her an identity. "Clark. She was the love of my life, but she had a lot of insecurities that were triggered by my actions. So, I went through a period of thinking she needed to change, when I really needed to just grow up and

stop blaming her for all of our issues. Then, in comes Jennifer."
He chuckled. "That's Nicole's mom. She was so laid back.
She rarely raised her voice. She was just cool." He nodded as
he reminisced on the good times. "It was a welcomed diversion from the drama that came with Clark." He smiled, obvious admiration for his ex-drama queen.

He shifted in his chair. "And I thought the nice quiet girl
was exactly what I needed. Not to mention, Jennifer was
biracial and she understood my insecurities."

I nodded anxiously. He put one finger up as if he was getting to the rest of the story. "Well, all that glitters ain't gold.
And what you see ain't always what you get. By the time I realized that I loved my ex-girl—"

"The drama queen, right?"

He smiled and nodded, but didn't really fully acknowledge
my sarcasm. "By that time, I was married to the devil and
Nicole was a little baby. It all happened too soon."

"Huh?"

He laughed. "You ever heard of the statement, a wolf in
sheep's clothing?" he hissed. "That was my wife."

"Why did it take you so long to figure that out?"

"It wasn't that long." He paused as if he contemplated
telling the rest. "Jennifer got pregnant almost immediately."
He sighed. "And I was raised to do the right thing." He
looked at me as if I had the answer. He huffed. "What is the
right thing?"

"It depends."

"When you're in your early twenties, you don't have a
clue."

Anxious to get the full story, I scooted closer. "Why do
you say your ex-wife was so sneaky? What did she do?"

"I don't like to tell the story, because I try to forget it."

I smiled. "You can tell me. You look like you want to talk
about it."

He huffed. "Almost two years into the marriage, I found

out that she set me up. She intentionally got pregnant. She knew that I would marry her if she had my baby."

That's the oldest sob story in men's history. They should know by now how not to get women pregnant. Why is it that *we* trapped *them* when we get pregnant? If we're the ones walking around with a big belly for nine months and eighty percent of the parental responsibility falls on us, who the hell is trapped again?

He laughed. "See, that's why I don't tell the story."

"Go ahead. I'm just messin' with you. So, how did she trap you?"

"She stuck my condom packets with needles."

"Devin, don't play."

"I swear I'm not lying."

"How do you know?"

"She admitted it."

My mouth stretched open. "Are you serious? I don't believe you."

"My divorce papers state fraud as the reason. If you want to take a look at them, be my guest."

See, hookers like that make it bad for good women.

"I love my baby to death and I don't regret her being here. I just wish I hadn't married Jennifer. You know?"

He swallowed the last of his drink. The situation was obviously still a sore spot. The waiter sat a refill in front of him.

"So where's Clark?"

He smirked. "Happily married."

"Do you think things would have worked for the two of you if it wasn't for Jennifer?"

He drew in a deep breath. "I dunno. I think about it all the time."

As I was in the midst of backtracking and righting my own wrong, I sympathized with him. "Do you think you'll ever let it go?"

"I like to believe that I have."

"Are you in a relationship now?"

"Nah, I'm a busy man."

I smiled. "You know that's an excuse, right?"

With an affirmative nod, he proclaimed, "That's the truth."

"How long have you been away from your wife?"

He squinted. "Five years. We've been divorced for four."

"Have you had a serious relationship since your divorce?"

"Ah . . ." He thought momentarily. "I've had relationships, but nothing major." He chuckled. "I'm married to my job and my daughter."

"Yeah, right."

"Seriously. I don't have time."

"Are you waiting for Clark to get a divorce too?"

"Taylor, no. What kind of man do you think I am?"

I told him that he was human, just like me. Then, I was comfortable enough to give him the brief synopsis of my nine-year regret and how I'd stolen him from his girlfriend. However, I left out the part that she was a live-in girlfriend that still lived with him.

"Wow, that's amazing. So does he live here?"

I nodded. It was hard for anyone to digest that I had a boyfriend that lived in another state with his ex-girlfriend. You had to be a part of the relationship to really understand.

"He was right in this area all along and you guys never crossed paths."

"Nope."

He chuckled. "Taylor, you know you were just taking inventory."

I squinted. "What?"

"Men have been doing it forever. Every year you take inventory of the people you dated and why you didn't like them or why it didn't work. Then, you start convincing yourself that they were really someone you could be with."

"Yeah, I agree. I've taken inventory before. But my relationship now is different."

"Why?"

I huffed. "Because I always knew it was a mistake."

"So why did it take nine years for you to pursue it."

I shrugged my shoulders. He chuckled. "As each year passed and you managed your inventory, he looked more and more like a king."

"Whatever."

He softly tapped down my hand that sat propped up defensively blocking his accusation. Then, he smiled. "Let me stop hatin'. Where's his old girlfriend."

"History."

"So, you took him from her in three weeks? That must be real love."

"Yeah, I think you only get one real love."

He tilted his head and smiled as if his love story played internally. "You think?"

"Yeah."

"So, I should go take Clark from her man?" He laughed. "That's ludicrous."

"Well it doesn't work out for everyone."

He nodded and raised his glass for a toast. "I'm glad it worked out for you."

Still a tad insecure about the whole thing, I nodded. "Thank you."

Obviously the Grey Goose had taken over as he began to sing softly. "What if we were wrong about each other? What if you were really made for me? What if we were supposed to be together? Would that not mean anything? What if that was supposed to be my house that you go home to every day? How can you be sure that things are better if you can't be sure that your heart is still with me?"

My heart reached out to him. Questions and regret filled his eyes. I'd been there. Nine years of blaming myself. He still loved whoever this Clark woman was. His emotions were all too familiar to me. When someone hurts you, you can get over it. But when you hurt someone that you love, you end up six years later, drowning in sorrow and singing Baby Face.

Hoping to lighten the mood, I joked. "You know, Devin, my best friend always says that light liquor makes you emotional. So, maybe you should try something dark."

"And what do you suggest I try?"

"I've actually been drinking Crown Royal lately. It's smooth and keeps your emotions in order," I said, laughing.

"You're trippin'. I'm not emotional, but I'll give Crown Royal a try and see how it makes me feel."

"I hope it helps you get over your ex-girl," I teased.

"I'm definitely over it, but I guess I'm still looking for that high. You know?"

"Yeah, I know, but do you think it happens when you're over thirty?"

"I dunno. But if it doesn't, I'm comfortable being a single man."

I wasn't convinced. His eyes told a different story, one of a man holding on to the past, with lost hope for the future, and burying himself in meaningless tasks. I nodded. He continued to attempt to convince me. "I spent the majority of my young years tied down. So, I'm really okay with being alone."

I raised one eyebrow and asked, "Really?"

He laughed. "Yes, Dr. Phil."

"I'm just curious, because I've been there." I shook my head. "For nine years."

"So I have a few years left to wallow in my misery."

I shook my head. "No. You just need to forgive yourself."

35

DEVIN

Taylor and I left the restaurant, heading for the MCI Center. It had been such a long time since I'd had good conversation with a woman that I found attractive. She was what every man was looking for. She possessed the right balance between beauty and brains. She tipped a nine on both scales. Her humor was an added bonus. It's just my luck that I meet someone who stimulates both sides of the brain and she's taken. Whoever the dude is who landed her is a lucky man.

We trotted over to the arena, and I subconsciously reached for her hand. She offered it freely. Her peaceful smile made me smile. Who would ever think that Taylor Jabowski was a beautiful black woman with so much personality? Based on the details of her situation, it seemed like four weeks ago I could have still stuck my foot in the door.

When we got into the game, we walked down to our floor seats. Taylor kidded. "We ballin' y'all."

"Yeah, we ballin'."

Once the game began, it slipped my mind that I was here with a chick. She was standing up, making calls, getting emotional. We slapped high fives. I couldn't stop thinking, *Taylor Jabowski*.

I got two 32-oz. cups of beer from the concession stand.

Instead of whining about it being too much or how she hates beer, she wiggled in her chair and cheered "Hey!"

She raised her cup and we toasted. She said, "To forgiveness."

That hit home because I'd been in the process of purging my negative feelings toward Jennifer. I nodded. "To forgiveness."

She gulped her drink. It was the sexiest thing I'd seen in a long time. I studied her. When she pulled the cup down, she looked at me. "Whatchu doing?"

I smiled. "Watching you."

She smirked. Then, she started singing, "If you want my body and you think I'm sexy, c'mon baby let me know."

She giggled. I just looked at her without cracking a smile. My intense stare forced her to pause. Our gaze connected. She turned her head to end the attraction.

We focused on the game and she didn't try me again. She stood up and cheered. I pretty much sat in my seat and admired her from behind, beside, and between. During commercial breaks, the music played and she danced. Hanging out with her was money well spent. Suddenly, I looked up and our faces were on the big screen. I pointed. She covered her face. Our one second of stardom felt like an eternity. So that I didn't look like a sucker, I reached over and moved her hands from her face and kissed her. Her head rested helplessly in my hands, as we continued to kiss. When the feeling resonated with her, she pulled back and glared at me.

"I'm sorry, Taylor. The camera made me do it."

She smirked. "Yeah, right."

"Don't be mad at me."

"I know not to hang out in a public place with you anymore."

"Does that mean we can still hang out?"

She folded her arms. "I'll keep you posted."

When the game was over, I didn't want to part. She was apprehensive as well. We both said, "Okay."

"All right then."

"All right."

"I had a great time."

"We have to do this again."

I wanted to invite her over to my empty place, but I decided against it. This was the best date I'd been on since I've been single. After walking Taylor to her car, I skipped back to mine. Though she was taken, I was hopeful. Good women aren't extinct. Maybe Jennifer was right, nothing good would come as long as I harbored bitterness toward her.

36

TAYLOR

I'd finally figured out what people meant by someone taking their breath away. I sat in my car holding mine. Devin Patterson had kidnapped it. As I even imagined how I wanted to be a great stepmom to his beautiful little girl, I knew I'd lost my mind. This man has baggage. He's bitter. That's too much for me to handle. I looked at the clock. 11:22 P.M. Would it be inconsiderate to call Scooter now?

Instead, I called Courtney. "Girl, why do I love 'I Love My People'?"

She cracked up. "I told you he was fine."

"Fine is a damn understatement. I don't remember him looking like that."

She laughed. "Whatever. You better start paying better attention to your surroundings."

"How about it?"

"I would do him."

"Would I?"

"Are you?"

"Nah, he has too many things going on. He's back and forth to New York. He's in love with his girlfriend before his wife. He's mad at his wife. You know the fine ones all have issues."

"I can't say you're lying."

I chuckled. "Plus, I got a man."

"Taylor, don't play with me. When he moves out, then you'll have a man. For now, don't tell me that bullshit."

"You'll be the first person I call when he moves out."

When I got to work the next day, I floated on a cloud. I wasn't sure who I was thinking about. I was just happy. Katherine came into my office. She smirked. "Hey, boo."

She waited for me to tell her that Devin was an asshole as were most of my dates. I frowned. She covered her face. "Oh no. What did he do? Did he say something stupid?"

I said. "Girl."

"C'mon Taylor. What happened?"

"We had a ball."

"You're lying."

"No, actually we had a great time."

My work phone rang. "Taylor Jabowski."

"I missed you last night."

I put him on hold and told Katherine I'd give her the details later. I picked up. "I missed you, too."

"How was dinner?"

My eyes shifted back and forth. "Uh, it was good."

"I hoped to hear from you when you got in."

"I'm sorry. It got late. We actually went to the Wizards game. Courtney's job gave her tickets."

Taylor, what the hell are you thinking? That was definitely a fumble. I shrugged my shoulders. He chuckled. "I'm jealous."

"Don't be. Of course it was no fun without you."

He laughed. "You're a trip. I can't wait to see you."

"You just left me two days ago."

"What does that mean?"

"Ah, nothing."

He laughed. "I'm off on Friday. I may drive down there post-call on Thursday."

"Is that too much?"

He chuckled. "Baby, I feel like I live in Iraq. Ain't nothing too much. Talking to you is like peace in the Middle East."

I laughed. "Scooter, you're crazy."

"I'm dead serious. Your voice keeps me focused."

I sighed. Why did I feel guilty? He was living in hell for me and I was out footloose and fancy free with some stranger with issues.

"It'll be worth it in the end," I told him.

"I know. It's just getting there."

After listening to Devin's sob story last night, I offered him a bit of advice. "It may seem hard now, but nothing is worse than marrying the wrong person."

"Why do you think I'm going through with this? This definitely ain't the easy route." He chuckled. "I've tried to stop plenty of my boys from making the same mistake that I was about to make."

"Aren't you glad I caught you before you fell?"

He chuckled. "Damn straight."

Katherine showed up at my door with a beautiful bouquet of yellow roses. I smiled and mouthed, "For me?"

She nodded. I blushed. For some reason, I knew they weren't from Scooter. She walked over to my desk; I gestured for her to take the card out. She smirked. I put my index finger over my mouth. She giggled and slapped my hand down. She mouthed, "I'm not stupid."

Devin jumped off of the little card before any of the other words. Scooter called my name. I turned my attention away from my admirer. "Yeah, baby."

"I'm getting paged. I gotta go. I'll talk to you later."

Devin's message said: *Thanks for a wonderful night on the town. Your man is very lucky. I hope he knows it.*

Katherine snatched the card. She put her hand on her hip. "Taylor, I am disappointed in you. You told his fine ass that you have a man. Have you lost your mind?"

"No. I do have a man."

"Taylor Jabowski. You have officially fell off."

I nodded. How was she using my lingo on me? I laughed. "Katherine, you're a mess."

I sent Devin an e-mail telling him I enjoyed myself as well and thanking him for the wonderful flowers. He responded very briefly. He was obviously not trying to push the envelope with someone who claimed someone else.

I decided to sit the flowers on the receptionist's desk. I didn't need a constant reminder of Devin staring me in my face.

37

DEVIN

I waited to hear from Taylor for two months after she sent that bullshit thank you message. As I sat in her building, I contemplated going up to her office. I tapped my pen on the conference table. Her pretty smile kept popping up on the projector. Why wasn't the old lady in this meeting?

We were finished meeting by twelve, so I asked one of the union guys if he knew Taylor Jabowski. He kidded. "Of course. Everyone knows Taylor."

"She's a friend of mine. Could you show me where she sits?"

"Sure." He looked at his watch. "I hope she isn't out to lunch."

We walked into her office spaces. He pointed. "Her office is right there."

"Thank you so much."

I nervously stood in her doorway. I'd never been flat-out rejected that way. I sent my signature flowers, and still she disappeared. She cackled on the phone.

Her office chair faced the opposite direction. I wondered who brought her so much joy on the other end. I cleared my throat. She took a few seconds before turning her chair around. Finally, she hung up the phone and looked at me.

I felt the vibration on the floor from her heart dropping.

Her eyes widened before she smiled. After she found her breath, she pointed to a chair. "C'min Devin. This is a surprise."

"I can tell."

"You could have called, you know."

"My gut reaction told me to just pop up."

She chuckled. "If I were mean, you could have gotten your feelings hurt."

"If I thought you were mean, I wouldn't be here." I smirked. "Nah, let me correct that. You are mean."

"No one has ever called me mean."

"I take you out, send you flowers, and I never hear from you."

"Whatever. If you want to talk, you know my numbers."

"Guilty as charged. So, how's your man? Is everything cool?"

She blushed. "Wonderful."

Damn. I hoped she'd tell me he was a jerk and she stole him back for no reason. Instead, she looked undisputedly happy. "That's all right."

"So, what's up with you and your love life?"

"Quantity and no quality."

Her eyes looked compassionate. "I can't imagine."

"I never imagined it either."

We laughed. "I know the feeling, though."

"So, you want to do something for lunch?"

She winced. "I'll be busy until around two and I have something to do at six." She looked at the time. "So maybe we can go for coffee or something."

"That's cool. I'll meet you outside at 2:30."

"I'll be standing outside of the building."

Like clockwork, she walked outside of her building when I pulled up. She hopped in and asked. "Where we going?"

"I scheduled a massage."

"A what?"

"I know you like massages."

She smirked. "Yeah, I do but . . ."

"It'll be fun. We can have our Dr. Phil sessions while we get our massages."

She raised her eyebrows. "So, we're going together."

"We won't see each other's goods." I chuckled. "I promise I'll close my eyes."

"You promise."

When we got out of the car, Taylor and I stood face to face. She couldn't pay me to believe that she wasn't feeling what I felt. She smiled. "Devin, you're funny."

"What did I do?"

"Nothing," she said, shaking her head.

When we got into the salon, I whispered to her, "I always get tense before I get a massage."

She chuckled. "Why is that?"

"I'm always afraid that I'll get aroused."

She curled her lips like she didn't want to visualize it. "Spare me."

I would spare her all right. I just hoped that opportunity arose. We were taken into a small transition room. Wine and brownies were there. I picked up a brownie and put it up to her mouth. She bit into it and I wiped the crumbs from her lip. She smiled. I wanted to kiss her, but didn't want to scare her off like the last time.

When the therapist came out, she told us we could change in the same room or separate rooms. We agreed on separate rooms, but to have the massages done in the same room. She looked like that was strange. I gave her the we're-not-fucking-yet eyebrow raise. She chuckled. "That will be fine."

When I entered the room, Taylor was lying on her stomach under a white sheet. My fear of being aroused crept up on me. I quickly lay on the table across from her. She lifted her head from the head rest. "Are you okay?"

"Yeah, I'm good."

When the massage therapists came in, they discussed different aromatherapy scents. Taylor requested Clairvoyance. She said, "Is that okay with you, Devin?"

I laughed. "Yeah, I need some of that."

"Me too."

As the sounds of nature began to play, we both settled. Water washing up on the beach forced me to imagine Taylor in a bikini, us sharing a private island in paradise. As I inhaled the aroma, I prayed that her vision was as clairvoyant as mine.

A relaxing fifty minutes with one woman massaging every inch of my body and one beside me who had been one of a few to massage my mind made me feel like a king. I didn't want it to end. When they told us it was done, I popped my head up. Taylor continued to lay with her eyes closed. One of the therapists said, "You guys can relax as long as you like."

"Hey, Taylor."

"Yes, Devin."

"Did you enjoy it?"

"It was exactly what I needed."

I swung my legs off the table and wrapped a towel around myself. I stood by her table. "I'm glad."

Without opening her eyes, she said, "Are you in a rush?"

"No. I'm just going to change and let you relax here alone."

"I thought we were going to talk about your issues."

I hopped back on the table. "Okay."

"So, tell me about your quantity."

I scowled. "Not worth discussing."

"How's your baby?"

"She's good. Remember we toasted to forgiveness. My ex-wife and I are actually working on being better friends."

"That's good."

"Nothing else too much."

I wanted to know more about her, but it was obvious she wasn't sharing. "Okay, let's get out of here. Maybe we can grab coffee before your six o'clock appointment."

When we got dressed and out of the spa, she looked so peaceful. I wanted to resist, but I didn't. I hugged her in the parking lot. She kissed my cheek. "Devin, you're a sweetheart."

"You seem more reserved than you did the first time we hung out."

I opened the car door. I kissed her lips. She smirked. "Devin, I have to stay away from you."

"Why?"

She sat in the car. I stooped down to hear her explanation. She sighed. "Because of this."

"You feel it. Don't you?"

She hung her head. "My boyfriend left a woman he planned to marry for me. I can't risk what we have. You and I have too much chemistry. I think it's best to stay away from you."

I stood up and closed the door. Disappointment loomed over me as I walked to the driver's side. When I sat inside, I respected her stance. "Taylor, your man is so lucky."

38

SCOOTER

After working thirty hours, I should be asleep. Instead, I'm flying down I-95 en route to Taylor. You'd think I'd be tired of the same routine after three months, but to make my baby secure this is what I do. She's a good sport considering my living arrangement. To get away from the war zone I live in, this seems like the lesser of two evils. My income tax return was deposited in my account three days ago. My new apartment was verbally approved and I could move in three weeks. We are so close to our destiny, I can smell it. Once I'm in my own place, Taylor can stay as long and as often as she likes without spending money. I'd hoped that I could surprise her with the approval letter this weekend, but the rental office didn't send it out yet. I'll give it to her on Valentine's Day, her birthday.

I swerved to avoid a pothole. Bang! I felt that one. Suddenly, my car felt like it was riding on a square wheel. Thump. Thump. Thump. This must be a joke. As my car drifted onto the shoulder, I shouted, "Fuck! Shit! Damn!"

I just wanted to lie in Taylor's fluffy queen-sized bed. Damn if I wanted to go back to Connecticut and sleep in that cheap daybed. Shit! I'm still in Connecticut. Rain pounded on the roof of my car. As it registered what was going on, I dropped my head on the steering wheel. Instead of calling for help, I called Taylor.

"Hey, boo-boo. Whatchu doing?"

"Sitting on the side of the road. I got a damn flat and I don't have a donut," I said dismally.

"Oh no! I'm sorry. Do you have AAA?"

I nodded.

"Do you?"

"Yeah."

"Why don't you call them?"

I nodded. Why did I even call her? What did I think she could do?

"Yeah, I'll hit you back."

"I hope you can still make it."

I huffed. "Yeah, me too. I'll call you back."

As I attempted to call AAA, a police officer pulled up behind me. He hopped out of his car and tapped on my passenger side window.

"You need help changing the tire?"

"Nah, I don't have a spare."

"You got AAA?"

With the phone up to my face, I nodded. "I'm calling them now."

"Do you have anyone to come pick you up?"

Anybody who could pick me up was at work. Akua is post-call, too. We barely speak. Damn if she'll get out of her bed after a long night of work to come get me. I prayed the tow company could drop me off somewhere to get a rental car.

When I spoke to the AAA representative, she asked if I'd be with the car when the tow got there. Where the hell else will I be? She checked on the trucks in the area.

"Sir, it's going to be about two and a half hours."

This is absolutely unbelievable. Trucks and cars sped past me going twenty miles over the speed limit. The slightest swerve around a pothole could slam one into the back of me. I had to get off of the highway. Putting my pride aside, I paged Akua. I sat there praying she'd call back.

When my phone rang, I jumped. "Ku."

"What the hell do you want?"

I sighed. "Are you asleep?"

"Do you think I would have returned your phone call if I was asleep? I don't fuck with you like that."

"No." I paused. "I need a favor," I said.

"From me?"

"Yes, from you."

"What do you want?"

"I'm on 95, right before Southport at Exit 20. I got a flat. I need you to come pick me up."

"Wait on me, nigga!"

She hung up the phone. I don't even know why I called her. Another officer came up behind me. He asked, "Is someone coming out?"

"Yeah, AAA. But they won't be here for about two hours."

I hoped he'd offer a solution, but he nodded. "Okay, I'll come back and check on you in about an hour."

This is bullshit! I leaned my seat back hoping I could at least get some rest while I waited. What a joke. A police officer tapped on my window every ten minutes or so. Don't they have some kind of walkie-talkie system to say that there's some dummy at CT-Exit 20 stranded in a Honda Accord? Don't bother him, he's okay. Obviously not. I pulled out an anesthesiology book and planned to study. My head nodded as my eyes glazed over. Headlights flickered in my car. A horn blew. I looked into my rearview mirror and saw Akua's Ford Taurus.

I quickly called her. "Hey, I have to call AAA to let them know where the key will be. Don't get out of your car. I'll be back there in a minute."

After I made arrangements for them to take my car to the

nearest tireshop, I hopped out. From my car to Akua's car, I got drenched. Unconsciously, I leaned over and kissed her cheek. "Thank you, Ku. I really appreciate this. I know you didn't have to do it."

"My father says a man should always have a spare tire."

I wanted to tell her to tell her father to go to hell. Instead, I nodded.

"Where is your spare?"

"My spare was a new tire. When I got a flat a few weeks ago, I put the spare on and didn't buy a new one."

"You never think, do you?"

"Nope."

She huffed. "I guess you were going to see your freak-ass girlfriend."

I nodded.

She chuckled slightly. "That's what your bitch-ass gets."

I felt like I hadn't seen her smile in months. We brush past one another in the house, barely sharing two words. We pretend we don't know each other in the hospital. I chuckled, too.

Her eyes inspected my expression. We paused. She turned to the road. "You must love her to ride in all this rain, post-call. Maybe she is the one."

I felt like I should lie. No. She's not the one. For the sake of not saying anything, I looked out the window.

We rode back to New Haven in silence. When we got in town, we stopped at Starbucks. I asked, "When my car is ready, will you take me back?"

She nodded. At the same small table we used to study at when we were interns, we broke banana bread. The rain trickled down the window. She smiled. "Today is perfect for sleeping."

I nodded. "Yeah. I should have gone home and gone to sleep."

"I had a pretty light night last night, so I was wired this morning." She curled her lips. "You're lucky."

"Thank you. I really appreciate it."

"Don't mention it."

I felt like I was sitting with a stranger. She obviously had come to accept it was over. She wasn't throwing out her usual slurs. She seemed peaceful. Maybe she's been this way for a while, I just hadn't noticed because I was so involved in my own life.

When we got to the apartment, I turned on the television and she sat beside me. We were zoned to separate rooms. What was up with this? I flipped through the channels. A reality show popped up. She raised her arm about to take the remote. Then, she relaxed. "I'm sorry. I was going to say, I like that show."

Since she'd rescued me from the highway, she could say and watch anything of her choice. I handed her the remote. "Go ahead. What's this?"

"A group of women that know they have some issues all go to this house and work on their issues."

As if I cared, I asked, "What kind of issues?"

She shrugged her shoulders. "All of them have different issues. Some are OCD. Some are irresponsible. Just like social disorders."

I frowned. "You like this show?"

"Yeah, sometimes I feel like I should go on there."

"You?"

She nodded. "I could lighten up a little."

"You could."

We laughed. She smiled more this morning than at some of the happiest periods in our relationship. Maybe she'd come to accept her flaws. I appreciated that. Why couldn't she have done this when we were together?

When they called to say my car was ready, Akua was in the kitchen. She asked, "Do you want a sandwich?"

I kidded. "So, am I allowed to have things labeled Akua?"

"If I'm making it, it's okay. But my stuff is still off limits to you."

I walked in the kitchen and my hormones pushed me up against her. I wrapped my hands around her waist. "Really?"

She tilted her head and looked at me. She smiled. I expected her to say, "Get the fuck off of me," but she didn't. Why did I feel a sense of accomplishment? Why did I like knowing that I could hit it despite all I'd taken her through?

I backed up. "I'm just playing."

"What do you want on your sandwich?"

After we had lunch, we got in the car to pick up mine. Before she started the car, she sniffed. I looked at her and tears started rolling down her face. I'd been in this position once in my life. The person in the passenger seat seemed so heartless. Tears like the ones streaming from Akua's eyes only fall for that one true love. Taylor was mine. I was hers. In all these months, she'd been angry. I didn't think she was capable of this type of emotion. I sat stunned.

"I love you. Please don't leave me."

It was too late. Why didn't she react like this at first?

"I know I have my faults, but I can change."

I was speechless. She pleaded, "I have never loved anybody like I love you. I don't care what anyone thinks of me. I don't care if my family never speaks to me again. I want to be with you."

Who was the girl beside me?

"I love you. I can't imagine living without you." She dropped her head in her hands. "It just hurts so bad. Please take the pain away."

I rubbed her back, and she whispered, "What did I do so bad to make you leave me for someone three hundred miles away? Tell me. What did I do?"

Finally, I spoke. "You didn't do anything. This was just something that I never resolved."

"Don't lie to me. I had to do something. I thought you were happy. I tried to do everything for you."

I stroked her braids. "I know baby. It's not your fault."

She started the car. I felt like shit. When she put her hand on the gear, I said, "We don't have to go. I'll stay here this weekend."

39

TAYLOR

Determined to make our relationship work, we were spending about five hundred dollars a week. I am a frequent Friday evening passenger on the US Airways flight number 977. It rolled out of Reagan National Airport at 5:25, and landed me in Scooter's arms by 6:30.

While I waited to board, I sent him a text message: GETTING ON THE PLANE.

He quickly replied: CAN'T WAIT TO SEE U. I MISS U SO MUCH.

The five days separating us always feel like an eternity. I was burning inside to see him too, but I suppressed the desire to tell him. Instead, I stared at the loving note on my screen. As I re-read the message umpteen times, my cheeks stretched closer and closer to my ears. When they called my row, I stood up, rolling my carry-on with one hand and my wide-open flip phone and plane ticket in the other. I bounced toward the attendant taking the boarding passes. He noticed the sunshine beaming on my face in the middle of winter. "Guess this is going to be a special Valentine's Day for you."

Feeling rather silly, I tried to justify my jolly expression. "It's my birthday. So every Valentine's Day is good for me."

He nodded as if he didn't ask for so much info. "Well, happy birthday and Happy Valentine's Day."

I strolled through the terminal in a daze and sat in my seat. Before I turned my phone off, I took one last glance at Scooter's message. As if it would make me feel closer to him, I rubbed the ball of my thumb over the screen. Then, pressed OFF. I snapped on my seatbelt and anxiously awaited takeoff.

My heart sinks each time I arrive in Connecticut. My feelings of anticipation flip-flop back and forth on the security spectrum. As secure as I feel when I'm with him, I feel just as insecure each time we part; knowing he goes to an apartment with his ex-girlfriend.

After I finally got off of the plane, I casually strolled to the airport in no rush, because Scooter will not arrive at the hotel until around eight. When I got out to the shuttle stand, I saw men carrying roses, women accepting them. No one is there to greet me. I take a deep breath. Insecurity again. How could I succumb to sneaking around with another woman's man? Why did it still feel like she was his woman? I stood in her town feeling like I deserved more. I did deserve more. I leaned onto my other leg and reminded myself of why I was here. Plus he was moving in two weeks. What more could I ask for?

Inside my coat pocket, my cell phone vibrated in my hand. My heart beat rapidly as I pulled it out to read my text message.

GOING TO THE MOVIES AFTER WORK. WILL BE THERE BY TEN.

My insides felt like three-hundred degrees in thirty-degree weather. Smoke exited my mouth as I stretched it wide open while re-reading the message. The phone vibrated again in my palm. I slammed the phone shut and climbed on to the shuttle. I plopped down in my seat. I didn't want to hear anything else he had to say.

My heaving caught the attention of the older lady beside me. She peeped at me through her big silver bangs. Her shoulders swayed, tapping her upper arm against mine. I huffed, not because of her, but because of me. I leaned my head on the window and watched the unappealing scenery.

She asked, "Do you live here?"

Swishing the left side of my forehead back and forth on the window, I said no.

"Me either."

I didn't comment. She continued, "I'm here to see my grandkids."

I smiled tightly and mumbled, "That's nice."

"I live in Ft. Lauderdale. It's too cold here for me."

I nodded absently.

"Are you here for work?"

I huffed. My eyes watered. "To see friends."

"That's always good. Where are you from?"

If she were ten years younger I would have ignored her, but I felt obligated to answer. I huffed again. "Maryland."

"Is it cold there?"

I nodded. She finally got the memo, because she stopped talking, and returned to rocking. We pulled up to my hotel, the driver announced, "Westin."

I got up to climb over the lady when the driver opened the van door. I gave her a fake smile. As if she could read my mind, she said, "Have a good trip honey. Every Valentine's Day won't be like this one."

I took a deep breath and nodded. "Thank you."

When I stepped into the hotel alone, I felt like eyes were scorning me. With my eyes lowered, I stepped up to the front desk. "I want to check in."

Before I could tell her my name, she said, "Taylor right?"

I looked up. The same lady from a few weeks ago smiled eagerly at me. I smiled. She reminded me, "I'm Taylor, too. Remember I told you last time."

She probably knew I was here every other weekend for a damn secret rendezvous. I felt like a hooker. My eyes begged her to understand this screwed up relationship I had become a part of and nodded.

"What's your last name Taylor?"

I hesitated. Stealing someone's man made me feel like a felon on the run. It was as if everyone I talked to was a security camera. I cleared my throat. "Jabowski. My last name is Jabowski."

She typed away at her keyboard for another two minutes or so. She tapped her fingers on the counter and smiled. I sensed compassion in her expression. "I'll just need your credit card for incidentals."

I opened my wallet. Initially, I tugged on my GW Alumni Platinum card, but stopped. How does a perfectly intelligent woman end up here? Instead, I handed her my debit card. She swiped it. As I scribbled my information on the card, she put my key cards in the sleeve. "Ms. Jabowski, you're in room 1015. I think you'll like your Valentine's Day gift."

Maybe Scooter wasn't being a jerk. Suddenly my anger switched to Taylor, the receptionist. Why did she ruin the surprise? My heart jumped with excitement. When I got on the elevator, I pulled my phone from the holster to finally read Scooter's second message.

I LOVE YOU.

I blushed. When I reached the tenth floor, I skedaddled to the room at the end of the long hallway hoping to find Scooter there wrapped in a bow. I put my key in the door and said, "Hello."

There was no response in the dark room. I flicked on the lights and entered a massive penthouse. Knowing that I hadn't upgraded anything, I was certain that Scooter was in on this. Thinking that I was playing a game of hide-and-seek, I tiptoed around the room. I looked in the closets, under the bed, in the shower. Out of desperation, I even looked in the dresser drawers. Maybe he wasn't here, but he left a gift. After I exhausted all possibilities, it was clear the only game being played was me. I slouched on the king-sized bed and mumbled, "I am so much smarter than this."

The answer was revealed to me as I unwound. Taylor, the

front desk clerk, knew nothing of Scooter, nor did Scooter prearrange this. She was giving her namesake a gift. Though no one knew my thoughts but me, I was embarrassed.

The Moët in my luggage was screaming my name. I pulled it out and began to celebrate my birthday. After the lecture Courtney gave me before I left, I didn't want to call her. So, I just sipped.

Eight o'clock came and went. Scooter sent his first message. IS EVERYTHING OKAY?

I wasn't ready to respond. Nine o'clock came and went. He sent the next message. ARE YOU MAD AT ME?

Finally, I responded. YES.

Again, he wrote. I LOVE YOU.

Ten minutes later he wrote. BE THERE SOON. WHAT ROOM?

Ten o'clock came and I paced the floor. At 10:30, my phone rang. At 10:45, the hotel phone rang. I contemplated.

I swirled the last of the Moët around in the bottle. In a lovely penthouse, alone, drinking his favorite celebratory drink on my birthday, I started to cry.

After an hour of ringing, I felt unsure of my motive. I looked at my cell phone when it rang again. It was Courtney. After a debate with myself, I answered. Attempting to sound happy, I said, "Hey girl. What's going on?"

She immediately asked, "What's wrong?"

"Nothing."

"Where's Scooter?"

I huffed. "Not here yet."

I paused to allow room for her ranting, but she just breathed. There were uneasy sighs of communication on the line. So I asked. "What'd you do today?"

"I worked late and Mark took me to dinner."

"Where's he?"

"Right here."

Her confidence made me feel worse. Tears rolled down my

cheeks, as the hotel phone rang off the hook. Courtney said, "I guess you're not answering, huh?"

I sighed. "No."

Instead of expressing her real feelings, she jumped to another topic. "This is the first Valentine's day in eight years that we haven't been together."

I inadvertently sniffed. "I know."

Mark spoke in the background. "Yeah Taylor, I was looking forward to having two ladies on my arm tonight."

Courtney shuffled around and I could hear her walking through her long hallway. The pitter-patter from her going down the stairs echoed through the phone. Finally she said, "You feel like talking about it."

I sniffed again. "How did I get here?"

Blatantly she said, "Arrogance."

"What?"

She cleared it up. "Confidence."

"Whatever."

She said, "Taylor, what happened?"

"He went to the movies." I huffed. "I'm assuming with his roommate."

She paused. "Did you think he wouldn't?"

"He claims that she talks to other men and they really don't communicate and . . ."

"But he didn't say he did not want to take her out, right?"

I sniffed. "No."

"Taylor, this stuff takes time. As long as she's in that apartment with him, she is his woman. No matter what he's told her, he hasn't left yet. She's still in first place.

"So when is he supposed to be out of the house?" she asked.

Emphasizing my doubt, I said, "*Supposedly* the end of the month."

I waited for her to analyze. She didn't. I added, "He supposedly found a place and was approved. And . . ."

"So why are you tripping?"

"I dunno," I said.

She continued, "Even when he moves out, it won't be completely over until June or July tops."

I snapped, "June or July?"

She chuckled at my impatience. "Yes Taylor. People don't break up that easy."

I pouted. "Why not?"

"Scooter is not going to be blatant about this. Scooter is not a player and never has been."

"You're right."

"So are you going to answer?"

"Whatchu think?"

"Taylor you're there now. You may as well."

When I finally picked up the phone, he sounded desperate. "Taylor, I'm sorry. Please forgive me."

My heart melted as always. I said, "Room 1015". Then, I slammed the phone down.

My cell phone vibrated. HAPPY VDAY BEAUTIFUL –D.

Devin? That was a surprise. If he was text messaging me at eleven thirty, he was obviously alone on this lovers' day, too. Then it dawned on me, maybe he was just taking inventory. Maybe I should be doing the same.

Scooter tapped on the door and took my mind off of Devin. A huge bouquet of roses hid his face. He handed them to me and smiled. I smirked. With the bouquet pointed south, I walked back to the sofa and plopped down.

"I'm so sorry. She . . ."

"Save it."

He stood in front of me. His eyes followed my eyes, hoping to gain access. I denied him by putting my head between my legs. He kneeled down in front of me and tried to lift my chin. I fought him.

He wrapped his arms around my folded body. "Taylor. I know you're mad. I'm leaving in two weeks."

I held back my tears. "I can't do this."

"Do what? We're at the finish line now. This isn't the time to give up."

"If we're at the finish line, why do you feel like you have to please her? Why do I still feel like the other woman?"

He gasped. "Do you know how hard it is to look in the eyes of someone who loves you, someone who has done nothing to hurt you and say I want to leave you because I fell in love with someone else?"

I shook my head. He sat up on the couch and rubbed my back. "Taylor, I had no idea that I would feel this way about you so soon. I mean, I was planning my life with her and you . . ."

I lifted my head. "So it's all my fault?"

"It's no one's fault. We can't help what we feel, but it doesn't make me feel good that I'm hurting her. I took her out today, because I felt sorry for her. That's all."

Why did I sympathize with him? I guess mostly it was my own guilt. I let another incident slide on my road to victory.

40

SCOOTER

Why did Akua wait until three weeks before my moving date to become vulnerable? My feelings were in too deep with Taylor. I pictured her in my life. I imagined spending Christmas and Thanksgivings with her family, not Akua's. Her tears began to wash away my confidence. We've been sleeping in the same bed again. She now tiptoes out in the morning to avoid waking me.

She asks every day, "Have you made a decision, yet?"

I wonder how long the stranger I've been sleeping with will be around. What if I miss my chance to be with my ideal mate? If I screw this up, will Taylor ever speak to me again? If I hadn't led her on for so long, things would be different. There was less than seven seconds left in the game. I looked left. I looked right. I weighed my choice. Do I shoot the jumper and get three points? Do I go for the guaranteed lay up, lying beside me? Two points, but it still puts me up a point. Three points will guarantee a win. As I compared my drama to basketball, Akua stared at me.

Her vulnerability was so beautiful. I found myself kissing her for no reason. When I sat up on the side of the bed, I sighed. "I have to pack."

She pulled up on me and rested her chin on my shoulders. "You're really leaving me?"

I shrugged my shoulders. Her wet cheek touched my back. "Why won't you give me a chance to change?"

I dropped my head. "Ku, I don't know what I'm doing."

"Why do you love her so much?"

I shrugged my shoulders.

"Why can't we figure this out?"

"I'm going to move out, so I can be clear about what I want." I turned to face her. "I think that's best. That way, I'm not leading anyone on."

"I'm afraid of losing you. I've always thought if I worked hard for something I wouldn't lose it."

I stood up. "You're not losing me."

She crawled to the edge of the bed. "Why do you have to leave?"

"Just let me clear my head."

I went into the other room and began to gather my things. The house phone rang. Akua answered, "Hey, honey. Yeah, we miss you, too. When are you coming to see us?"

I stood at the door frowning. She mouthed. "It's my other boyfriend."

I didn't correct her and tell her I was not her boyfriend anymore. I nodded and knew she was talking about my best friend. Maybe he received the subliminal S.O.S. that I sent out. Ripping and running up and down the road has prevented me from sharing my drama with anyone. I've been primarily figuring this out in my own head. I was too afraid that someone else would push me in the wrong direction.

After a few moments of conversing, she told me to get the phone. I stepped into the room and mouthed. "You didn't tell him anything, did you?"

She glared like it was a stupid question. I picked up, "What's up, Dawg."

"Yo, I haven't seen you or Ku in a minute. Y'all usually come through to see a brotha."

"Man, things have been hectic around here. I'm working like crazy. She's working like crazy."

"I'm just as guilty as you man. Working is my middle name."

I stepped outside of the apartment. "Yeah, I got some other drama going on around here, too."

"Like what?"

"I'll give you the short version."

"Go ahead."

"You know Akua's crazy, right?"

He laughed. "That's my girl. She keeps your ass straight. That's all."

"What would you do if you could have your ideal mate?"

He sighed. "Man, are you talking about me or talking about you?"

Between clenched teeth, I said. "Nigga, I'm talking about if you were in my shoes?"

"How do you know it's ideal? Are you checking it from afar? Or are you dealing with the person?"

"Dealing with the person."

"Leave that shit alone. A chick that will mess with you while you got a girl, will end up leaving your ass for somebody else. That's the way that shit works."

I frowned. "Man, that's crazy."

"You asked me. I told you. Shit. You got a good woman. If you leave Akua, let me know."

I laughed. He said, "I'm not playing with you. That's a diamond right there."

"Her smart ass?"

He laughed. "Yeah, I rather have a smart ass any day than a chick that's letting any dude pop game on her and falling for it." He paused. "I don't do those weak chicks, and a chick that's down for you while you have a girl is usually somebody you can tell anything."

I leaned on my front door. He'd missed too much of the story and it was too hard to explain that Taylor was a strong woman with a weakness for me. He'd see what I meant once we were together. I chuckled. "Man, you got some crazy hang-ups."

"Call it whatever you want to call it, but don't be stupid."

"We gotta hook up."

"Yeah, I was thinking about coming through next week."

How could I explain all the packed boxes? "I'm coming to Maryland next week."

"Well shit, I'll catch you down this way."

I hung up the phone and walked in the house. Akua sat on the couch. "Did you tell him?"

"Not everything."

"If you can't tell your friends, maybe you're not sure about your decision."

41

TAYLOR

The days leading up to the move left me empty. The night before he was scheduled to move, Scooter didn't call. I figured he was packing. I sat in my house alone with my fingers crossed the entire moving day. Finally, my phone rang.

As we sped down the highway of love going 100 mph, the sound of brakes screeching pierced my ear. The phone call I wanted, but feared. I let it ring. I waited for the message that he didn't leave. Ten minutes later, he called again. I answered. He sighed, "Tay-Bae."

My heart floated in my stomach. My intuition warned me of bad news. I took a deep breath and swallowed the last of the martini I was sipping.

He continued, "We need to talk."

My eyes watered. The expected/unexpected was about to occur. My voice trembled, "I'm listening."

He cleared his throat. "I still love her. And I've decided to stay."

The last five months flashed through my mind. Then, everything went blank. As if he'd kicked me out on the highway into oncoming traffic with no warning signs, I wrapped my arms around my body to shield me from the collision. Tears poured from my eyes. The shock locked my jaws shut. My shielded heart cracked into tiny pieces, as he continued to roll the bulldozer over it back and forth.

"We were happy until I started seeing you again," he reminded me.

Each time I would open my lips to respond, the words would disappear. He continued to stab me. "Tay-Bae, you and I were a big mistake. She loves me. I can't do this to her."

The multiple stab wounds left me curled up in my bed, bawling like a baby. Finally, I was forced to defend myself from the attack. I yelled, "Why Scooter? Why did you wait until now? You knew you were going to stay! Why did you do this to me?"

He sighed. "Taylor, please believe me. I love you. I never meant to hurt you."

I wailed, "Why *are* you hurting me?"

"It's even harder to hurt her."

After he'd kicked me out on the highway and stabbed me several times, he now pointed a loaded gun at me. Before he could cock the trigger and shatter me for life, I ended the call. The only words I could think of to hurt him rapidly fled from my lips. "I hate you. I hope you have a miserable life."

I slammed the phone in the helpless receiver. Over and over again, I slammed it, wishing Scooter could feel the effect. I released one scream. Then another. I yelled, "Why me?"

This could not be real. My olive-colored room circled around me, washing me with its dull luster. My high ceilings stared down at me. I was belittled. Humiliated. A mistress alone in my own castle. I had been robbed of my pride and dignity.

Waterfalls poured from eyes. I fiddled with the charm bracelet dangling from my wrist. Blurred visions of the future I had imagined hung from every charm. I grabbed the phone from the receiver. Then, I quickly hung up. Instead, I turned the ringer off. It was too soon to tell the world how dumb I'd been. How could I explain his actions? What could I say?

Was there some way for me to share the blame? Unanswered questions. Frightening realities. My chewed-up nails clamped to my hair. I was lost. Dumbfounded.

All the warnings from people reappeared as neon signs posted on my bare wall. THIS WON'T BE EASY. HE'S NOT LEAVING HER. BE CAREFUL. I HOPE YOU DON'T GET HURT. THESE KINDS OF SITUATIONS NEVER END PEACEFULLY.

I resigned to hibernate until I was woman enough to acknowledge they were right. In the midst of my insanity, I chuckled. Four years ago, I had the pick of the litter. As thirty whispered softly in my ear, piss was being tossed at me from a rusty bucket. I tucked my head under my flannel sheets to cover the embarrassment.

42

SCOOTER

When I opened the door to our bedroom, Taylor had packed everything. She sat on the side of the bed, staring into space. My head tilted to internalize this distorted picture. We'd been married less than a year. What was going on? I'd done everything to make her happy. I'd moved back to the DC area. Her stoned face crumbled my heart. She huffed. "This was a mistake from the start."

I walked toward her. "What? Us?"

She nodded. Her lack of emotion resembled the same nonchalance as when we were teens. This was different. We are grown. We own a home. I knew we were having problems, but had it really come to this. My mouth hung open. "Taylor, what are you trying to say?"

"I'm going back to my townhouse."

"What about the tenants?"

"Their lease was up two weeks ago."

"I thought you said . . ."

As I attempted to tell her the lie she'd told me, I stopped. She had this planned all along. She never loved me. She wanted to be in a relationship and I was just the likely candidate at the time. I've always loved her more than she loved me.

As I stood before her and unscrambled my life, I tackled

her. My anger controlled me as I shook her. "You ruined my life. Akua loved me. I left a good woman for you. You never loved me."

That same premonition flashed before my eyes when I hung up the phone. It hurt me to hurt Taylor, but a piece of me knew she'd get over it. Akua sat on the bed beside me, rubbing my back. She sniffed. "Thank you," she whispered.

I didn't respond. I stood up and headed to my car to bring in the boxes. When I came back into the apartment, I replayed the scene that led to my final decision.

Akua was on her knees at the front door. Her arms wrapped around my legs. She wailed. "Please don't leave me. Don't leave me."

When I tried to pull away, she tugged harder. Tears flung from her eyes. Snot dripped down her nose. I turned toward her so that she wouldn't appear so desperate. When she loosened her grip, I kneeled in front of her. Obviously embarrassed by her reaction, she covered her face and shook her head. "Please."

Her voice trembling, she said, "I love you. I need you."

I peeled her arms from her face and wrapped mine around her neck. "Ku, baby. I thought you were okay."

She choked on her spit. "I don't want you to leave. I need you." She yelled, "Please! Please, don't leave me. Please don't sign that lease. Please. I need you."

I sniffed back my own tears. My heart ached. Nothing good would come to me if I left her here like this. This is a good woman with issues. What did she ever do to me, except love me with all her heart?

She wept on my shoulder and I tried to say what I'd been trying to for the last two weeks, "It doesn't mean we're not going to be together if I move. I need to make sure this is right."

She sobbed. "It is right. She doesn't love you like I love you. I'll do anything."

On her knees, she pleaded. Watching this soldier disarm

before me robbed me of my strength. No woman has ever loved me this much. As I held her in my arms, I surrendered. "I'll stay, baby. I'll stay. I love you, too."

I wiped her face. Exhausted from her battle, she stretched out on the floor. I lay beside her and wondered how and when I would conjure up the nerve to tell Taylor my decision. It took me seven hours to do it, but it was over now. I knew she hated me, but as I watched Akua unpack boxes as I fast as I could bring them in, I knew Taylor could never love me the way Akua does.

43

TAYLOR

The last month faded into the worn canvas I call life. I walked around like a zombie. What was my motive? Did I love him? Did he love me? A piece of me always knew he wouldn't leave. Maybe my quest for Scooter was to kill the notion that I could only stay in a relationship for two months. So what if the relationship was with someone else's somebody. I reached deep and chuckled.

Although I knew she never approved of the sneaky operation, Courtney cried with me. She came to my house every day after work. I sat in my pajamas, acting normal when she came to the door. She was stronger than me. My pity party had neared her threshold for compassion. I wiped my tears and hoped she didn't notice the obvious.

She hugged me. "How do you feel, boo?"

"It still hurts."

She plopped down beside me and rubbed my back. "I know."

She consoled her friend, not the woman out to steal another woman's man, as I started with my daily question, "Why me?"

She didn't respond after the first ten times. Finally, she asked, "Do you think you're the victim?"

As if the words were lodged in my throat, my mouth hung

open. There was no sympathy in her eyes. I was the mistress. The tears stopped dripping from my eyes. She rationalized the situation while I sat stunned.

"Tay-Bae, you went to the reunion to get Scooter. You didn't give a shit about his situation. You wanted him at all cost. As much as I hate to say this, this is the price you had to pay."

My eyes shifted back and forth as I watched the distress in her every expression. I bit my lip and batted my eyes. Where was her sympathy?

"You are not the victim here, Taylor. If Scooter didn't tell you he had a girl that would be one thing, but he told you up front."

I sniffled as the tear that got stuck in my eye from the initial shock fell. She wiped my face and continued to tell me about myself. "You put yourself in this predicament." She paused. Then, she called my name as if I wasn't listening, "Taylor!"

I lifted my head. My face was wet all over again. I nodded. Her voice softened, "You're not the victim here. A victim is an innocent person. Shit! You're an accomplice, if not the damn mastermind."

I chuckled despite my pain. She rubbed my back. "I know it hurts, but I can't keep sitting here letting you think you're the victim." She dabbed my face with tissues. "You're going to move on and forget all of this. You'll find a new man. A new relationship, but you may have killed their relationship. The trust in that relationship will never be the same."

Akua was the woman. I was the other woman. She sympathized with her. I tried to understand me. "But their relationship was on the rocks when we hooked up."

"Are you high?"

We laughed because I knew better. I told myself whatever I needed to get me through this situation. An *I-don't-believe-you-believe-that* expression sat posed on her face for moments. It forced me to smile. She laughed. I laughed. "I know you know better, right?" she asked, shaking her head.

I wanted to believe that Scooter and I had something special. It wasn't the typical everyday act of infidelity. Judging from Courtney's expression, I was as stupid and naïve as any other woman in a love triangle.

She said, "Is any man really going to approach you and say, 'I'm not leaving my girl. You down for a booty call?' " She chuckled. "It just doesn't work like that."

I nodded. She rubbed my back as she continued to preach. "When a man makes it his business to claim his woman that should be enough." I sniffed and she patted my tears with tissue again. "The next time a man mentions anything close to having a girl, I want you to run as far and as fast as you can."

I laughed again. She made sense. I decided not to interject. If he loved me, I wouldn't be here crying. I needed to accept it was a lie from both ends.

Courtney smiled cautiously. "It's no rush. Your turn will always come. It may not be when you want it, but . . ."

I gave her a high five and said, "It's always right on time."

She nodded. Based on the smile on my face, she knew her wisdom seeped in. I closed my eyes, hoping to block out the vision of naïveté. I opened up to Courtney smiling. I smiled back. "I hope I didn't upset you, but I felt like you needed to hear it," she said.

"I did."

44

TAYLOR

When the invitation to Devin Patterson's 30th Birthday Bash appeared in my in-box, I blushed. He remembered me. After the downward spiral I'd taken with Scooter, I have been on a dating hiatus over the last few months. I had to clear my mind and decide if it was my age driving me into a relationship or if it was what I really wanted.

I called Courtney. "Hey, girl. 'I Love My People' is having a party in New York in two weeks. You want to go?"

"Hell yeah. I'll be anywhere his fine ass is."

"You're silly."

"Did you call him or something?"

"No. Why?"

"I'm thinking if he sent you an invitation, then he's probably still single."

I huffed. I wasn't in the mood for analyzing his status. If nothing more, fine single men know other fine single men. Birds of a feather flock together. We would definitely have a good choice of men to dance with. "I don't know what he is, but we're going."

She laughed. "Tell me when and where, so I can have an alibi."

"And an outfit."

"True."

I contemplated calling Devin before responding to the invite. Instead, I sent an RSVP for two people. Later that afternoon, he sent me an e-mail, asking if my other guest was my boyfriend. I responded that it was Courtney. In his response, he asked, "Courtney with the ring or Courtney without?"

I called Courtney to share the joke. She said, "Tell him Courtney without the ring and he better have some cute friends."

"Very funny."

I responded while she was on the phone. He sent a response back immediately. I said, "He said . . ."

Courtney laughed. "His ass is single. His ass is responding real time." I laughed. Courtney joked. "Taylor, he is feeling you. Big time."

"He did ask if he could call me."

"Hell yeah!"

I interrupted her. "Calm down. I'm typing my numbers down."

Shortly after, Devin called. "You know I thought I would never talk to you again."

"I know."

"I couldn't do anything but respect you for trying to be a good girlfriend and stay away from temptation."

"Good thinking."

"So, how's your relationship?"

"Over."

"What?"

"Yes. It's over."

"Are you okay with it?"

I chuckled. "Yeah. Yeah. Yeah."

He laughed. "I'm just asking, baby. I'm concerned."

"Yeah, right."

"I am. Let's hit a happy hour. Maybe I can play the role of Dr. Phil this time."

I whined, "I don't like role playing."

"Honestly though. You want to hook up and chat?"

"Are you in town?"

"Yes, I have a few phone calls to make. Then, I'm heading over to the Grand Hyatt for happy hour."

"What time are you getting there?"

"I'll be there around five. I'm going to stop by the crib and change my clothes. Then, I'll be there."

I brushed off my khaki suit and figured it would have to suffice because I didn't have time to change.

He called before I got to the hotel. I forgot to warn him that I'm always a fashionable fifteen minutes late. When I picked up, he chuckled. "Are you looking for parking?"

Since I was still driving up New York Avenue, I lied, "Yes."

"Can you come scoop me up? I'm right outside of the Convention Center. I had to pick up something."

As I sped through lights to get there, I said, "Okay, I'll be around."

I hung up the phone. He called back. "I'm the guy standing on the corner, looking like he got stood up."

I laughed. "I'm coming Devin."

"Are you even in this area?"

As I sped up to the light at Seventh Avenue, I said, "Yes, I'm across the street. I'm driving the Lexus . . ."

The light turned green and I saw him. I drifted through the intersection. With my phone still pinned to my ear, I admired the man flagging me down. My taxi was definitely available.

I pulled over to the curb. We smiled at each other as he walked to my car. He tried the door. It was locked. Finally, I snapped out of my trance and unlocked the doors.

When he sat in the car, he leaned over and kissed my cheek. I blushed. "Good to see you."

"Good to see you too." He pointed. "Go this way. You still want to go to the Hyatt, right?"

I shrugged my shoulders. "I'm with you."

"Good, because I'm with you." He laughed. "You have the cutest facial expressions."

"What do you mean?"

He pointed. "Like that little look you're doing now." My eyes shifted. He pointed again. "Your eye movements. You're so funny."

He looked around my car. "Looks like you've had a hard time with the breakup."

I laughed. "Leave me alone. My car is always junky."

When I stepped out of the car, he stared at me. My A-line, knee-length skirt bounced as I trotted toward the hotel. He smiled. "You look nice."

He wore a navy suit. Prada shoes. Crisp dress shirt. I nodded. "You too."

As we walked into the lounge, he said. "I'm dying to hear about what happened with you and your man."

When I sat at the bar, Devin stood behind me and briefly massaged my shoulders. Finally, he sat beside me. He picked up the menu. My eyes gravitated to his watch. He had on a damn Breitling. Ten thousand dollars for a watch. I smiled. My kind of guy.

He studied the bar menu and finally asked for two glasses of Crown Royal Special Reserve on the rocks. He smiled, acknowledging that he'd taken my advice. I smiled back and said, "So, has it worked?"

"I'm not sure it worked, but I like it. It's actually my new drink of choice."

"Good. But can I tell you something?"

"What?"

"I don't drink mine straight. I have to mix it with a few things. I'm not that much of a soldier. Thanks for thinking of me though."

"You are definitely something else." He checked his expensive watch. "We have reservations at Oya at seven."

Did I tell him that I planned to hang out with him all evening? He squinted. "So we either plan something to kill time or have our Dr. Phil session until then."

"It doesn't matter to me."

"So what happened?"

"It just didn't work out."

"Now, Taylor. I thought we were better than that."

I laughed. "What?"

"When we first met, you made me unveil all my issues." He shook his head. "Now, you're acting like you don't want to talk about yours." He tapped his knee against mine. "That's busted."

"Well, I told you that he had a girlfriend when we hooked up again, right?"

He nodded.

"Well he went back to her."

"When you told me about it, I was hoping he wasn't still messing with his old girl."

"Why didn't you say something?"

"It wasn't my place. Especially at that moment. You just met me. I was obviously attracted to you. You would have thought I was hatin'."

"You're right."

After two gulps of his Crown Royal, he asked, "So, do you think you're over it?"

"Without a doubt."

"Are you sure?"

"Yeah, actually it's kinda scary."

He shook his head. "You didn't love him."

I frowned. He repeated, "You didn't love him."

"Why would you say that?"

"I could tell when you were telling me about him. You loved the thought of winning him back. You were holding on to this relationship from ten years ago that you walked out of when it was ideal. But what's ideal when you're nineteen ain't ideal when you're twenty-nine."

I nodded. He laughed. "Dude made the right decision. Y'all were destined for failure."

"I agree."

"So, now can you answer my question?"

I raised one eyebrow. "What question?"

"Did you feel it?"

When he asked, the invisible wire connecting us electrocuted me. I nodded. "I think so."

"I never thought I'd feel it twice."

Why was he giving *it* an identity? "What do you mean?"

"I guess I've always been more of a romantic than most men. I believe in chemistry, connection, soul mates or whatever you want to call it. That was the way it was when I fell in love with my ol' girl from Hampton."

I nodded. He could have said her name because I sure hadn't forgotten it. I took the privilege. "Clark, right?"

He smiled. "You're so funny. Anyway, after going on countless dates, meeting so many women and never having that instant attraction"—he squinted—"I started to believe I was crazy. That was until I met you."

"Really?"

"Really. I wanted to call you but I didn't want to call you. God knows I wasn't trying to be a part of another love triangle."

I smiled. "I understand."

"When you said that you and your man broke up, I felt like it was a sign."

"A sign for what?"

"A sign to let you know I'm interested in spending time with you and seeing if this goes somewhere." He shrugged his shoulders. "You down?"

I nodded. He held his glass up. We toasted.

45

TAYLOR

Courtney and I arrived in New York hours before Devin's birthday party. When we walked up to his building, the doorman opened the door for us. Devin stepped off of the elevator and kidded. "Hey, Courtney-without-the-ring."

He stretched his arm to hug me. He kissed my forehead. "Taylor Jabowski."

Courtney shook his hand. We hopped on the elevator. Devin said, "Y'all look nice."

"We're wearing this to the party."

"It doesn't matter to me."

Courtney smirked. "Nah, we don't get down like that."

We stepped off of the elevator into this full-floor apartment. I looked at Courtney. She looked at me. We stood speechless with our bags.

He gave us a verbal tour. "The guest room is down there." Looking at Courtney, he said, "You have your own bathroom in there." Continuing to point in the same direction, he said, "My little girl's room adjoins that one through the bathroom."

He nodded in the opposite side of the apartment. "My room is this way." He smiled at me. "There's a bathroom in there, too."

I pointed to the guestroom. "I'll get dressed in here with my girl."

"Some of my boys are staying the night, too. They might try to get you."

Courtney laughed. "Ooh. That sounds fun."

Devin shook his head. "You're a trip."

"She's all bark and no bite," I said.

"I believe you."

He walked towards his stainless steel and granite kitchen. "Do you guys want something to drink?"

We nodded. He said, "What do you guys want?"

Courtney asked, "What do you have?"

"None of that fruity stuff. I have Grey Goose, Crown Royal, and any wine of your choice."

We looked at each other and said. "Wine."

"What kind?"

Our eyes consulted, I said, "Cabernet."

"You guys can take your stuff in the guestroom and get comfortable."

Courtney followed me to the living room. "He is paid and he's fine. He must be DL or something."

I laughed. "I think he's just a little bitter."

"He doesn't seem bitter to me."

"I think he masks it well."

"They all have issues. If you don't think he's DL, you better holla."

I gestured that it was time to go to our room. She grunted. "If I were single . . ."

I nodded and put my index finger over my lips. We laughed. Devin came in, asking, "What are you guys laughing at?"

We laughed harder. "Nothing."

He handed us our glasses and went back to get his. He held it up. "To getting older."

I laughed. "You're the only one getting older." His expression dimmed. "Psyche. I'm just joking."

He nodded. "Okay."

When we finished drinking, Courtney decided to get ready, leaving Devin and me in the living room alone. He poured a little more wine for me.

"Why don't you get your things and get ready in my room?"

"Why are you trying to get me in your room?"

"I know how long it takes for women to get ready. I'm just trying to help you out. I'm leaving here no later than eleven."

I laughed. "All right."

When I walked into his massive bedroom, I looked at him. He stood at the door with a cocky grin. *Yeah, I know my place is tight.* A king-sized bed. A 55-inch, flat-screen Plasma television hung over the fireplace. I smiled. *Okay, you got me. I'm staying in here with you.*

He kissed me. The wine conquered my balance as I fell on his bed. He climbed on top of me. I rubbed his back to condone his aggression. He painted paisley prints on my neck. I moaned and touched his arms. Ooh. There wasn't an ounce of fat on him. I lifted his shirt. My fingers raked the ripples in his stomach. He lay in between my legs as we dry humped.

He mumbled, "Lemme close the door."

Instead, he continued to roll around his bed with me. I held him closely. His warmth was inviting. If he stood up, it would interrupt our moment. Then, I'd have time to think. He whispered, "Wrap your legs around me."

Clamped together, we stood and he kicked the bedroom door closed. We fell back on the bed. He pulled my shirt over my head and made love to my breast with his mouth. I whispered, "Do you have condoms?"

He nodded. He jumped out of his sweatpants and peeled my jeans off. Trojan Man opened the wrapper and slid the condom on faster than I could say, "Get one."

He climbed on top of me. The tip tickled my rim, as he stared into my eyes. I whined, "Devin . . ."

He rubbed my hair from my face. He kissed me. Still his stiffness teased me. I squirmed. "What's wrong?"

"I'm glad you're here."

Not now, Devin. Put it in. Finally, I said, "Please."

He plunged inside of me. Was it that moment of anticipation that made me feel that this was the best first-time sex I'd ever had in my life? He thrust his tongue in my mouth. *Ooh.* He was so passionate. He stroked gently, then vigorously. It felt too good to hold back. I couldn't stop myself. He sent sparks through me and I released. After a few seconds, he collapsed on top of me. The sheets were soaked and we momentarily lay motionless, absorbing each other.

I'd never considered myself to be sprung after the first time, but he definitely had me twisted.

As if we'd known one another for years, we showered together and I got glamorous in front of him. When I put on my jeans, he chuckled. I looked at him. "What?"

"Your body is like 'whoa'."

We giggled. He pulled his T-shirt over his head. I read the chocolate writing on the crème shirt and smirked. RESPECT THE D.

Hell, I more than respected it. I would honor it. He smiled. "You like my shirt?"

My eyes lowered as I imagined the D inside of me. "And I like the D."

He hugged me. "You are so funny. D stands for Devin."

"Oh my head was in the wrong place," I said laughing.

He pulled me tighter. "Mine was in the right place."

We laughed. He slipped on his chocolate blazer and brown Gucci shoes. Damn. Why did I wait so long to entertain him?

When we walked into the 40/40 club, Devin held my hand and Courtney lagged behind. We'd parked Devin's BMW 645 in valet and I felt like I could claim him. One of his friends was already sitting in the designated area for his birthday. Devin shook his hand and said, "What's up man? This is my girl, Taylor. That's her girl, Courtney. This is my man, Lamont."

We smiled and spoke. Courtney whispered in my ear. "Does he mean girl like girlfriend or girl like home girl?"

I chuckled and shrugged my shoulders. Between clenched teeth, she said. "You better find out. So, you know if you should or shouldn't get numbers tonight."

"I know."

We laughed. I said, "I think I'm straight, though."

Around eleven-thirty, Devin's friends began to pour in. He whispered in my ear as a biracial chick and white guy approached. "That's my ex-wife."

"You didn't tell me you guys were that cool."

"We're working on it."

He reached out to hug her. He shook her fiancé's hand. Then he said, "Jennifer, this is a very special friend of mine, Taylor."

Jennifer shook my hand and appeared ecstatic to meet me. "Oh, what a pleasure to meet you Taylor."

I smiled. "Good to meet you, too."

She put her hand on my back. "Taylor, this is my fiancé, Aaron."

We shook hands. She chatted for a few minutes longer. Then, they found a cozy corner near the party. Devin and his friends indulged in cigars. He walked up and kissed me. "I'm sorry."

"Why?"

"You probably hate cigars."

I chuckled. "No, I actually like them. I was wondering why you hadn't offered me any."

He handed a cigar to me. "You're all right with me."

I took a puff and handed it to Courtney. Devin smiled in amazement. "I knew you were cool when I first met you."

I danced in front of him. "How did you know?"

He chuckled. "Cause you was backing that thing up."

I turned around and wiggled my butt on him. "Like this."

With his arm wrapped around my waist, he nodded. "Yeah, like that."

I twirled on him until I felt his nature rise. Watching him from my peripheral, I smirked seductively. Finally, he handed the cigar to Courtney who was flirting her ass off with his friends. We danced harder than the first night we met. As I worked my Soul Train moves on him, he grabbed my waist. "Wait, Taylor. My nigga is in the house."

He backed away from me. I wiped my forehead with the back of my hand. He exclaimed, "J Dawg!"

I turned to see who had stolen his attention from me. He was embracing Scooter. I looked at Courtney. Her mouth moved a mile a minute. I stood stunned. If I were smart, I would have run to the bathroom. Scooter glared at me. His girl scrutinized the familiarity in his stance. The moments leading up to Devin's introduction left me baffled. The cigar smoke suffocated me. My eyes refocused. Maybe this wasn't who I thought it was?

Devin said, "This is my best friend Jason."

Ain't this some shit! Where the hell do they know each other from? Why hadn't Scooter ever spoken of Devin? Hell, why hadn't Devin said anything about Jason aka Scooter?

Devin bent down to kiss Akua. They rocked side to side. He said, "Ku, baby. What's going on girl?"

She whined, "Hey, honey."

Scooter and I stared at each other like we'd seen a ghost. We both tried to decide how to proceed. I looked at Courtney. She was shooting herself in the head with her index finger. Damn right! *Just shoot me.* Devin turned around, "Jason, this is my girl . . ."

46

SCOOTER

His girl? How did she get to be his girl without me knowing they even knew each other? Did they just meet at the club? Even my pride refused to let me front as I completed his attempt to introduce us. I said, "Taylor?"

Obviously noticing the tension, Devin yanked his neck back. "Y'all know each other?"

Akua rolled her neck and pointed. "Who is that?"

I ignored her and answered Devin, "Yeah, we went to high school together."

Taylor's eyes shifted from my mouth to his. She blinked hard and rapidly like somehow she wished she could disappear. Finally, she closed them and took a deep breath. "How do y'all know each other?"

Devin smiled. "This is my back, this is my line brother."

She covered her face. Thankfully Akua stood a foot below because she couldn't hear the entire conversation. Devin was so into my lady on his arm that he didn't fully understand what was occurring between us, either. This was the first we'd spoken since my dreadful phone call. She mouthed. "Line brother?"

I nodded. Devin kissed her cheek and wrapped his arm around her waist and bent down. "Akua, this is my girlfriend, Taylor."

They shook hands. I thought, *girlfriend?* Akua tugged my arm. I bent down. "Is that your Taylor?"

I shook my head. She squeezed my hand. "She sure looks like the girl on that prom picture." She glanced at her again. "Jason, that is her." She frowned. "What the fuck is going on here?"

I bent down. "Baby, I'm trying to figure this out now. I didn't know they even knew each other."

She gasped like she didn't believe me. Devin wrapped one arm around my shoulder and the other around Taylor. "My favorite people."

Devin is pretty much a private guy, but damn! His favorite people? Was she dealing with him when she was coaxing me to leave my girl? She whispered something in his ear and wiggled away. I still couldn't internalize what was going on.

Akua yanked my arm. "What the fuck is going on?"

"Shit. Hell if I know."

"You mean to tell me that that is the Taylor you were leaving me for and she is now Devin's girlfriend and you don't know what's going on?"

I snapped, "No, I'm just as shocked as you."

She grunted. "Why does Devin always end up with the sneaky bitches?"

I looked at Akua. She'd figured it out. This was Taylor's attempt to make me jealous. How did she find Devin, though? I thought it was ironic that I never heard from her after we broke up. She had this in store. Rage boiled in me. Why my man? He didn't deserve to be involved in this. He watched her walk over to Courtney. I knew him well enough to know he was digging her.

He chuckled. "Small world, huh?"

"Tell me about it. When did you meet Taylor?"

"Last September."

"September!" I shouted.

He shrugged his shoulders. "Yeah somewhere around that time."

She was playing me all along. Anger and jealously rushed to my head, giving me a splitting headache. I huffed. "Why didn't you tell me anything about her?"

"It wasn't anything to tell. We just started hooking up on the regular a few weeks ago." He tapped my shoulder. "Have some drinks. We have Grey Goose, Moët . . ."

As he ran down the bar list, my fury convinced me this was a personal attack. "Did Taylor tell you she knew me?"

"Nah, man. Damn. Have some drinks and relax."

How did he not see the friction between us? Was he naïve or just caught up? I wanted to smack him in the back of his head. I turned to find Akua sitting in Devin's designated area sipping a drink. I smiled. She rolled her eyes. *C'mon, baby, not now.*

While Akua greeted my other friends, in sign language, I gestured to Taylor, "Meet me in the bathroom in ten minutes."

She stormed over to me. "I don't remember that shit anymore." She tilted her head. "What are you trying to say?"

I huffed. "Meet me in the bathroom."

"I'm not meeting you anywhere. We don't have anything to talk about."

Her neck rolled. My shoulders bucked. Anyone with a brain knew we were in a lover's quarrel. I grabbed her shoulders. "You're with my line brother and you think we don't need to talk?"

"Scooter, get out of my face. You never told me about your damn line brother. And damn if I plan to leave him alone because you know him," she growled.

"You know he's a Que. You know I'm a Que. You know we both went to Hampton. It don't take a rocket scientist to ask if we know each other."

47

TAYLOR

I shouted. "Hampton?"
His head bobbed. "Yeah, Hampton."

"You went to Prince . . ."

Oh my God! He flunked out of Princeton after we broke up and transferred to Hampton. I hung my head. I tried to suppress that it was me who robbed him of his dream of being an Ivy League Alumni. I'd convinced myself that he graduated from Princeton. How will anyone believe that I just have selective memory and that I'm not some vengeful witch?

Akua interrupted us, "Baby, what's going on?"

I glared at her. She rolled her eyes and looked up at Scooter. I sympathized with Devin, because he was enjoying his party and had no clue this altercation was occurring.

Courtney came to join me. I assume to provide some added protection. After looking at Scooter and his cute little chocolate drop up and down, she smirked. "Hey."

Akua scrunched her face. "Hello."

Courtney tugged my arm. "Let's go to the bathroom," she said.

When we walked to the bathroom, I screamed. Courtney yelled, "Taylor! What is going on?"

I huffed. "It's a small fucking world."

"You didn't know that they knew each other?"

With one hand on my hip and the other leaning on the sink, my eyes questioned her. "What do you think?"

"Devin said Scooter was his best friend."

"Well, obviously Devin is not Scooter's best friend, because in the five months we dealt with each other, he didn't mention Devin."

"Are you sure?"

"Yes, I'm sure." I paused to recollect. "I mean, he used the terms like my boy or my line brother, but it didn't seem like he had a lot of friends to me." I used my fingers as quotations. "Especially, 'best friends.'"

As my best friend cross-examined me, it appeared that even she doubted the validity of my story. How could I expect anyone else to understand?

I looked up and Akua slung her long braids back and went into the stall. Courtney mouthed. "Let's go."

We walked out of the bathroom and danced a few feet away from Devin's party. He came over to me, "You hiding from me?"

I shook my head. We began to dance. When Akua came back out, she danced in front of Scooter. He rocked side to side, with his cigar in his hand. He stared at us and I stared at them. Our lovers stared at us.

We argued with our dance moves. Here, take that. Back and forth, we challenged each other and my dance partner didn't even realize he was in a battle.

48

SCOOTER

Akua said, "It's so unfair that Devin gets all of the deceptive women. He's such a good guy."

"I know baby, but I'm going to stay out of it."

She cupped my face into her hand. "You just said the other day that as we get older, good friends are what's most important. You stayed out of it the last time and he ended up marrying that crazy hooker." She nodded in Jennifer's direction. "Don't let your boy go into something with someone who intentionally set out to play him."

I bent down and kissed her cheek. "You're right, Ku."

A part of me wanted to tell because I couldn't bear the love of my life fucking my boy. Then, I wanted to tell because I couldn't believe that she could be so conniving. How could I even think about leaving this honest woman on my arm for her evil ass? I shook my head. We always love the wrong women more. There is no way in the world this highly educated woman could not play the African-American who-do-you-know game.

I asked Akua, "What should I say?"

"Call her ass out."

I huffed. She was Taylor's enemy and she wanted her busted at all cost. I, on the other hand, noticed how happy Devin looked. I hadn't seen him that free since undergrad. I struggled with my decision. Out of obligation, I stopped dancing and told my man that we needed to talk.

Akua coaxed me with a head nod as Devin and I headed to one of the cigar rooms. I contemplated. *This is his birthday.* Devin looked agitated and I was compelled to say something. He chuckled. "What's up, man?"

"Remember you gave me an obligation."

He smirked. "Man, what the hell are you talking about?"

"After you broke up with Jennifer, you said that people see shit better from the outside looking in."

He nodded.

"You told me to watch your back and you would watch mine."

He smirked. "Man, why the hell are you all sensitive tonight?"

"A couple of months ago I told you I was faced with the opportunity to be with my ideal mate. Do you remember what you said?"

"Yeah, I told you I'd bang you in the mouth if you left Akua."

I laughed. "You also told me that the other woman was no good if she could mess with me while I had a girl." I took a deep breath and prepared for the blow. "The girl I was seeing was Taylor."

He frowned. "Taylor? *My* Taylor."

"Yeah, your Taylor."

As it resonated, he stared into space. "She told me about her man who she'd taken from his girl." He winced. "But she said he was in DC and . . ."

He stopped and shook his head. Before I could tell him the entire story, he asked, "Do you think she knew that we knew each other?"

"How could she not? I'm sure she knows we went to Hampton. What do you do when you find out someone went to a school?"

He hung his head. "You right, man. Come to think about

it, she never said your name, ever. She always called you her boyfriend or old boyfriend."

"Maybe she's slicker than I thought."

He looked like I had crushed his spirits. He dropped his head. "Women ain't shit." He stood up. "I got a party going on downstairs."

I patted his back as we headed out of the cigar room. "Man, I just wanted to tell you before you got in too deep."

He nodded. Did I really believe that she could be so spiteful? Or was I more concerned with my own happiness? Devin shook my hand. He chuckled. "I'm glad you didn't wait until my wedding day this time."

I laughed. "You ain't lying."

49

DEVIN

I stood at the top of the stairs watching her dance freely, as if she didn't have a care in the world. How did I make a 360 degree turn right back to my starting point? Here I was comparing Taylor to Clark when I should have looked at her similarities to Jennifer instead. I swore I would never date another attorney. What would make me believe that she would be any different?

Since we had consummated the relationship less than four hours ago, I didn't owe her an explanation. Jason walked beside me as we got close to Taylor. She turned around and rolled her eyes at Jason. I looked at the two of them. This wasn't even about me. She wanted to hurt Jason and I ended up being the victim.

Jason went to join Akua in the corner. Taylor leaned her weight on to one leg. She ran her hand down my disgusted face. I smirked. She wasn't prepared to confirm or deny what she wasn't positive I knew.

She asked, "What's wrong?"

I huffed, "Nothing, man,"

"Did Scooter, I mean Jason, tell you anything?"

I smirked. "Nah, was he supposed to?"

She sighed. "No, but you seem different."

"You don't know me like that."

She frowned and attempted to speak. Then, she hung her head. "You're right. I don't know you like that."

I walked away from her and continued partying with my friends. I envied my boys that had their girls on their arms, girls that were down for their men. For a second, I even looked at Jennifer and thought we could have worked it out. Who told me to be a hot head and run out of our marriage, chasing a feeling that may never occur again?

Taylor and Courtney hung out on the opposite side of the club. From my frequent observations, they seemed to be enjoying themselves. And they say a good man is hard to find. I shook my head and found myself sipping more Grey Goose than usual. Just to think when I made my wish, I wished to be in a serious relationship by my next birthday. Oh well, back to the drawing board.

When Jason was about to leave, Akua gave me a hug. Obviously translating the hopeless feelings inside of me, she whined, "Bye, honey."

"Thanks for coming, baby."

Jason and I shook hands. "Yeah, man, we're about to drive back. We both have to work in the morning."

"Thanks, man. Thanks for everything."

He sighed. "Sorry about ol' girl."

I waved my hand. "Whatever, man. It ain't heavy."

He looked around at all the other young ladies that came to join my party. "I know you ain't trippin." He joked. "Ladies love the D."

"You know it. Hit me up sometime next week."

Jennifer and Aaron followed shortly after. Jennifer hugged me. I kidded. "You gone, wifey?"

She nudged me and whispered, "You know Aaron hates when you say that."

"I'm just fucking with you. When you become his wife then I'll stop saying it."

"Well you have one month left." She smiled and looked

around. "I wanted to say bye to your new little friend. She seems really nice. Where'd she go?"

I shrugged my shoulders. "I don't know."

Damn if I needed the two devils conspiring. They might set me on fire. I chuckled. "She may be gone."

I shook Aaron's hand. This corny white boy must love her ass. He stood around, looking out of place all night at her ex-husband's party. As much flack as I give him, he is a cool dude. "A'ight, man. Y'all have a good one."

I went over to the bar to find my houseguests. "Hey y'all, we're going to leave in a few."

On the ride home, one of my boys hopped in my car. It gave me another few minutes or so to decide how I should proceed with Taylor.

When we got into the apartment, she looked dumbfounded, as I asked, "Where you sleeping?"

My boy said, "Dawg, you know I'm sleeping on the couch."

I walked to the linen closet to grab him a blanket and pillow. When I returned Taylor and Courtney were in the guestroom. I knocked on the door.

Courtney said, "Come in."

When I walked in, they were both fully dressed sitting on the edge of the bed. Taylor smirked. Courtney began, "Devin, I know you don't think Taylor was trying to play you for a fool."

"Why would I think that?" I looked at Taylor. "We cool, right."

Taylor huffed. "Devin, don't bullshit me. I know Scooter told you that I intentionally tried to holler at you to upset him."

"Did you?"

"Hell no. You tried to holler at me."

"But you never told me you knew him. You told me the dude you were seeing left his girl. Scooter and Akua never broke up, at least not that I know of."

Her face sagged. "Well, he told me he did. I wasn't lying."

I nodded. "Just hiding the truth."

She curled her lips, and said, "Why am I even explaining? Fuck it. You're going to believe what you want to believe."

I put my hand on the doorknob. "Are you sleeping in here?"

The Grey Goose I'd sipped all night made me horny. When she nodded, I knew I had to lighten up. I wanted her in bed with me. Who gave a damn if she was a liar? I'm a man on my birthday with a fine-ass chick in my house. I planned to hit it again.

I said, "You know you have to get your stuff from my room."

She smirked. "I'll just sleep in my bra and panties."

"C'mon and get your stuff. Stop acting like a poor sport."

50

TAYLOR

My game was definitely done. It was time to retire. I dragged behind Devin. His boy, Byron, or B, as they referred to him, was knocked out on the couch. If men didn't think they were so slick and used initials for names, I probably wouldn't be in this predicament. Devin held my hand as he pulled me into his room. When we got into the room, I bent over to get my luggage. He walked up behind me. When I stood, he kissed me passionately. I pulled away.

"What's wrong?"

"You've had a stank attitude since Scooter talked to you. Now, you want to kiss me."

He kissed me again. "I'm not tripping about that. Shit happens."

I curled my lips. He held my face up to his face. He stared into my eyes and kissed me. "You came all the way up here to hang out with me. I don't even want to talk about you and Jason anymore."

Trying to ignore the hormones raging in my jeans, I turned my head. "Good, because I'm sleeping with Courtney."

"Can you at least help me change the sheets that you wet up?"

"Fuck you, Devin."

He pulled my waist closer. "I like it when you talk like that."

He flicked on the fireplace and turned on his Bose system with the remote. I squirmed away from him. "Stop Devin. I'm going to help you change your sheets and I'm going in there with Courtney."

He pulled my arm and began unbuckling his jeans. I asked, "Where are your sheets?"

He pointed to the bathroom. I walked into the bathroom and opened the neatly organized linen closet. After grabbing the first sheets I saw, I closed the door and walked back into the room. Devin's jeans were off. He lifted his RESPECT THE D T-shirt up far enough for me to see the D poking out nearly a foot from his body. He looked down. I gazed at it.

He smiled. "Are you going to leave the birthday boy like this?"

"Put the sheets down," he said, laughing.

Reluctantly, I stepped closer to him and lay the sheets on the bed. He grabbed my hand and guided me to stroke him. His lips grazed my lips. "Devin, we shouldn't."

"We already did."

He slipped his hands down my panties and my knees buckled. He said, "I got you, baby."

To assist him in his effort, I pulled my jeans down farther. He helped me to the floor and turned over to his back on the fur rug in front of the fireplace. I pulled my blouse over my head and tossed it on the clothes pile beside us. He said, "Get on top."

I climbed on him, letting his steeple sink deep into me. I shouted over the loud music. "Ooh, this D is good."

My dirty talk motivated him. He rose on to his elbow and wrapped the other arm around to get a better angle. Raising one knee up, with his foot flat on the floor, he slightly tilted me and sank deeper. "You respect this D."

I nodded. He thrust harder. "I can't hear you."

"Yeah."

"Say it," he demanded.

"I respect this D."

He flipped me all the way over and started taking longer strokes. He retracted as far as possible. Then, he'd plunge down vigorously. Over and over again, until my body trembled uncontrollably. What the hell was he doing to me?

He collapsed on me. "Taylor, you made a mess again."

I giggled. "You keep making me do it."

"I'm sorry."

"It's okay."

He kissed my cheek. "You like it. Don't you?"

I nodded.

"C'mon. Let's change the sheets, so we can get in the bed."

When we stood up, he joked. "I'm going to have to put that rug in the cleaners now."

I pouted. "It's all your fault."

Once we got settled and in the bed, he lay on his back. I snuggled close to him on my side. My hand traced his biceps as I wondered what he thought of me. How he perceived us now that Scooter opened his big mouth? I kept trying to shake the feeling. So what his sex is good? So what he's fine? So what he's paid? Finally, I rose up on my elbow. "Devin."

When he didn't answer, I looked at him. He peacefully slept. I lay on my back. *Taylor, why are you tripping on this man?*

Devin's phone rang and I popped up. He stood at the nightstand fully dressed. I rubbed my eyes. He picked up the cordless phone. "Good morning, princess."

His daughter's voice came through the receiver, "Did you have fun at your party, Daddy?"

"Yes, baby. What are you doing?"

"Playing. Am I going to see you today?"

I chuckled, thinking how early we began to ask that question of the men in our lives.

"Ah, I dunno."

She called his name several times. Even I looked at him to see if he was going to answer. "Yes, baby."

"Are you coming to get me?"

"I'll call you when I'm on my way."

"Bye, Daddy."

When I sat up in the bed, he looked like he was ready for me to leave. He smirked. "What do you have planned for today?"

Okay, I'm in his town for his birthday weekend. Obviously, our plans did not coincide. I shrugged. "I guess Courtney and I are going to hit the road."

"Yeah, I forgot that I told Nicole we'd hang out today."

He didn't realize I could hear her through the phone. "Yeah, I know how it is. Duty calls."

He chuckled. "Basically."

I put on my pajamas and went back to the guestroom. Courtney smirked. "I guess you changed your mind."

"I shouldn't have."

"Why?"

"He got issues."

"He just has to get over the shock. What did he say?"

I frowned. "That's it. He didn't say anything."

She lifted her eyebrows and asked, "Well, how the hell did you end up sleeping in his room?"

"Our bodies did the talking."

She burst into laughter. "Well at least you got some to hold you over. You never know when you'll get a good piece again."

I gave her five. "You ain't lying."

After we got dressed to leave, Devin walked us to the parking garage. We said our farewells and I knew that both Devin and Scooter were history. As we parted, I felt like I was leaving a small piece of my soul behind.

51

SCOOTER

Unconsciously, whenever I spoke to my boy after his party, I was jealous. Had he talked to Taylor? Were they seeing each other and hiding it from me? I argued with myself. Why didn't I tell Devin sooner about what was going on? Why didn't I assume they would meet somehow? How stupid could I be?

A huge block of ice sat in between our conversations. I didn't want to seem pressed. Knowing Devin, neither did he. Although the carefree look on his face that night warned me that my boy and I were in love with the same chick. When I rolled over, Akua handed me a birthday card with a certificate for eighteen holes and a cart at Yale's Golf Course for me and one other person. The card said some mushy things, but all I was concerned about was when I was going to play golf. She interrupted my thoughts, "Baby, Devin's coming up today to hang out for your birthday. I have to be to work at nine."

Normally, that would have made me happy. A whole day drinking beer, riding around in a golf cart with my boy, and talking shit. For obvious reasons, I felt I'd rather golf with Akua. I huffed. She rubbed my arm. "What's wrong, baby?"

"Nothing. What time is he coming?"

"He said he'll be here around eight. I think he reserved your time at the course already."

I covered my face. I hate surprises. Tell me when you plan a whole day for me. That makes everyone's life much easier. As I thought about what I'd rather do for the day, the phone rang.

"Hey, honey. Yes, he's up. Yes. Yes. No. No. Yes."

What's up with all the questions? I sat up in the bed and reached for the phone. She shrugged her shoulder like the call was for her. I rested my elbow into the pillow and waited for the two of them to finish their conversation. Finally, she handed me the phone.

Devin chuckled in my ear. "Damn dawg. You gettin' up there."

"Whatever man. I'm still not as old as you."

He laughed. "Yeah. Whatever. I'm on 95. I'll be there in like twenty minutes."

"All right dawg. I'm getting in the shower now."

I hung up and I wrapped my arms around Akua's waist, leaning into her lap. "Can we get breakfast baby?"

She pushed my forehead. "I guess that's the least I can do for your birthday."

"Yeah. How about it?"

She put her robe on and headed to the bathroom. I hopped out of bed and followed behind her. "Baby, let me hop in there with you."

She smacked her lips. I snickered. When I walked in the bathroom, she had begun brushing her teeth. Her question was muffled, "Why you got to get in here with me?"

I shook my head and turned the shower on. "Maybe because I want to."

She rinsed her mouth out and took off her robe and under-clothes. Knowing she'd complain, I jumped in and stood at the front. She stepped in behind me and tried to wrestle me to stand behind her. I joked, "C'mon Ku. It's my birthday. It ain't fair that you always get to stand right under the spout and I gotta stand back there and freeze."

She took the bulldog tactic and tried to bite me. I yanked my arm away. "All right. You win."

As I slid behind her, a smirk of victory graced her face. "Thank you, honey."

"Whatever, man."

She grabbed my washcloth from the shower caddy and began washing me up. She stood on her tiptoes. "Give me a kiss honey."

Reluctantly, I bent down to kiss her. As her soft hands touched all over my body, my nature began to respond. I massaged her shoulders and pushed up against her. She wrapped her arms around me. Just as I was about to make love to her, she sighed. I asked, "What's wrong?"

"Do you love me?"

I frowned. "What?"

"Don't act like I'm crazy."

"Akua, what the hell are you talking about?"

"Do you still think about Taylor?"

As my nature wilted and lost all sensitivity to Akua's touch, I knew that Taylor still had an effect on me. As if I was offended, I rinsed the soap from my body and hopped out of the shower. While I dried my face, I ranted, "I don't believe you gonna bring something like that up on my birthday."

The water stopped running and still she stood in the tub. I snapped, "Are you making breakfast or what?"

"Do you?"

I huffed. "No. I don't think about Taylor. Where did that come from?"

Finally, she slid the shower curtain back and looked into my eyes. "I think about it every day."

I dried my face and asked, "Why?"

"I just do."

Initially, I was angered by her accusation, but suddenly I felt sorry for her. I reached out to hug her. She stepped out of the shower and leaned into my chest. I stroked her back. "Akua, I love you."

She nodded. "Sometimes I wonder if Taylor hadn't been with Devin, if you would have tried to go back to her."

How was she so sure that Taylor had been with Devin? It's funny that Devin's visit was triggering a bunch of what-if emotions in her as well. I kissed her forehead. "Akua, I'm happy with my decision."

She backed up. "Are you?"

I leaned in and kissed her mouth. "I can't imagine how I could have been so stupid in the first place."

An assured blush sat on her face. I nodded. "My bad, baby."

As her esteem resurfaced, she chuckled. "Yeah, your bad."

I kissed her again to affirm my feelings. "I love your crazy ass." Then, I twirled my towel and hit her bare bottom. "Hurry up. Devin should be here in a minute."

As she scurried out of the bathroom, she mumbled, "Don't rush me."

I looked in the mirror to see if Taylor was written on my face. Hoping I could erase the vision of her sleeping with Devin, I washed my face again. The doorbell rang and I yelled to Akua, "Baby, you ready?"

She dashed past the bathroom door, already dressed in her scrubs. When the door opened, I heard smooches and my mind automatically reverted to him locking lips with my other girl. Attempting to suppress my irritation, I yelled from the bathroom, "What's up, dawg?"

"Nothing man. You got me up early enough this morning."

As I headed into the bedroom to get ready, I said, "Akua told you to get up here this early. You know she's a hater."

She laughed. "Whatever Jason. I was trying to do something nice for your lazy butt."

"You're right, baby. Anybody who doesn't wake up at the crack of dawn is lazy."

"Go to hell Jason."

Devin shook his head and I joked, "Sometimes, I wish I could tape her smart-ass mouth shut."

52

DEVIN

I studied the interaction between the two of them. It was if their relationship never had a ripple. What kind of spell did Taylor put on him to make him believe he could leave?

I took a deep breath. Obviously, the same one she put on me, because I have yet to stomp her innocent smile out of my memory. We exchanged casual conversation while eating breakfast.

Jason and I were barely out the door when I asked, "Yo, what happened?"

He chuckled. "Whatchu talking about?"

"Man, we've been dancing around this shit for weeks. How did you and Taylor get together? When did you leave Akua? Shit nigga, what happened?"

"Yo, I was in love with Taylor."

"When did y'all hook up?"

"At our class reunion." He smirked. "That was my boo in high school." He shrugged his shoulders. "She's the girl that you never forget. I guess I was just vexed that she was still single and that I could possibly have everything I ever wanted."

I smiled as I visualized her. "Yeah, I know."

He snapped from his gaze. "Man, whatever. It's a good thing I didn't leave my girl for her ass."

A part of me felt like he didn't believe that, but I let him slide. He saw what I saw in her. The burning question remained though. Is she really a shady person?

Finally after a few rounds, I asked, "Are you really glad you stayed with Akua?"

He laughed nervously. "Yeah. I know she loves me."

"Who do you love?"

He sighed. "I love both of them, but Taylor is no good for me."

"Do you really think she's no good though?"

He grabbed his golf bag and headed to the cart. Before answering, he gulped his beer. "Taylor's a good girl." He took a deep breath and looked at me as if we'd be rumbling if I even considered taking it further with her. "I definitely don't want to see her with my boy."

I squinted. "Whatchu saying, dawg?"

"Yo, after your party that shit bothered me. I kept convincing myself that she did it on purpose, but I don't think she did."

"Why didn't you say something?"

He chuckled. "I didn't want to look like a little bitch."

"What nigga?"

He laughed. "If y'all get together, I'm not going to be happy about it."

"I feel you, dawg."

I made a promise to myself to stay away from Taylor Jabowski. Jason had been through some rough times with me. She probably wasn't worth losing a good friend over. I shook his hand and thought back to when we were on line and we all identified the girls on campus that were off limits to the bruhs. Of course, Clark was the only chick on my list that I would have to shoot someone over. The look on Jason's face told me he felt the same about Taylor.

Though it was a relief to know that I wasn't totally wrong about her, it was rather disheartening to know I couldn't even consider pursuing her.

*   *   *

Traveling to DC was a constant reminder of what I couldn't
have. Late as usual, I rushed into Penn Station trying to hop
on the 7:00 A.M. train. Luckily, I skipped onto a car just before the doors closed. My heart beat rapidly as I walked
through the train searching for a seat. The conductor announced. "Today is make-a-friend day. There are no single seats
on this train. Please clear the seat next to you. Passengers
searching for a seat, please sit at the next available seat. Again,
there are no single seats on this train."

I huffed and tossed my jacket overhead. I spotted the back
of a brother's head and it appeared he was sitting alone. I
plopped down beside him and slightly glanced at him. It wasn't
until I got situated that I realized who was beside me. I started
to change seats. Do I pretend I don't know him?

I looked down the aisle searching for another available
seat. Finally, he said, "Devin?"

I turned to face Clark's brother. The last time we'd come
face to face was when we fought in a nightclub. He never
thought I was good enough for his younger sister. Though it
has been over six years ago, I tensed up and nodded. "Yeah.
Reggie, right?"

He extended his hand. I was baffled. This was the most
self-righteous bastard I'd ever met in my entire life. We shook
hands. He smiled. "How you been man?"

From what I recalled, this was probably more than he'd
said to me through the entire course of my three-and-a-half-
year relationship with Clark. I nodded. "Good."

He asked, "You still in New York?"

"Yeah. You?"

"Yeah, I'm trying to get out."

"Are you still in banking?"

"Yeah, man. I'm going down for an interview today with
Smith Barney."

I nodded. I wanted to ask about the love of my life but I
figured I'd allow him to offer the information. He has two
kids by Clark's best friend who also lives in Baltimore. How

was he able to be away from his kids so long? Maybe he was finally growing up. I chuckled. "I guess your little man is getting to that age where you gotta stay on his heels."

He nodded. "Yeah. You know I've had him since . . ." He paused and frowned. He took a deep breath. "Since, Tanisha died."

If he said what I thought he'd said, it would be too painful for him to repeat. I squinted. He nodded. "Yeah, he's been with me for six years."

My stomach balled in knots. Finally, I said, "What?"

"Tanisha's boyfriend took her life about six years ago."

He and Tanisha had an on-again, off-again love affair until he got engaged to a chick named Sheena in New York. Then, Tanisha found some flunky to take his place. I couldn't even remember the guy's name. I sat stunned. "Yo, he killed her?"

"Yeah, it wasn't until she was gone that I realized how hard life was without her."

He took a deep breath like he didn't want to discuss it anymore. I dropped my forehead into my hands. Tanisha was probably one of the sweetest people I'd ever met. His expression looked like he agreed. All I could say was, "Damn, dawg."

He nodded. "Yeah, if it wasn't for my kids, I would have taken my own life."

My mouth hung open. This had completely humbled him. I repeated, "Damn, dawg."

"Yeah, a part of me definitely died with her." He sighed. "That was my baby."

It's a damn shame that it took him until she was gone to realize how much he loved her. As I pitied him, I calculated in my head when this had obviously all occurred, and I wanted to throw up. Clark lost her best friend around the same time she lost me. Why didn't she attempt to contact me?

I couldn't hold back anymore. "How's Clark?"

He had always adored his sister. As I watched his dim eyes

brighten, I imagined he felt the same for her as I felt for my own daughter. He nodded. "Clark is doing well. She's happy."

As much as she deserved happiness, it hurt to hear that she found it without me. I nodded. "She got married, right?"

"Yeah. She married a good brother."

"He must be a good dude if you approve."

"Yeah."

We both laughed. "Does she have any kids?"

"She's a stepmom and she has custody of my daughter."

The wicked side of me was thankful that aside from a ring and a document there was nothing more connecting her with her husband. Hell, divorces are a dime a dozen, especially over thirty. A grin must have begun to peep through the cloud on my face, because Reggie felt the need to add, "Yeah, she's good with both of the girls. They love her to death."

How could anyone not love her to death? I nodded. "Yeah, I'm sure."

"I'll have to tell her that I saw you."

"Yeah, tell her that I asked about her."

He nodded. "I certainly will. She'll be happy to hear that." He laughed. "I think."

I forced a chuckle. "I hope."

"You're still married, right?"

I took a deep breath. Clark obviously didn't share with him that I tried to contact her after my divorce. They used to be so close. She must have really been through with me by that time. I shook my head. "Nah, I've been divorced for almost five years."

He chuckled. "That's everyone's story."

I frowned. "You?"

"Separated."

"That's the rough period."

"My whole marriage has been rough."

I laughed. "I know what you mean man."

"Yeah, it's crazy."

I felt sorry for the brother. "Yeah, a lot of us have made the same mistake, though."

He shook his head. "If I could do it all over again, I would have married Tanisha. She would still be alive and I'd probably be a much happier man."

"I feel you man."

"Next time, I'll go with my instinct."

Instinct? That was a strange choice. "As opposed to what?"

He sighed. "As opposed to all the other superficial stuff that we think will make us happy." He paused for a second as the words seeped in. "Life is too short. You have to go with your instinct."

My instinct told me to stay with Clark. My mind forced me to marry Jennifer. My instinct said that Taylor was the one to help me forget about my past mistakes and brighten my future. My loyalty to my homeboy forced me to suppress the attraction. Who'd ever think the best advice I'd heard in years would come from a man I used to consider my enemy?

53

TAYLOR

I decided to celebrate my birthday at Ozio's on M Street. We rented the loft that overlooked the club on the Friday after my birthday.

As I got fly for my night, I absorbed my world. There was no reason to complain. Thirty. Flirty. And fly. Hell, you can't have everything. I squeezed into my tight black T-shirt that I had made in honor of that damn Devin Patterson. Our two-week relationship still crosses my mind. Anyway, the T-shirt had PROVIDING QUALITY SERVICE SINCE 1977 stitched in white.

Thirty gave me a sense of accomplishment. The world should know that now they have to respect me. When I strutted in the club, my confidence was obvious.

Courtney laughed. "Oh, I guess that's your new mature walk."

"Yup, love me or leave me alone."

We slapped five. I said, "You'll see how it feels when you turn thirty."

She rolled her eyes, saying, "Ho, now you taking this shit too far."

We laughed at my overconfidence. As we danced the night away, several of my other friends rolled in. After the waiter seemed to bring a constant stream of appetizers out, she finally brought the carrot cake. Courtney gathered everyone from the dance floor to sing "Happy Birthday." I sat on the couch, with my knees clenched together, my hands folded on my lap, while my friends sang to me.

The big three-oh flickered on the cake. Finally, it was time to blow out the candles. I sucked in all the emotions that plagued my late twenties. How was I to turn thirty without a prospect?

I blew out the candles and it seemed like the flame of desperation was finally extinguished. I was thirty and I felt damn good. So what, there was no prospect. I inhaled a feeling of freedom. Everyone clapped. I clapped too. I celebrated my life.

When the loft emptied, Courtney and I stayed there dancing. I looked over the ledge. Oh shit! Devin Patterson. Assuming his presence was coincidental, I huffed. He smiled. He walked toward me. Butterflies lined my stomach. His black blazer covered one of the white letters on his T-shirt. My eyes refocused when I saw the letters, "AY". As I fantasized about him trotting up on a white horse, wearing a shirt with my name on it, he walked up the stairs. The abstract picture of Ray Charles and the letters R-A-Y struck me back down to earth.

Courtney whispered in my ear, "I invited him."

I wish I could say I was mad at her, but I wasn't. I was just happy he decided to come. He hugged me and kissed my cheek. "Happy birthday, lady."

I smirked. "You're late."

"But I'm here."

"I'm glad you came."

"I wouldn't have missed it for the world."

Considering he hadn't responded to any of my e-mails or phone calls since his birthday party, he could have fooled me. I cleared my throat. "Now, you wouldn't just happen to be taking inventory."

He laughed. "Okay. You got me." Then, he leaned his body close to me. I smiled and he kissed my cheek. "Yeah, I am."

"So am I the best of the worst?"

He chuckled and his lips grazed my ear. "Nah, you're the best thing on the market."

"You could have fooled me."

He rested his arms on my shoulders. "Taylor, you know what happened."

Not really wanting to explore the whole Scooter dilemma, I shrugged my shoulders. "Do you want some cake?"

"Can I eat it, too?"

"Devin, don't be silly."

The DJ obviously knew I was celebrating my thirtieth birthday, because he was spinning all the old-school hits. BBD's "Poison" blasted through the speakers. Devin and I burst into laughter. He sang the lyrics. "It's driving me out of my mind. That's why it's hard for me to find. Can't get her out of my head. Miss her. Kiss her. Love her."

He landed a kiss on my lips when he finished his singing episode. He looked into my eyes. "Taylor, I didn't want to mess up again."

"Did you really have to act so ugly?"

He shook his head. "Taylor, I'm sorry."

"Are you really sorry or are you just tired?"

"Nah, I want you in stock." He kissed my cheek. "I want you to be the only product on my shelf. I knew it from the moment I met you. As much as I wanted you, I still was scared. So, when everything went down, it was just an easy out."

I frowned. "What?"

"Get out before you get in. That's how you protect your feelings."

As I thought of how often I'd used that strategy, I nodded. He smiled. "You feel me?"

"But, what about . . ."

He kissed me before I could mention his loyalty to Scooter. Obviously, it was no longer an issue. After landing a few soft pecks on my face, he asked, "Can you give me that chance?"

"Um . . ."

He kissed me again. "Taylor, we ain't getting no younger, we might as well do it."

As his corny lines continued to make me laugh, I knew I wanted to pursue something further with him. I surrendered. "All right, dawg."

He held me tightly and exhaled, like I'd done him a favor. My hands cupped his face to reciprocate the gratitude. My brain instantly fast-forwarded to visions of us sharing a happy future together. We proceeded to rock to the beats serenading our reunion. As we twirled on the dance floor, I suppressed the fantasy and lived in the moment.

TAPPIN' ON THIRTY

CANDICE DOW

ABOUT THIS GUIDE

The suggested questions are intended
to enhance your group's reading
of Candice Dow's book.

DISCUSSION QUESTIONS

1. Do you think turning thirty forces most people to reevaluate their lives? Why?

2. How do you think Taylor's family indirectly influenced her decisions throughout the story?

3. Who do you think was the best person for Taylor? Why?

4. Were you at all sympathetic to Taylor's reasons for dating Scooter?

5. Were Scooter's issues with Akua justified?

6. Would you describe Scooter as a strong man?

7. Did Devin seem like a player or was he genuinely interested in finding love? What about Taylor?

8. Did Scooter make the right decision?

9. If you were Devin, would you have followed your heart or remained loyal to your friend? Why or why not?

10. Why shouldn't people put an age on finding love?